JOHN F.D. TAFF'S

LITTLE

DEATHS

BOOKS of the DEAD

Collection Copyright 2012 by John F.D. Taff

For more information, contact: Besthorror@gmail.com
Visit us at: Booksofthedeadpress.com

LITTLE DEATHS
FIRST EDITION

Cover Art by Diego Candia
Book Design by James Roy Daley
Graphic Design by Derek Daley
Edited by Ashley Davis

10 9 8 7 6 5 4 3 2 1

Great titles from:
BOOKS OF THE DEAD

BEST NEW ZOMBIE TALES (Vol. 1)

BEST NEW ZOMBIE TALES (Vol. 2)

BEST NEW ZOMBIE TALES (Vol. 3)

BEST NEW ZOMBIE TALES TRILOGY

BEST NEW WEREWOLF TALES (VOL. 1)

BEST NEW VAMPIRE TALES (Vol. 1)

CLASSIC VAMPIRE TALES

GARY BRANDNER - THE HOWLING

GARY BRANDNER - THE HOWLING II

GARY BRANDNER - THE HOWLING III

GARY BRANDNER - THE HOWLING TRILOGY

JAMES ROY DALEY'S - INTO HELL

JAMES ROY DALEY'S - TERROR TOWN

JAMES ROY DALEY - 13 DROPS OF BLOOD

JAMES ROY DALEY - THE DEAD PARADE

JAMES ROY DALEY - ZOMBIE KONG

TONIA BROWN - BADASS ZOMBIE ROAD TRIP

MATT HULTS - ANYTHING CAN BE DANGEROUS

MATT HULTS - HUSK

TIM LEBBON - BERSERK

PAUL KANE - PAIN CAGES

ZOMBIE KONG ANTHOLOGY

For My Parents
Thomas & Kathleen Taff
Because of Whom
I am a Better Person.

TABLE OF
CONTENTS

BOOKS of the DEAD

BOLTS

I can hear them coming up the stairs, the pounding feet on the treads, the quiet, gathered whispering of their voices. It swirls up the stairwell like the hiss and sputter of torches.

I can smell the smoke, the papers burning in my office.

I can hear her in the bedroom, sitting on the bed, rocking. I can hear the mattress squeaking. I can hear her strange, deep muttering, her thick moans.

What have I done? Oh god, what have I done?

I need to let her go.

My worst fear, though—the fear that dulls my brain, that slows the blood in my veins to a crawl—is that it's too late.

* * *

I saw them online, the bolts.

I bought movie memorabilia: props, costumes, little knickknacks. I'd turned it into an online business over the years, buying pieces from studio auctions, estate sales, filmmakers whose lives had taken bad turns, other collectors like me. I had my own website where I turned around and sold them. It was fun, easy, and it provided a decent living without an office, a commute, or a whiff of anything even approaching actual work.

As an added benefit, I could do it from home in the little office in the apartment that I shared with my girlfriend, Rachel... well, Rachel *and* the stuff that I chose not to sell. The trouble was, at least according to her, that I chose *not* to sell way too much.

We shared a three-bedroom apartment, one of those lofts downtown where the space is open and the rent is steep. Still, we were 17 floors up with a great view of the city, and a balcony where we could sip drinks and feel cosmopolitan in the summer.

The only problem was that almost every square inch was filled with stuff. One bedroom served as my office, another as storage. The rest of the place was lined with glass cases displaying all sorts of geeky stuff—the uniform cap Leslie Nielsen wore in *Forbidden Planet*, "hero" prop phasers and tricorders from various incarnations of *Star Trek*, a Jedi robe from *Star Wars*, even a fedora worn by Bogart.

I replaced a lot of the toys I had had in my youth and lost—Major Matt Mason, Planet of the Apes figures, Ultraman, and Speed Racer. All for a lot more than my mom and dad paid for them back in the day.

My absolute weak spot was horror movies. Rachel knew that if I happened across some piece from an old Universal or Hammer horror flick it would most likely *not* be put up for sale but instead would join the massive collection that threatened to overwhelm our apartment.

I had Bela Lugosi's neckpiece medallion from the 1932 *Dracula*, one of Lon Chaney's set of werewolf teeth, the dagger Karloff carried as Ardeth Bey in *The Mummy*. I had a stake and mallet used by Peter Cushing on Christopher Lee in one of the cheesy Hammer *Dracula* films, and Vincent Price's costume from *The Mask of the Red Death*.

That's just the tip of the iceberg.

I find it easy to acquire things.

I find it hard to let them go.

I found the bolts on eBay one morning. The several thousand dollars I had in my Paypal account from a recent sale was burning a hole in my pocket.

I sat in my office, still in my bathrobe, still unshowered, a cup of cooling coffee on the cluttered desktop. As my fingers lingered over the keyboard, I felt a warm pair of lips smack the back of my neck.

"Going to work, ace," she said. Yeah, she called me names like Ace and Sport.

"Have a good one, Rabbit," I replied without turning. Yeah, I called her Rabbit. She was small and had big ears. Don't judge.

"Doing business or adding to the clutter we call home?" she asked, her head bent next to mine, her words, her breath tingling in my ear.

"Can't say just yet."

"Well, no more superhero dolls for a while. I hate the way they all stare at me when I get out of the shower."

"That's because you have a hot ass," I said, nuzzling her cheek. "Superheroes are notorious ass men."

She laughed, and it tickled down my spine. "Still…"

I held up my hand. "I make no promises, woman!"

Rachel kicked the back of my chair playfully.

"Try to shower and dress before I get home."

"Again, no promises!"

Footsteps across the carpet, the front door opened.

"I love you, Ace!"

"Love you, too, Rabbit!"

The door closed, and I saw it.

The listing headline read: 'Actual Prop Neck Bolts from Karloff 1931 *Frankenstein*'.

The auction came up straightforward enough. A pair of the neck bolts that Boris Karloff wore as the creature in the iconic film. The little bolts that conducted the electrical charge that brought all the dead pieces of the monster back to life... a kind of life, anyway.

The description said that the pieces were made of hard cast rubber. Painted dull silver, in great shape. A certificate of authenticity was included, an actual letter signed by Jack Pierce.

Pierce was a make-up artist who might have gone unnoticed except for his work on the Universal monster films. The actors brought the parts to life, sure, but Pierce's make-up brought the *actors* to life. What you see in your mind when you picture these horror icons is not the *authors'* descriptions, but Jack Pierce's *vision*.

Dracula's pasty complexion, cape, and widow's peak? *Jack Pierce*.

The Mummy's wrinkled skin, and slack eyes? *Jack Pierce*.

Frankenstein's flat head, green skin tone, and neck bolts? *Jack Pierce*.

I knew—even as my fingers typed out my bid—I knew I wouldn't be selling these.

* * *

They arrived late in the afternoon, while I was busy selling two of my less popular action figures. I thought this would make Rachel feel good... particularly when I told her about the life-size *Battlestar Galactica* Cylon I'd just bought.

As I was packing the two figures, Rachel came in from work. She slammed the door, tossed her keys onto the table, dropped her purse, and flashed her eyes over to me. Bad day at work, bad day in traffic, or just a bad day. I didn't know which, but I knew it didn't matter.

There I sat in the living room, still in my underpants and t-shirt, in a sea of packing materials.

Shit.

Rachel took a deep breath, expelled it in a loud, long sound that was half decompression, half pressurizing for the second round of whatever bout she'd been fighting that day.

"More shit, Ace? *Really?*" she said in a voice where every word gained steam, gained volume.

"Actually, these are..." I tried to begin.

"Actually, why don't you just sit around in your fucking tighty-whiteys and your fucking Punisher t-shirt all day and just buy, buy, buy. I mean, let's pack this place like a warehouse! We don't need a bedroom. And you evidently don't even need a bathroom!"

She lifted her purse from where she'd dropped it, looked at it as if she had picked up a snake, tossed it to the floor again.

"I didn't..."

"No, you didn't," she said, cutting my words off as expertly as if she'd done so with a knife. I could almost see them hanging there, dripping meaning or blood or whatever it was that truncated words drip.

"You didn't get dressed, you didn't shower, you didn't clean the place like I asked. You didn't do jack shit. What is it again that attracts me to you, can you remind me?"

I shrugged, threw my arms wide. "My irrepressible charm?"

Rachel narrowed her eyes, prepared to say something, then stomped off into the bedroom instead, where she slammed the door but missed the satisfaction of several action figures arranged on shelves outside the bedroom toppling to the floor.

I took the opportunity to quickly clean the place, picking stuff up, lightly dusting with an old sock, putting dishes into the dishwasher and giving everything in the kitchen a light spritz of Windex and a rubdown.

Then, I jumped in the shower in the second bathroom in my office, brushed my teeth, pulled on some real clothes and went back into the main room.

She still hadn't come out, so I made a quick call to her favorite Thai takeout, opened a bottle of chardonnay, set out some dishes and candles.

When the food showed, I paid the delivery guy, took the brown paper bag reeking of deliciousness to the table, lit the candles.

And did what I should have done from the very beginning.

Waited.

After a while, the aroma of the food seeped under the door, yanked at Rachel's nose as in one of those cartoons. The candles had burned halfway down, and my chin was slumped against my fist, elbows on the table.

I heard the door creak open slowly, a small, dark figure standing in the dark wedge of the bedroom.

"Dinner?"

I jerked awake, jumped to my feet.

"Rabbit, you okay?"

She lingered in the dark, one of her small hands grasping the edge of the door. "Yeah, pretty sorry, though."

"Sorry?" I asked, as if struck by momentary amnesia. "For what?"

"For being an asshole, for dumping on you as soon as I got home without even saying hello." She considered this for a moment. "You know, that kind of stuff."

"Already forgotten," I said. "Apartment is clean. Boyfriend is clean. Dinner is served, though probably a little cold by now."

I saw her face peer out through the darkness, saw the smile that had attracted me to her originally. The bedroom was in total night, the dining room lit only by candlelight.

But, man, her smile lit the room, every corner of it.

We ate dinner, me finally giving her the space to say what she needed. It was relatively tame stuff, the normal ingredients in your run-of-the-mill bad day.

"I didn't really mean it," she said after a while, staring at the pile of cold Pad Thai on her plate.

"Listen, I know you're pissed about all the stuff I buy..."

"Silly boy." She smiled, and it totally, I mean *completely* removed any sting from what she'd just said. "You make your own money, you can buy whatever you want. It's just that... well... you can't let go of things. Why can't you let go?"

"I sold two pieces today."

"And how many pieces did you *buy*?"

I thought about that life-size Cylon and took a deep breath.

"Let's start house-hunting again. You've been wanting to do that."

"Sure, let's find a nice, new place so you have even more square-footage to fill," she said, then immediately looked at her plate. "Sorry."

I bit my lip. "So what are you saying?"

Slowly, she raised her head, gave me a shy version of the flashier smile.

"I'm saying that I'm sorry. And if you could let go of some of this stuff, if you could let a little of *me* into this apartment, that'd be great."

I felt something tight and nervous within me deflate, and a smile floated to my face. "Are we talking chintz and wicker and old country roses? Or candles, hippy beads, and patchouli?"

"Neither, fuck-face," she said, another pet name. "Now take me to the bedroom or lose me forever."

I did, and we made the kind of love that told me it was all okay.

* * *

For a while, at least.

Then, as they say in the movies, she died.

Well, they don't actually say that in any movie I'm aware of.

Yet, still, she died.

* * *

Rachel and I seemed to move past some barrier in our relationship. I sold more things than normal... especially after the Cylon arrived.

One night a few weeks later, we went to bed, turned off the lights and snuggled in the warm sheets. The sounds of the city through the open window were comforting—police sirens, the blat of car horns, the squeal of tires. All far enough away to sound strangely soothing, like crickets in the country. Sleep came quickly.

The next morning was Saturday, and I got up, left Rachel to sleep a little. I snuck into the kitchen and rooted through the cupboards and found the stuff to make banana pancakes.

I had a few stacked on a plate before I looked at the clock again. Nearly 10 a.m., and it seemed strange that she wasn't awake yet. Turning off the gas, I placed the last pancake onto a plate, slid the pan into the sink.

The bedroom was quiet, still. A picture-perfect beam of golden sunlight shafted through the slats in the blinds, fell all dusty-sparkly onto the comforter.

I sat on the edge of the bed, and moved my hand through the spray of dark hair that fell across her pillow.

"Rabbit? Breakfast is ready."

I smoothed away her hair. It wanted to drape her cheek. I kissed her there, with my hand holding her hair to the side.

Cold.

"Rabbit, come on." I moved the covers aside, rolled her over.

She flopped bonelessly onto her back, one arm flailing out and striking the headboard hard enough to have hurt.

Her eyes were closed. Her mouth was closed, too, and I couldn't hear her breathing.

I was holding my own breath now, wanting to say her name but unable to articulate one word, one sound. My hand, shaking badly, went to her forehead, her cheeks, her throat. Each time I called her name in my head, *Rabbit, Rabbit, Rabbit!*

Then, "Rachel!"

It came from my mouth, strangled and dry, as near a wail as anything I had ever uttered.

She didn't stir.

My shaking hand went to her chest, palm flat against her sternum.

Nothing stirred beneath it. Her skin was as cold and plastic as a doll's.

I swallowed something dry and raspy that lodged in my throat, blocked my airway.

She was dead.

I scooted across the bed, fell to the floor with a thump.

I sat there for a few moments, sat and didn't move, sat and didn't think. My brain ran, just ran, like a runner who didn't know when he'd crossed the finish line, didn't know where to stop, how to stop.

I swallowed the bolus that seemed to clog my throat, and my heart lurched into motion again with a tremor.

Pulling myself up, I leaned over the bed.

She was mostly uncovered, my Rabbit. She still wore her t-shirt from the night before. Her limbs were thrown across the bed, her hair sprayed across both our pillows.

Her skin was blue—light, unnatural blue. The warm morning sunlight falling through the window had given it the illusion of life, but there was none.

My Rabbit, my sweet Rabbit.

My brain thoroughly disengaged, I shuffled into the kitchen and drank a cup of coffee, picked at the pancakes.

I waited for my brain to tire itself out, come back from wherever it was, and tell me what to do.

I could not make the call, could not *imagine* making that call, the call that would bring men who would come and take her away on a metal gurney.

As I sat there, her body cooling in our warm, early morning bed, I looked around the place, looked and saw all of the stuff, *my stuff*, staring back at me.

Without thinking, I launched myself from the chair, sent it skittering back across the tile floor, into the kitchen. I grabbed the nearest glass case, five feet tall and filled with memorabilia, and toppled it over, screaming in anger.

The entire case shattered, spraying the floor with shards of broken glass, figures, broken bits of irreplaceable items.

Breathing heavily, I went into my office, kicking, arms thrashing, sending things into the air, across my desk, clattering to the floor. I shrieked, wordless and raw, and I stomped and threw and tore papers until I was exhausted.

Finally, I slid on some papers; fell to the floor amidst the carnage.

I looked around the room, panting like an animal, stunned at what I'd done.

Then my eyes caught them there on the floor, atop a flutter of papers, sealed in a plastic bag.

Frankenstein's bolts.

I realized two things instantly.

I hadn't yet cried.

I had completely lost my mind.

* * *

Spirit gum... I can remember the smell of it filling the room as I uncapped the small, brown vial of the stuff.

Spirit gum... strange name, considering my intentions.

I stood in the doorway to the bedroom for a long time, the vial in one hand, the plastic bag with the bolts in the other, stood there as the sun climbed up the blinds, watching her, my Rabbit.

She seemed so small in our bed, so tiny, so forlorn with her arms thrown open and hair tousled, her eyes closed, her face drawn into a small *moue*, like she was frustrated or annoyed with me.

My brain, understand, was still gone, still moving into the distance.

Kneeling at the side of the bed, I carefully brushed aside her dark hair, exposed her neck.

I unsealed the plastic bag, knocked one of the bolts into my hand. The two were slightly different. One had a blunt cap, like the head of nail; the other was just a flat rod. Each had a little L-shaped wire that angled out like a tiny antenna.

There was a thin circle of rubber around the base where it attached to the neck, which was then was covered with makeup.

I remembered from pictures of Karloff as Frankenstein that the capped bolt was on the right.

With trembling hands, I applied a smear of spirit gum to the rubber seal.

Taking a deep breath, I placed the bolt on Rachel's neck, guessing about where it should be.

The spirit gum stuck immediately, but I held it in place until I was sure.

When I finished, I looked at her. The bolts seemed to be in the right place, seemed to make a straight line through her neck.

I nodded, pleased with the work I had done, then collapsed in the chair at the foot of the bed and waited... *waited.*

* * *

After an hour or so, I stood and tried to rouse her.
Nothing.
Then, it struck me.
Of course...
They weren't *bolts* at all.
They were *electrodes.*

* * *

In the end, I ripped the electrical cord out of a lamp on the nightstand, peeled it apart, stripped both ends with a paring knife.

I wrapped each bare wire around one of the bolts, careful not to pull them from her neck. The Y shape of the cord draped her unmoving chest as if she had fallen asleep wearing a pair of earphones, listening to music.

I closed the blinds against the sun, and the room swam in darkness.

My hand, holding the plug, hovered over the outlet.

My brain, exhausted from its long run, was making its way back, bringing with it the first slivers of doubt.

But I plugged it in.

And... well... *nothing.*

There was no Frankenstein's laboratory scene of arcing electricity and showers of sparks. No crazy flashing lights or breakers popping.

She didn't suddenly seize on the bed, her teeth clenched. Her hands didn't tighten, her toes didn't point.

My hand moved to pull the plug, when I saw it: subtle, beautifully eldritch.

Thin arcs of violet-white electricity zagged across the tiny gap between the antennae and the bolts. A soft sizzle accompanied this, an electric razor heard from a distance. The smell of ozone reached my nostrils, as fresh and clean as the air after a spring shower.

I thought of how the bolts, made of rubber, couldn't possibly conduct electricity.

I knew that they would melt, would have to melt.

I saw her chest expand suddenly, rise.

I heard a strangled breath escape her suddenly open mouth, the intake of another, sounding as if it would never end, never draw enough breath to fill her lungs again.

I cried, finally.

Not just because she was alive.

But because she was crying, too.

* * *

I helped her into the shower, where she slumped in my arms as the water fell over her.

Her hair went lank, plastered her face.

She was jabbering, incoherent. It wasn't just that she didn't make sense: she wasn't making *words*.

Her eyes were dull, vacant, staring right through me, no sign of recognition, of awareness.

I thought she might have had a stroke, must have had a stroke.

A hospital. I needed to take her to a hospital.

I held her slippery, trembling body in the crook of one arm while I prepared to remove the bolts from her neck.

How to explain those?

She must have been alive all along, had to have been. I mean, Christ, I wasn't a doctor.

How could I be sure that she hadn't *actually* been breathing, that her heart hadn't *actually* been beating?

What had I been thinking?

Gluing those bolts to her neck, zapping her with a lamp cord?

Shit, I might have *really* killed her.

As my hand neared the bolt on the right side of her neck, made ready to peel it off, fling it across the room, she flinched, and her eyes rolled in their orbits, focused on me.

I saw two things in those eyes.

The first was sadness, an almost wistful sorrow.

The second was fear tinged with revulsion.

My hand paused, fell away.

Her skin was a pale, luminous blue. More disturbingly, there were patches of deep green that looked as if they were floating on her skin like algae on a lake.

Her flesh was no warmer than it had been, even though the shower was hot.

She hadn't been alive earlier and she wasn't alive now.

A single finger reached out and touched the bolt on her neck.

I was rewarded with a brief, light shock, like walking across a carpet and touching a doorknob.

As I jerked my hand away, she moaned, thick and full of grief, slumped in my arms and began to weep again.

* * *

I eventually wrestled her to the bedroom and put some clothes on her. She was shivering, icy cold. It was like trying to put clothes on a human-sized doll. She didn't help, didn't *try* to help, didn't seem to *know* how to help.

It was all I could do to get a t-shirt and a pair of shorts on her. When she was dressed, I led her to the kitchen, step by lurching step. I lowered her forcefully into a chair. She was unwilling or unaware of how to bend, to conform her body to that shape. Her hands gripped my arms tightly, sank her nails in my flesh, but she eventually sat, rigid, straight backed. I sat beside her, looked at her.

Her dark hair was still wet, still adhered flatly to her head. Her skin was a mottled bluegreen, so pale, devoid of anything red or pink, the colors of health, of life. Her eyes were pale, too, as if the lens had fogged over with a green-yellow mist.

And the bolts... they completed the look, jutting from her neck, spidery electrical arcs jumping intermittently across their antennae.

Rachel looked at me, dull and sad; each move of her eyes, her head, her body was ponderous, slow, even when she blinked. She was still crying softly, her sobs thick and garbled, as if coming from deep within her.

"Rachel," I said, touching her arm. "Rabbit, it's okay... it's okay. You're okay."

Her eyes fixed me and the look I thought was uncomprehending suddenly took on a horrible clarity. She tried to speak, to say something, but it just came out as a long, grunting *nnnnnnnnnn.*

Her head shook, slowly at first, from side to side, then more powerfully.

No!

I reached out to embrace her, but she pulled away, her eyes tracking down to my arm, then widening in fear.

"NNNNNNNNNNNNNNNNNNNN," she growled, trying to grab my arm with fingers that didn't work. Her head still shook from side to side, spraying spittle across the table.

I looked down at my arm, the arm she had grabbed as I had forced her into the chair. There were four perfect half-moon cuts from her nails in the meat of my forearm, each weeping blood that had run down to my wrist and dripped to the floor. They were deep, and they bled profusely.

She continued to hold my arm with one hand, while the other found its way to her mouth, wedged inside and muffled the already impenetrable sounds of her distress.

* * *

I cleaned myself up, applied some Band-Aids while she looked on, propped against the bathroom doorframe, still muttering.

When I finished, I showed her the arm, told her it was okay, but she looked away, groaning.

I took her back to the kitchen table, sat her down, this time more easily, and sat myself, trying to figure out what to do.

If you're wondering: yes, there was a tiny, annoying voice at the back of my brain that was screaming, in the mad voice of Colin Clive:

It's alive! It's alive! It's alive!

When I looked up from my reverie, she was stuffing cold banana pancakes inexpertly into her mouth. Gobs of chewed pancake coated her lips, fell onto her t-shirt.

She smiled then, smiled with teeth coated in gummy yellow, her greenish tongue lolling like a happy puppy's.

My Rabbit.

Dear lord…

* * *

A few days passed. Then a week.

The phone rang off the wall, her office, her friends, her family.

I didn't answer, didn't know what to say.

Rachel? She's fine. Well, she did die, but I glued some Frankenstein bolts to her neck, real ones, and she's getting better.

I helped her dress every morning, helped her eat, helped her bathe. I brushed her teeth and hair… both of which started to come out. A few clumps of hair in the brush, another tooth in the sink every morning.

I helped her use the toilet, but I don't want to talk about that *at all*.

She didn't like to be away from my side or out of sight of me, so we spent the days mostly sitting in the main room watching television or reading. Well, I read. She mostly stared into space or at me.

All the while grunting at me in her strange, guttural new voice.

Neither of us slept much. I'd wrestle her into bed and she'd lay there as stiff and unmoving as… well, as a dead girl, muttering through the night.

' I was able to sneak out a few times to get food, groceries.

Each time when I came back, she had destroyed some new section of the apartment. Not deliberately, mind you, just staggering around in anguish looking for me, waiting for me to return.

When I did, she shuffled to me, weeping as she often did, hugging me tightly and moaning, her eyes both sad and reproachful, like a dog disappointed at its master for leaving but overjoyed at his return.

After a couple of weeks, the knocking at the door began. First the gentle, tentative knocks of family and friends, then the more forceful knocking of the police.

I didn't answer, didn't know what to do.

* * *

The landlord called, threatening, letting me know the police had been by. The other tenants had been complaining about the loud noises, the midnight shrieks, the crashing and banging that occurred at all hours.

And the odd smell.

It couldn't go on.

I couldn't go on.

Not like this.

Late on a Sunday night, we sat on the couch together, watching television.

By chance, *Frankenstein* was on one of the classic movie channels.

I hadn't seen it in a long while, so I let it play, despite some misgivings over how Rachel might react. But her rocking and moaning seemed to subside a little, and I thought she might actually be watching it.

Towards the end, that's where I got the idea—after the villagers chased down the good doctor and his creature, torches blazing, cornered them in a windmill, set it on fire with the monster inside.

In the movie, the creature hurled his creator out of the windmill, where he was saved by the villagers.

I didn't expect, didn't want that for me.

I simply can't let go.

She knew this.

* * *

The room is warm now. I can feel the heat.

There's knocking at the door, pounding.

I ignore it as best I can. The door is solid steel. If they break it down—*and they might be able to*—it will take some time.

I sit on the bed and hold her hand, her cold, cold hand.

She turns to me, and her face is blank.

She mouths words, but they're just sounds really, deep, guttural.

Her free hand paws the air, finds my face as if by accident, strokes it roughly.

Her eyes lock on mine, but they aren't *her* eyes anymore, not the eyes I remember. These are a spoiled, poisonous green, limned with yellow.

Her mouth moves again, her lips twitch and grimace, her tongue twists thickly around words that I finally understand.

Silly boy.

So I hold her hand, rest my head on her shoulder and feel a trickle of her cold drool drip down my neck, pool in the hollow of my collarbone.

And let go…

CALENDAR GIRL

It was at the reception that Josh spoke the first words that truly scared her.

The wedding, like the rest of Melinda's courtship, moved with a dreamlike cadence.

People drifted in and out of perception, events passed like objects whirling around the heart of a hurricane. Time, rather than connecting these happenings, separated them, split them into odd, unconnected vignettes.

Here she was, as if just awakened, getting married to a man she hardly knew.

It was only five months ago that they'd exchanged their first words across a conference room table.

Josh, the bright, new supervisor brought in from the company's Chicago office.

She, the eager, dynamic account executive just out of college.

Josh had handled his first meeting as if he knew every intimate detail, spoken and unspoken, about the clients and their business.

"I love an organized man," Melinda had said to break the ice after the clients left, and the others applauded her effort with nervous, restrained laughter.

Except Josh.

He'd looked at her with that baby face, those light brown eyes, looked seriously at her.

"Of course," he finally said. And that was the beginning.

Melinda had been surprised when, only a month later, Josh produced his ubiquitous black date book, bulging fat around the tiny clasp that held it shut, opened it and said:

"March 4. That's the day you'll marry me."

His handwriting was firm and clear even in the dim light of her bedroom.

"Oh, Josh," she sighed, burying her face in his neck. "*I do*."

* * *

As they finished their first dance, they were stopped by Melinda's aunt and uncle.

"Well, we've got to leave," said the uncle, hitching up his unnaturally brown polyester pants, his gaping shirt exposing flesh the color of suet.

"We're so happy for you, honey," cooed the aunt, pulling Melinda in dizzily for a too-tight hug. "You'll have to get your address to us when you settle in. Do you know yet where you'll be living?"

"We haven't had time to think about that."

"Well," said the uncle, who had been eying the exit. "You're both young. Take your time."

"I'm not worried. I have it all planned," Josh broke in solemnly, hooking his thumb back over his shoulder.

Melinda followed his aim as he said his goodbyes.

The head table lay in that direction, cleared of the dirty dinner dishes.

The only things left were two champagne flutes, an open bottle of Dom.

And Josh's date book, like a dark window in the tablecloth.

A chill scurried through her body.

Then, the whirlwind took hold of her again, tugged her along after it.

* * *

"So, it's been nine months," began Jeannie, shoveling in a forkful of pasta during her annual Christmas lunch with Melinda. "Are you still getting any?"

"*Jeannie!*" Melinda squealed, taking a small bite of her salad.

Melinda noticed sourly that, as she did every year, Jeannie had ordered the most fattening thing on the café's menu. She was one of those women who looked good no matter what she ate or how much.

In fact, given her masculine table manners, Melinda suspected that Jeannie looked good no matter *how* she ate.

"Come on! Everyone's taking bets on whether you two schedule it in advance."

"He's not as bad as that," Melinda said, picking at her salad. "He's just ... *organized*. And no, we do *not* plan that!"

"He carries that book with him everywhere," Jeannie said, slathering a hunk of bread with butter.

"Not everywhere," interrupted Melinda, beginning to feel uncomfortable.

The fact was, Josh *did* carry it everywhere, and, yes, she was aware that everyone whispered about this particular eccentricity. Melinda had even joined in before they started dating seriously.

"What does he write in there that's so important?" Jeannie continued, unabated by Melinda's interruption or even the food in her own mouth. "Have you ever looked?"

"No, that's private. I would never do that."

"It kind of takes the spontaneity out of things, doesn't it? What does he do when things don't go as planned?"

"It's funny. Everything seems to go just as he plans. Always," Melinda said, spearing a lettuce leaf and chewing on it thoughtfully.

Melinda dropped her fork, took a drink of water.

"Hey, sorry," said Jeannie, reaching across the table to grab her hand. "I didn't mean anything by it. Josh is a great guy, a real catch. He's just a little strange, that's all. But all men are strange, aren't they?"

Melinda, lost the thread of Jeannie's lunchtime ramblings, was mired in her own thoughts.

Exactly what *was* Josh writing in his little black date book?

* * *

The next morning, Josh rose before her and padded into the adjoining bathroom.

Melinda snuggled into Josh's depression, pulled his scent-laden covers over her. As she wriggled into a comfortable position, she felt a lump pressing up through the sheets.

Annoyed, she flopped onto her other side.

The lump was still there, bulging like a tumor in the mattress.

She got out of bed, glancing at the closed bathroom door, and knelt.

The sound of the shower started as she ran her hand between the mattress and the box spring, felt the object, drew it out.

The date book's leather surface bore the quilted imprint of the mattress that had pressed down on it.

She ran her hand across the cover, tapped the straining clasp that held the book shut.

Glancing at the impassive bathroom door again, she unsnapped the clasp, opened the book.

She noticed something strange right away. There were no pencils or pens at all in the date book, nothing, in fact, with which to write.

In a way, that didn't surprise her. Josh always seemed to be without a pen, as she'd learned on countless trips to the grocery store, where he was never able to find one to write a check.

Not knowing what else to do, she flipped to that day's date.

The shower stopped.

She saw three lines of Josh's neat, blocky handwriting before she closed the book, shoved it back underneath the mattress.

December 19
7 a.m.
Mel peeks—shame on her!

10 a.m.
Get an X-Mas bonus today!

Then below that:
7 p.m.
Mel and I go out to dinner.

As the doorknob turned, Melinda slid quickly into bed, tousled the bed covers around her.

Josh walked out with a towel tied around his waist.

"Hi. Getting up?"

"Sure," she answered nervously.

He bent and kissed her, tousled her hair.

"Come on, sleepy head, rise and shine, or we'll both be late."

Melinda stood, acting sleepier then she was, and shuffled to the bathroom.

"If you're that tired, maybe you should wake up a little earlier in the morning, have a cup of coffee...

Catch up on a little reading."

She turned, too shocked to pretend otherwise.

Josh smiled at her, a gentle smirk.

She said nothing as she entered the bathroom and closed the door.

* * *

"So, you finally did it," laughed Jeannie, on the other end of the phone.

"My curiosity got the better of me," sighed Melinda. "I figured a quick peek wouldn't hurt anything."

"Anything juicy?"

"He'd written 'Melinda peaks—shame on her!' and something about a Christmas bonus and a surprise dinner tonight," she answered, goose bumps rippling across her arms. "He gave me a funny look after he got out of the shower. As if he had seen me do it."

"He's pulling your leg, Mel, playing with you because you won't ask."

"I don't know..." she said. There was something so confident, so knowing in the way he looked at me.

"Why don't you just ask him? I mean, you two are married. No secrets and everything, right?"

"No, that's none of my business."

"So, you'll peek, but you won't ask?" Jeannie snorted. "I still say he's playing a joke on you. You should get back at him. When he tells you about dinner tonight, tell him you don't want to go."

"That would be cruel."

"You'll go. But let him stew a little, just like he's letting you stew. Have a little fun, for god's sake."

"Maybe you're right," said Melinda, relaxing. Josh's look this morning had been playful. Maybe it was a joke.

"And if you're still curious about what's in the damn book, ask him. Oh, gotta go! Here comes my boss. Merry Christmas!"

* * *

"I have good news!" Josh beamed as he walked through the door of their apartment that evening. He set the date book down onto the table in the foyer, shrugged out of his topcoat.

He pecked her on the cheek, and she flinched imperceptibly at the touch of his lips.

Melinda repeated the words coldly in her mind as he said them.

"I got a Christmas bonus today! A pretty big one!"

She told herself that it could still be a joke. Josh could have known he was getting a bonus for weeks and written it in the date book.

But he hadn't said anything, never even hinted at it.

And that wasn't like Josh.

If Josh were to play a joke, Melinda realized, this was not the kind of joke he would play.

"I thought we'd celebrate a little—the holidays and the bonus. I made reservations at Carta Blanca at eight."

She suddenly felt very manipulated, joke or not.

"I don't think I feel like going tonight."

The look of sheer incomprehension that spread across his face almost made her laugh.

Almost made her cry.

"I made plans." He shook his head as if trying to dislodge something.

"I don't feel like going out to dinner tonight. Maybe tomorrow."

Josh stood there for a moment with his mouth open, and Melinda noticed his face begin to flush. He didn't seem angry, just shaken.

You don't get this upset just because someone doesn't want to go to dinner, she thought.

'You've got to go. I mean, I planned it," he said softly.

Unconsciously, like a child reaching for a favorite blanket, he grabbed the date book behind him without turning, clutched it to his chest, fumbled with it.

"I'm sorry, honey, but not tonight, okay?"

Josh merely stared at her, and Melinda almost wavered.

But she saw again how he hugged the date book to his chest, how his fingers stroked its leather binding.

Melinda went into the bedroom, left him standing in the hallway staring at where she'd been standing.

* * *

The next morning, Josh rose early and left for work without her, a sure indication, she supposed, that he was angry. Melinda had never really seen him angry, probably because life had never given him a reason to be.

His departure left her without a way to get to work, but she felt a little queasy anyway—and it was only a day or two before Christmas. So she called in sick and spent the morning in bed.

He had a right to be mad, she told herself. *Josh has never done anything to hurt me, to deceive me. If the only thing that comes between us is a date book, I'm lucky.*

And besides, she heard Jeannie's voice in her mind, *if you're that goddamn curious, ask him!*

Melinda rose about 10 a.m., showered and dressed quickly. On her way to the kitchen, she noticed the Christmas tree lights were on. That softened her heart, because she knew Josh must have done that for her before he left that morning. He knew that she loved to stare at the flickering, colored lights on the tree. Josh always joked that it would have to do until they had a fireplace.

In the kitchen, she made coffee and sat looking at the twinkling Christmas tree.

Maybe I am beginning to obsess about his date book.

But another part of her, and it was becoming more strident every day, told her that something was going on.

Something was not right.

She wondered if she'd done the right thing in marrying Josh so quickly. How much did she really know about him?

He'd come from Chicago, that much she knew. His parents were dead, and he was an only child.

Aside from that, she realized, she *didn't* know very much about him.

And, my, wasn't it beginning to get cold in here?

When they got married, everything Josh owned was packed into about a dozen boxes and tucked away in a corner of the storage area in the basement of their apartment complex.

Melinda put the coffee down, bit her lip.

Maybe there was something in those boxes that would shed a little light onto whatever was going on.

That wouldn't be as bad as peeking into his date book, she rationalized. Because whatever was in those boxes was just stuff.

And now his stuff, as Jeannie would say, was her stuff.

* * *

Melinda entered the storage area through a heavy, locked door.

This was not a place she came to often; they kept little here of any real value. Besides, it scared her to be in this dark, dank and windowless chamber.

A small corridor wound around a maze of tiny rooms walled in chicken wire. The bare bulb cast just enough light to create vague, ominous shadows.

Couches whose prints were woefully out of style; ancient, hulking TVs; moving boxes filled with goods long forgotten; and anonymous shapes draped with yellowed sheets were the common items here. In several of the rooms, exercise equipment peeked from their owner's embarrassed attempts to hide them here, away from everyone's sight, like the family's deranged aunt.

Melinda felt the heat of the small key she clasped, walked quickly to their enclosure. The key slipped into the padlock, and the warped door lurched open. Inside were Josh's old mattress and box spring, a few broken lamps, and a stack of boxes marked '*Josh's Things.*'

Melinda rocked the top box on one of the stacks to test its weight. It wasn't very heavy, so she brought it down to the floor.

The box was thick with dust and sealed with wide, overlapping strips of packing tape.

The key's jagged teeth ripped through the tape quickly, and she peeled back the box flaps onto wadded newspaper. Plunging her hands inside, her fingers closed around something so unexpected that she felt around for a moment longer before drawing it out into the insufficient light.

A brick.

She stared dumbly at it for a minute before setting it atop one of the other boxes and searching through the newspaper again.

Another brick.

Then a third.

She picked the box up—it was very light now—and dumped its contents. Nothing but crumpled paper.

Suddenly, the room seemed much smaller, the air close and heavy.

She pulled another box from the stack—funny how the weight shifted uncertainly inside—and dropped it to the floor.

It, too, was filled with newspaper and three bricks.

"Shit."

Grabbing another box, she shook it.

It felt like the first two, so she tossed it aside.

And the next.

And so on through the next five boxes, until she reached the bottom three boxes.

The first one was very heavy, and she knew she had found something important.

Wielding the key like a razor, she split the box open. Unlike the others, this was filled to the top with something dark. She reached in, touched something cool and smooth and slightly veined.

A familiar smell, soothing and earthy, drifted out.

Leather.

Her dumb hand lifted what her quicker mind already knew was in the box.

Date books.

Dozens of them, all neatly and compactly arranged inside. All alike, all clad in black leather, just like the one Josh carried.

Each book had a date stamped on its spine.

The box was stacked two deep with them, dating back to 1989.

Melinda selected a year at random—2003—and pulled it out, rifled through it.

Hundreds of entries in Josh's precise handwriting filled the narrow-ruled lines of the book, some interesting and some mundane, as one would find in any such book.

Then, she saw something that made every hair on her body stand straight up.

It was an entry dated August 24, 2003.

Melinda has her first interview with P&S.

She dropped the book, pushed away from the boxes.

In August 2003, right out of college, Melinda replied to an ad in the newspaper for a position at Pratt & Singer. She had three interviews before she was hired.

This was two years before she met Josh.

Melinda took a deep, gulping breath, pressed her hands against her temples.

She took the job at Pratt & Singer a few days after their offer, which came about a day after her final interview.

Scooting back over to the book, she counted forward mentally, flipped through it to find the date.

When she found it, she began to cry.

Melinda accepts job—of course!

28

She sat there, covered with dust, and cried for some time, her stomach a trembling knot inside her.

How could he have known?

When she had collected herself enough to continue, she looked at the other two boxes.

A chill swept through her, made her teeth chatter.

She crawled to the two unopened boxes, hesitated.

Selecting one at random, she scored the tape with her key, ripped it open.

Inside, she accepted what she saw in a numb, matter-of-fact way.

Of course, these date books each bore a year on their spine as well.

Beginning with next year.

Calmly, Melinda extracted a book from the box, flipped it open.

Of course, it already had entries in it.

She dropped the book back into the box, knelt before it, thought of two things.

The look on Josh's face when she decided not to go to dinner last night.

Shock. Disbelief. As if something fundamental had shifted, gravity ceased to function or the sun no longer rose in the east.

The night of her wedding, at the reception.

I have it all planned.

She looked at the boxes, two opened, one still sealed.

"You certainly did."

Melinda glanced at her watch. 1:30 in the afternoon.

Josh would be home around 6 p.m.

Realizing that she needed time to think about all of this, she grabbed a few books at random out of the second box and quickly left the storage area, locking the mess behind her.

* * *

Upstairs in the kitchen, Melinda had another cup of coffee and a few more surprises.

The ones that stayed with her the most, though, burned their dates into her mind.

March 17
4 p.m.
Melinda finds out we're pregnant! (It's a boy—of course.)

October 30
10:31 a.m.
It's a boy! Kevin Michael Brandeis. 8 lbs. 6 oz. 23 inches.

November 17
7 a.m.
Mel's doctor appointment—bad news. Cancer.

November 24
9:30 a.m.
Cancer has metastasized. Mel doesn't have long.

January 3
8 a.m.
Stay up all night with Mel. Slipping fast. Chemo not helping.

January 15
9:47 p.m.
Mel dies.

Melinda read about her own death next year with a curious, detached shock.

Just like that, occupying no more room or emotion than a lunch meeting or an appointment to have the car's oil changed.

Written in a date book more than a year in advance.

Something else caught her eye, too.

Something that, even after reading about her own death, struck Melinda as much more sinister.

April 16
8 a.m.
Rachel has her first interview with Braxton-Montgomery Inc.

When Melinda first read this entry, it aroused a twinge of jealousy.

Then, however, she remembered an entry she'd read earlier downstairs.

August 24
8 a.m.
Melinda has her first interview with P&S.

He planned them. Planned them all.

Right here in the pages of these damn date books!

She would love him, marry him, bear him a son, die.

Meanwhile, unbeknownst to either woman, wife No. 2 waited in the wings.

If, indeed, Melinda was wife No. 1.

But was Josh causing these events by writing them down? Or did he write them down because, somehow, he knew they were going to happen?

Neither of these explanations was satisfactory; neither was believable.

For a long time, Melinda simply held her cold coffee cup tightly and stared at the flickering lights of the Christmas tree in the living room, wondering what to do.

Confront him? Ignore it all? Divorce him?

The whirlwind that had been their relationship seemed like it was collapsing in on itself, spinning onto its center.

It was all too much to ingest in one afternoon.

When she looked at the clock next, it was 4 p.m.

Josh would be home in two hours.

That mess needed to be cleaned up before he returned.

Stacking the books in a pile, Melinda was struck by a sudden thought.

What if I wrote something in one of these books?

She returned the books to the box they were in originally, carefully resealed them all with packing tape.

The bricks, too, were replaced in their nests of wadded paper, sealed in their boxes.

When she left the storage room, the heavy door booming shut behind her, Melinda had only one thing in her hand.

The book for next year.

* * *

The party swirled around the house, spilled out onto the wide, Spanish-tiled patio, skirted the edges of the pool.

People mixed and mingled, laughter erupted here and there over the locust-drone of conversation, liquor and food were abundant, and the music was too loud.

All and all, it was a great party.

Outside, on the edge of the motion, Melinda stood alone, nursing the same margarita she'd held onto all night. A black dress, slim and made up of more cutaways than silk, shimmered in the reflected light of the torches.

Her eyes moved slowly around the expansive backyard, following a single figure as he made his way through the throng, talking, drinking, laughing.

Josh.

She smiled when she caught his eye.

I love you, he mouthed.

"I love you, too," she said aloud, though he was too far away to hear.

He disappeared into the crowd, and she stared at the spot where he had stood.

Five years, she thought. *Has it really been that long already?*

The promotions, the cars, the new house...

"Great party!" said a voice, whispering directly into her ear.

Melinda jumped a bit, sloshing margarita away from her onto the tile.

31

"Sorry," laughed Jeannie, grabbing her arm to steady her. "Didn't mean to wake you up."

"No," Melinda answered quickly. "Just snuck up on me, that's all. Having fun?"

Jeannie paused in mid slurp, gestured with her glass back to the house. "Rich is inside keeping a group of people either totally enthralled or mindlessly bored with his views on health care litigation—it's hard to say. You tell me."

"Well, I think it's going well," Melinda answered.

"Was he surprised? I know I'd be, if Rich did anything half as romantic for our fifth anniversary."

"Oh, he knew about it. I scheduled it way in advance. Even wrote it down in his date book just to make sure he wouldn't forget," Melinda said, draining the lukewarm, salty remains of her drink and setting the empty glass onto a nearby table.

Screams and laughter erupted from a knot of people gathered around the pool.

"Ahh, yes. The date book," intoned Jeannie. "I've always wanted to know how you got that away from him."

Melinda smiled at the question, at the memory.

"It wasn't easy. I take care of all of his appointments, his meetings, everything. He's got me, so he doesn't need to worry."

From the slightly overlarge, sequined evening bag she held like a football in the crook of her arm, she produced a date book that looked like every date book Josh had carried with him.

"He might not carry it with him anymore, but you certainly never seem to be parted from it," Jeannie laughed, swiping a flute of champagne from a tray that bobbed past them. "Well, he's a changed man, that's for sure. Ever since you got that thing away from him, he's been so... fun."

"Yes," said Melinda, her eyes finding Josh again in the crowd. Hands were grabbing him, lifting him. He was laughing hysterically, trying to escape.

"But I'm worried about you, though," Jeannie said softly.

"Hey, don't worry about me. I've got it all planned, remember?"

In the distance, Josh arced above the light of the tiki torches scattered around the patio, fell into the pool tuxedo and all with a tremendous splash, more screams, and a round of applause.

Melinda smiled again—too broad, too much teeth—lightly punched Jeannie's arm, moved away to get another drink.

Jeannie was quick to notice that Melinda had unconsciously gathered the date book to her as she left, enfolded it in her arms where it melted dark and seamless into the black of her dress.

* * *

Later, much later, that night, Melinda sat before a mirror at her vanity table, gathered her hair in a bun, rubbed her makeup off.

Josh came out of the bathroom, snuck up behind her, shook his wet head like a dog's.

"Hey!" she cried, jumping as droplets of cold water fell onto her.

"Surprise!" he yelled, kissing the top of her head. "Happy anniversary, and thanks for the party."

"Thanks, yourself," she huffed in mild annoyance. "Now, go and dry yourself off."

Josh moved back into the bathroom, came back out with a limp and sodden clump of clothing.

"I don't know if we'll be able to salvage this," he said, smiling at her in a naive, boyish way that melted her heart, as it always did.

It was good, she had decided long ago, to see him this way.

He'd always been so serious, too serious, she thought.

It had taken a great deal of time, patience, and pencil erasers to go through all of those old date books. But she had decided back then that her marriage, as new as it was, was definitely worth fighting for.

And changing those passages may have saved my life.

Admiring him as he stood naked in their bedroom, his hair slicked back, holding the sopping remains of his tuxedo, she knew she had done the right thing.

"You're dripping. Just hang it in the shower, and I'll take it by the dry cleaners tomorrow and see what they say," she said, rising and shooing him away. "And hurry up. It's getting late."

"I'll just be a minute. I want to dry my hair first."

Melinda removed her robe and climbed into bed.

It was a large bed, the kind she had always wanted. Their apartment had been too small for such a bed, but not so this house. She had seen to that.

The covers billowed around her as she made herself comfortable, the whine of the hair dryer coming from the bathroom.

She stretched, rolled over, frowned.

There was a lump in the bed, an ever so slight upraising of the mattress, more on Josh's side than hers.

She rolled back and forth over it, hoping to flatten it out.

It did not flatten.

For a moment, she thought it was the remote, a pair of socks, a misplaced book...

Melinda's heart stopped as she threw the covers off, bounded to the floor on Josh's side.

There, between the mattress and the box spring.

There, cool and textured to the touch.

There, the tiny, straining clasp.

There, when she drew it into the golden light of Josh's reading lamp, the date.

This year.

Her hands shaking, she unsnapped the clasp, fumbled through the pages.

There, the familiar, blocky handwriting.

March 5

2 a.m.

Melinda peeks again. Now, she knows. I've got it all planned. And the plans haven't changed...

Behind her, the sound of the hair dryer had stopped.

The bathroom door opened, and a shadow fell over her.

BUT FOR A MOMENT...
MOTIONLESS

December 31st, and I remember walking... walking the sidewalks of the great city, a great city, any great city.

It is dark, cold, but the lights of the city are remarkable, as colorful as a carnival. People are everywhere, crowding the sidewalks, jostling, moving— always moving.

I have been here before. It seems familiar, even as its unfamiliarity wraps itself around me. I wander as if lost, yet something guides my feet.

The wind is cold, a blunt, frigid wall that pushes me; fingers that tug at my long, dark overcoat, numb my cheeks, my hands. I see other rosy-faced people pass me under the lights, clinging to each other, clutching bags, gifts, bottles. They hold hands, smile as they pass.

I don't truly know where I am, what I'm doing...

... *who I am.*

So, I walk the streets, walk the streets and hope that something will jog my memory, tell me where to go, what to do.

In my mind I see the sky... endless seas of blue, clouds, storms...

I see fire...

I see water...

* * *

January 2nd, and there are no smiling faces to greet me now.

A light snow falls, adheres to the sidewalks, the streets, the dead bodies lying where they fell, sprawled across each other, limbs twisted. It's been two days, and they still aren't rotting... is that right? I mean, does that sound... *natural?*

They're... they seem to be... *drying*... desiccating. Their skin is taut, stretched over bones as the flesh inside dehydrates. They're taking on the look of yellow parchment in old books: stiff like starched shirts. Dried like toads in the sun.

And everywhere, everywhere there is a spicy smell, almost aromatic... of chili peppers and cinnamon.

* * *

Magazines and newspapers flutter in the deserted newsstands, faces on their covers stare back at me with empty, accusatory eyes. I give them no heed. Theirs was a dying medium before any of this happened.

Some places still have power, still have water. I have no idea how long that will last. But while it does, I find myself a nice penthouse apartment on the top of the highest building I can find. From there, I can look over the entire city, stretched below me like a flat, lifeless painting.

It is tastefully, minimally decorated; it was probably the home of a joyless, sexless, childless older couple who had money but little else. Still, the bed is comfortable, the sheets are clean, and the refrigerator is fully stocked, as is the wine cooler.

And there are no dead bodies to dispose of.

When I sleep, I have two dreams.

I am water, and I cover everything.

I am fire, falling from the sky, incinerating all before me.

I just don't know what I am *now.*

* * *

For everything that occurs in our world, large or small, good or bad, there are only two positions available.

You either make it happen or you let it happen.

Sounds harsh, but there it is. If something is important to you, you make it happen.

Everything else, then, you let happen... by inaction, lack of knowledge, lack of importance.

That, then, is what haunts me...

Did I make this happen?

Or did I let this happen?

Either way, I bear the full brunt of its responsibility, the entire burden of its guilt.

For I am the only one left.

* * *

Walking the city that night, December 31st, I remember going to a bar. I met a few people there, young, smiling. We struck up a conversation, and they invited me to a party they were headed to.

New Year's Eve... I told them it sounded fun, and I followed them into the night.

We walked for a long time, down city streets cold and dark and faceless, until we came to a brownstone. People spilled from its doorway onto the steps, onto the street. They were drinking, talking, smoking.

Elbowing our way through the crowd, we entered the house. I was introduced, accepted without question. Drinks were pushed into my hand. The music was loud, unfamiliar, thumping through the air, the floor, up my legs and into my body.

Midnight...

On TV a glowing ball made of lights dropped and people cheered. I kissed a few women, their lips soft and sticky, their breath sweet, patinated with alcohol.

I went home with one of the women I had met in the bar. I held her up part of the way, and she gave me slurred, indistinct directions. I helped her inside, and she pulled me in after her, kissed me, led me to her bedroom.

I kissed her back, and we fumbled with our clothing. The catches and zippers and buttons of what I wore seemed unfamiliar to me.

But I let it happen, let her coax me to her bed, to her...

This I knew... *this* I remembered...

Later, she slept and I could not.

I heard the furnace rushing warm air into the room. I could smell her on the heated air, on my skin, my fingers, my lips.

When I finally did sleep, curled next to her, I dreamt of water: rushing, covering water.

I knew that I was the water.

And I had made it happen before...

* * *

She was dead when I awoke, dead and already smelling of cinnamon.

I tried to rouse her, but she would not awaken.

I used her shower to wash myself, my hair. I brushed my teeth at her sink, with her toothbrush.

In her mirror, I did not recognize my own face, my own body.

I went into her small kitchen, checked the fridge. A few eggs, a quart of milk, some butter, and a lot of little tubs of yogurt. I hardboiled a few eggs in a small pan I found, drank the milk from the container, ate two cups of yogurt.

I cleaned my mess in her kitchen, washed the few dishes I'd used, put them in the rack near the sink. Before I left, I went back into the bedroom, kissed her cheek lightly, told her I was sorry, *so sorry...*

Outside, January 1st, the morning was cold and grey.

On the streets again, I saw that everyone was dead...

... everyone.

* * *

January 18th, and I still have not seen one living person.

I've walked all over the city, from Bedford-Stuy to Manhattan, from the Upper East Side to the Lower West. Nothing. No one.

Almost three weeks in, and most of them are mummified. The dead sprawl on park benches, sit in cars in traffic that will never clear. They clog the restaurants, the bus stops, the subway stations. They block the streets, the sidewalks. They litter the rooftops, the museums, the stores.

The smell, the spicy-sweet smell is everywhere.

But there is no one alive... no one, except me.

Only me.

I realize that what I miss the most, what haunts me the most, is the lack of sound.

There are none of the sounds of the city, the honking cars, the sirens, the feet, the voices, the shouting, the music.

It is silent, deadly, empty silent. Not even the birds chirp.

I long to hear a sound not made by me. The sound of a single voice, the squeal of tires, a few notes of music, even the patter of rain on the sidewalk.

But there is nothing...

* * *

January 30th, and, as always, I am absorbed with a delicate thought.

It is how poetry has indefinite sensations to which end, music is an essential. Since the comprehension of sweet sound is our most indefinite conception.

Music, when combined with a pleasurable idea, is poetry.

Music without the idea is simply music.

Without music or an intriguing idea, *color* becomes *pallor.*

Man becomes *carcass*.

Home becomes *catacomb*.

And the dead are, but for a moment, motionless...

... *motionless*.

These are not my words, I know... I don't know whose they are; that is lost in the recesses like so many other things, so many other pieces. But they have risen in me, risen in my memory...

They seem to fit; they seem to tell me something.

* * *

February 10th, and it has now been 40 days and 40 nights since it happened.

I leave the penthouse, bundled against the cold, for the café.

Inside, I get a start.

There is someone inside... *alive*.

I smell coffee, rich and black... toast... bacon...

He sits at my table, two plates before him.

Turning slowly, he smiles, and my heart warms instantly, as if plunged into hot water. My bones thaw, my cheeks flush with blood. I close my eyes and wait for the sound of his voice.

"Good morning," he says, and his voice is low, rumbled, deep. He gestures to the seat opposite his, and I remove my coat, let it drop absently to the floor, sit.

On the plate are two fried eggs, several strips of perfectly done bacon, two pieces of toast, cut diagonally. He'd even arranged a sprig of parsley and a slice of orange on the plate. A mug of deep, black coffee sits nearby, steaming.

"I like to try my hand at things every once in a while," he says, lifting a slice of bacon from his own plate and eating it. "Who knew bacon was so tricky? I must have burned an entire pound before you got here."

Saying nothing, content to hear him speak, I begin to eat. He watches me intently, the smile never fading.

"It's hardest on you, I know. I apologize. I know I don't have to, but I do anyway."

He looks at me, and his eyes are gray and moist.

"There are some who bear much of the burden of my work on themselves," he said. "And for that I am sorry... but there is no other way. No other way that I can conceive."

There was something about his voice, something other than the thrill it gave me to hear another's voice after nearly two months.

Then I realize what it is...

I've heard it before.

"Do I know you?" I ask, putting my coffee cup onto the table.

He smiles. "As well as any. I know you, though… better than anyone. I made you."

At that, he lifts his own cup, drinks a swallow, looks from me to the cup as his eyebrow twitches in wonder.

"Father?"

Almost sadly, he nods.

"Yes."

Suddenly the food is tasteless, unwanted.

"Why am I here? Where is everyone? What happened?"

Then, after a pause: "What is the secret I carry?"

"Ahh, dear, you carry too much for one soul to bear. So I cloud it from you so that it doesn't destroy you," he replies, his sad eyes never leaving me.

"You are the water that washes the world, the fire that burns it clean," he sighs. "You are the cover I pull over my work when I cannot look at it any longer. You are my… eraser… my reset button. My knife in the dark."

I shake my head, have no idea what he is saying.

… a horribly clear idea of what he is saying.

"I require a Word to make and another to unmake. You are that final Word, the Omega. The Word of the End."

"Did you give me a name, Father?"

"I call you Uriel. But you have other names… Abaddon, Apollyon, Ragnarok, Armageddon, Apocalypse, Revelation. It is all the same."

"I prefer Uriel."

He smiles ruefully. "So do I, dear, so do I."

I sit for a moment, trying to decide what to say, what question to ask.

Finally: "Did I make this happen? Or did I let it happen?"

He leans in close to me. "What a question… what a discerning question, Uriel. It never fails to amaze me how my Words take on lives of their own, endowing what I have uttered with a richness, a deepness I never anticipated. You transcend my intent."

"You didn't answer my question," I reply, after a long moment.

"No," he agrees, reaching to pat my cheek with his hand. "There is no answer to your question. You are my Word, you see, the articulation of my need, my creation. You were uttered for a single purpose, and you fulfill that purpose as intended."

"That is still no answer, Father."

He nods, takes another sip of his coffee. "The question implies a starkness that cannot be answered directly. You are a paradox, in your design, in your intent, in your purpose. You both make and let, if you will."

"I *made* this happen… *this?*" I ask, throwing my arms wide to indicate all that was around us.

"Yes, you are the Word of the End, and you made this. *Unmade* this, at it were. As you have done before… as you will do again."

"But I also *let* this happen?" I say, tears coming to my eyes unbidden, unwanted.

"Yes," he answers, softly. "Yes, you let it happen, too."

"How?" I wept now, tears streaming down my face, dropping onto my half-eaten food.

"Into each of my Words, I must allow for free will," he said. "Every Word I utter has within it the ability to decide for itself what to do, how to enact my will. It is the only way that I can achieve what I desire for my creations."

"And I... I was water once, I was fire?"

"Yes. Water, fire, ice. You have been these things for me and more. You have allowed me to begin again, to hone my creation, to breathe new life into it. Yours is a purpose greatly to be desired... greatly to be mourned."

I scrub my tears away, suddenly ashamed.

"And this time?"

"This time a small thing: a virus. You traveled the world, infecting all whom you met, touched, passed. They took that part of you and passed it on, a torch lighting other torches."

"Until all the world was aflame."

"Yes."

I hang my head, try to clear my thoughts, organize them.

"And now?"

"Now, I wait. I bide. Time will pass, the earth will forget, and I will start anew. See what I can achieve this time," he answers, drinking the last of his coffee.

"And me?"

"You carry my secret, the secret of the Word of the End. You carry it, and it is you."

"I am a tool?"

"You are my Word... one of an infinite number."

"And you will... utter me again?"

He nods.

"But you say I can choose... choose... to not *let* it happen again... to not *make* it happen?"

Again, he nods.

"And if I do?"

"All things serve my purpose in the end. It is the nature of the Word, and the great paradox of free will."

"I had a choice this time?"

"Yes."

I shake my head, and the tears fall again.

"This is why the Word is secret to you. Its burden comes at a price too dear. Oh, Uriel, if I could, I would lift this from you, take it upon myself."

"Why don't you then? Why curse me with this terrible purpose?"

"I cannot *un-utter* what I have uttered. And I cannot take your purpose upon myself. If I reached in to perform your purpose, I would destroy everything... not just this, but the All. That I cannot do."

I lower my head to the table and weep.

I feel his hand upon my head, stroking my hair gently.

"But I can keep the secret, Uriel. I can take away its knowledge from you, remove it. And you can return or stay here, unhindered by the truth of the Word. I can do this for you."

I lift my head, look at him through blurry eyes.

"And you have done this for me before... after each time?"

"Yes."

I thought a moment. "No. I wish to keep the secret of the Word. I wish to know its purpose and decide for myself the next time."

He smiles at me, knowingly, and wipes my tears away.

"Dear Uriel," he says. "What will you do now?"

I consider that, having not considered it before.

"I will stay," I answer, not terribly sure of my answer, whether he will allow this.

"You will be lonely," he says. "Until I speak the new Word... the Word of Making. Again."

He stands, takes my hand, lifts me to my feet. Then he draws me into an embrace, and I feel his breath against my neck. It is the breath of the Word, the breath of creation.

Releasing me, he steps back, looks once, wistfully I think, at the coffee cup, then leaves, walks out the door, down the street.

I go to the front window and watch him walk two blocks, then turn a corner.

I step outside, and it is warm, sunny. No longer January, no longer winter, but spring. I hear birds sing, feel a cool breeze tousle my hair.

And all the bodies are gone, vanished, removed.

Cleaned away...

Their stuff remains... the cars, the roads, the buildings... but I know that these, too, will disappear over time. He's merely tidied up the place a bit.

For me.

I step onto the sidewalk, breathe in, feel refreshed, renewed somehow.

The knowledge of the secret energizes me, while it also causes me guilt, pain.

I am his Word... yet I also have free will to do what I choose.

In a way, I am my own Word, too.

I decide, on a whim, not to head back to the penthouse apartment I'd been staying in.

I will leave this city, seek another... see the world once more as it was.

A flash catches my eye, a movement to my right.

My reflection in the café's plate glass window.

My aspect has come upon me with the knowledge he's bestowed.

I unfurl them to their entire span, and they burn white in the sunshine, each feather iridescent, pearly white. The *whoosh* of the air as they move, the jump of my muscles is intensely familiar to me.

Lifting slowly from my feet, I soar into the air, climb above the great, dead city, see its immaculate design, its layout, its straight-edged form, its organic sprawl. I see the way the sun plays on the buildings, how shadows fall in the canyons between.

I made this.

I let this be.

I go higher, arc my body toward the west, toward newer cities, distant cities.

And promise myself that next time, it will be different.

Next time I will choose.

I give my word on it...

THE
WATER BEARER

Jim was the kind of neighbor who never said too much; a wave when he saw you outside, maybe a few polite, friendly words at the mailbox, or when you caught him outdoors as he puttered in his well-kept yard, but little more.

The year is 1947, and Jim, oh, he must have been at least 80 years old. Never married but in good health, his back slightly stooped, his legs bowed.

My wife and I live in newly built suburban home, bought with money from a GI loan. That was supposed to pay me back for the year I'd spent tramping through the muddy fields of France and Germany, living with an ever-dwindling group of men, sleeping wherever I fell, and shooting at—and being shot at by—people I couldn't even understand.

Now here I was with three suits in my closet, a new Chevrolet in the garage, a kid who had been born while I moved through the dark trees of the Ardennes, and a young wife I barely knew. It was an adjustment for all concerned.

This spring, though, we had begun to settle in, to make our peace with our long separation. We had begun to find a rhythm.

The young, tender grass was taking root, the few trees just sending out their first, tentative leaves. Yet, for the most part, the defining color was still brown.

The only green at all was a small pond that lay in a natural depression in the middle of the common ground, which our house—and Jim's—backed up to. A ring of trees surrounded it, and its banks wore a mane of cattails and waterweeds that rustled in the wind.

I said the neighborhood was mostly brown, but that wasn't all true. Jim's yard was the exception. It was a dazzling green jewel amidst the rough. The grass was lush and thick in his yard, flowerbeds burst with unexpected color, and he had planted trees—*real* trees, taller than a man, as a tree should be—and they provided the only pools of shade on the entire street.

Jim spent about an hour every morning when the sun was cool watering his plants, pruning, mowing with an ancient push mower, clipping this and clearing that. Then, he'd disappear into his house.

It was on a Friday, as I recall. I had just closed a pretty good sale and phoned Sarah to tell her to start the grill. I picked up a couple of expensive steaks and a good bottle of wine, and we were going to celebrate.

I swept into the house, kissed Sarah and little Billie, then took my station out in the backyard to grill dinner. A few beers before, some wine with dinner, and we were pretty loose.

Sarah and I were still making up for lost time, and we didn't even try to make it back to our bed. We turned off the lights, fumbled with buttons and hooks and belts, and I pulled her to me there on the living room couch.

When I awoke, I was confused for a moment, uncertain of where I was. I didn't move for fear of a bullet. After a minute, I decided I was home.

I pulled myself from Sarah without waking her, dressed, found my pack of cigarettes and a book of matches. I crept outside in bare feet to smoke.

The night was brilliantly lit by a three-quarter moon low on the horizon. Its muscular light swept away the stars.

Cupping my hands against the evening breeze, I struck a match, lit my cigarette, took a few deep puffs. Exhaling, I saw another star, this one close to the ground and glowing red-orange.

A lean shadow sat on the steps of Jim's back door, rolled the star between its fingers.

"Evening," he said in his gravelly, amiable voice as he saw me. "Fine night for a smoke."

"Sure is."

"Just thought I'd come out here and stare at that old pond. It's been preying on my mind, you know."

What he said was so unexpected, so enigmatic, that I found myself walking the short distance between our yards to stand near him.

He looked at me with rheumy eyes, and I smelled tobacco, beer, but mostly musty age.

"That old puddle bothering you, Jim?"

Pulling on his cigarette, he looked away. "Yes, sir. Why tear out everything that took so long to *grow*, and leave something like that; something that just... *filled up?*"

He took three long drags from his cigarette and let the smoke gather around his head, blue and diaphanous.

"It's just a pond, Jim. It's not even that deep."

"Doesn't matter," he growled. "Water is water, and that's all there is to it."

I began to feel that maybe it was best that Jim never spoke much. He was getting on in years, and maybe he was a bit senile or becoming peculiar in his ways. I began to regret my decision to walk over and talk with him that night.

"Mosquitoes in spring. Bad smells in summer. Ugly in fall, frozen over in winter. You got kids, don't you?" he asked, fixing me with a hard stare.

"A little boy."

"That's the worst. Little boys are into everything. He'll be over there like a shot. Should have it drained."

I shrugged noncommittally. I mean, the pond was no more than three maybe four feet deep, and that's after a heavy rain.

Jamming his cigarette back into his mouth, he inhaled. The ember flared, lit his craggy face. "You're too smart to believe that's the real reason, though. Well, you're right. I have another reason, a *real* reason, but that's another story."

He stubbed the fading butt onto his steps, dropped it into an old coffee can at his feet. I could hear his joints creak as he rose, held out his hand.

"Good night," he said, and I shook his hand. He gave the pond one last, disgusted glance, turned to go inside.

Sarah still slept on the couch, the moon shimmering on her naked skin. I closed the door quietly.

As I did, I saw the moonlight sparkling on the water of the pond.

And for a moment, brief and shivery, it was bone-white beautiful.

* * *

"Do you believe a *place*, a spot of earth can be bad? Like a person, I mean."

This was two nights later, when I had awakened and felt the urgent need to pee and smoke, in that order. Pulling on a pair of pants and a t-shirt, I tiptoed outside and lit up.

Jim had been out there a while, and, again, he waited until I noticed him to call me over.

44

"Sure, I believe that," I answered in surprise, as he popped open a beer and handed it to me. It was this simple, neighborly act that surprised me, not the question.

I *had* been in such places—*felt* them—several times during my war years; in a back alley of a Paris slum, in a little clearing near the edge of the Ardennes, and again as I filed past the ruins of the Reichstag in Berlin, even after the Russians had systematically destroyed it.

There are places that, like canker sores or abscesses on the face of the earth, both breed and attract evil.

Jim nodded his head gently. "You also believe there are places good for balance. Everything in life is a balance. And that's the old part of me talking."

"I suppose that's true, as well."

"Now what if I were to tell you that it's possible to hurt a good place, just like you can hurt a good person?"

"How could you hurt a place?"

"Same way you'd hurt a person… spurn it. You can't hurt a bad place or a bad person. They're as hurt as they'll ever be. Oh, you can piss 'em off."

"Okay," I answered.

He gave my dubious response a dubious look, as if he might suddenly clam up; as if getting me to see this connection were vital. But he obviously wanted to tell his story.

"When you hurt a person deeply enough, even a very good person, sometimes that person will want to hurt you back," he proceeded after a minute. "It's just so with a place, even a very good place.

"I knew such a place once. It was a pool of water very much like that one over there," he said, swiping his hand toward the dark little smudge that was the pond.

Then he opened up like some terrifying night-blooming flower.

And he told his story, scattering it like dark pollen, just as I have set it down here.

* * *

It was 1923, the height of Prohibition and bathtub gin, Irving Berlin and jazz.

Already Hollywood was flickering across America, and radio was beaming to homes everywhere. The last great agricultural century, the momentous 19th, had finally given way to the gleaming, ferocious 20th.

For men like Jim, men who'd been boys during the country's reconstruction, who had participated in the great mythic West, it was a sad time, a lost time.

Old even then, Jim had been moving from flophouse to flophouse for several years, taking temporary jobs, all the while unconsciously moving east.

He stopped moving for a day or two when he reached Bonne Terre, a mining town south of St. Louis. He'd been born in St. Louis, and, like a salmon, I suppose, he had made it his goal to return there before he died.

While in Bonne Terre, though, he heard of a wealthy gentleman seeking to hire a man to maintain his house and grounds. Outdoor work had always appealed to Jim, and he went out to the man's property, a few miles from town, and applied for the job with a Mr. Krieger, the lawyer who was managing the man's affairs.

He was hired on the spot, paid a week in advance. That afternoon, he moved his meager possessions to the groundskeeper's cabin, set off from the main house behind a copse of dense evergreens.

The owner of the property, he was told by Mr. Krieger, was a young doctor, recently widowed. Wealthy by the measure of the day, the doctor had simply quit his practice, bought this land, and come out here to rebuild his shattered life.

Krieger gave Jim a tour of the house, not overly large or opulent, but seemingly a palace to Jim, introduced him to Grace, the housekeeper and cook.

"What about the owner?" Jim asked. "Will I meet him?"

Krieger gave Jim a sympathetic look. "Dr. Wilson is... a very private man. I'm sure you'll see him sometime, but as to when, I wouldn't guess."

* * *

It was an entire month before Jim saw Dr. Evander Wilson. Jim had made friends with Grace and had settled into a routine of having his meals with her, working alone, retiring early to his separate living space.

Jim didn't take long to get the lawn and garden in order, either. He spent a day or two organizing everything in the work shed, then another few days planning what plants he'd need and where he'd put them.

Two weeks later, everything was planted, the lawn was freshly clipped, and Jim was pruning hedges and bushes near the house.

He stopped to drink from a glass of lemonade Grace had brought him earlier.

A shadow fell over him, though, startling him enough to slosh cold liquid down the front of his shirt.

"Sorry," came a quiet voice, and Jim turned to see Dr. Wilson.

The doctor was young, not much older than 30, with pale skin, brown hair, and large, brilliant eyes behind wire spectacles. He was dressed simply in a pair of khaki trousers and a white shirt with the sleeves rolled up.

Thin and sinewy, Dr. Wilson still seemed puffed up to Jim—not with pride or vanity, mind you, but with something held in.

"Dr. Wilson, sir," said Jim, holding out his hand. "A pleasure to meet you."

Wilson took Jim's calloused hand in his own smooth, elegant hand, shook it lightly. "Yes, Mr. Krieger told me about you. You've certainly done a splendid job with the lawn."

The doctor left him to his work, walked slowly around the house and into the woods, where he vanished in the mid-afternoon shade.

Jim did not see him again for a week.

* * *

When he did, Dr. Wilson nearly ran him down.

Jim was preparing to trim the lawn, when Wilson bounded around the corner and into him.

"Good lord, man, I'm sorry," he apologized, grabbing Jim by the shoulders and holding him steady. "Are you okay?"

"Yes, sir," breathed Jim, but the truth was that Dr. Wilson had startled him.

He wasn't the same man Jim had met a week ago. He was energetic, ebullient.

"Well, catch your breath, Jim," Wilson said, still gripping his shoulders. "It looks as if I didn't break any bones."

"No, sir."

"Then I'm off. Good day to you!"

And with that, Wilson dashed off into the woods.

Jim noticed, as his breathing returned to normal, that the doctor wore a bulging backpack, and he remembered Grace telling him several days ago that the doctor had been returning from God only knew where with wet clothing.

Probably found himself a swimming hole, mused Jim, then returned to his work.

* * *

Off and on for the next few weeks, as late spring gave way to the heart of summer, Jim saw Dr. Wilson a few more times. And each time, it seemed as if he were more alive, more energized, more *there,* in a fundamental sense.

Dr. Wilson even began taking breakfast and dinner at regular hours in the dining room. Most evenings he sat reading in the parlor before retiring to bed early.

But always in the afternoon he disappeared, his pack bulging with a change of clothes and a lunch put up by Grace.

And the longer this went on, the more curious Jim grew.

The truth was that Jim was beginning to find life there dull. His duties were easy and quickly accomplished, leaving him with much of each day to himself. He'd begun reading books from Dr. Wilson's library, but increasingly he felt the need to stretch his legs... and satisfy his curiosity.

So one morning after breakfast, he asked Grace if she wouldn't mind putting up a lunch for him, as he was determined to take a hike that morning.

Jim knocked around in the yard until he saw Dr. Wilson leave for his afternoon excursion. Quickly putting away his tools, Jim dashed to the house, grabbed his lunch, and set out after the doctor.

He stayed well behind the doctor as they made their way through the dark, cool woods, but he didn't hide. Dr. Wilson never once turned, though, never slowed, just pushed forward at a leisurely pace, whistling as he went.

Following him over the rolling, densely wooded land, Jim quickly found himself out of breath, sweating. Pacing himself, he let the doctor pull ahead of him a little way, as his joints began to protest.

Down a small, rocky slope and around a stand of trees thickly clogged with young saplings, Jim drew to a panting halt. Cursing and wheezing, he turned around, but the doctor was nowhere to be seen.

Just then, there came a loud whooping cry, followed by a splash.

Jim spun and heard the glissando of raining water from behind a hillock dotted with wildflowers. Cautiously, he moved toward it, climbed to its crest.

There below him, nestled amid a circlet of massive, old trees, was a small pond, no more than 20 feet across. The trees hemmed it in closely, but all around there was a narrow, grassy bank wide enough to sit or lay upon.

One side of the little pool was crowned with cattails. The trees, twisted, gnarled and moss-slicked, dipped their roots into the pool like tentative bathers.

The pool must have been fed by a spring, for the water was burnished silver, not at all stagnant or green or weed-choked.

Within the pool, Wilson floated, occasionally ducking below the surface, rising again in a blast of spray and breath.

Jim hunkered behind one of the trees, watched the man drift lazily atop the water. Clouds sailed around him, mirrored on the water, so silver it almost seemed a pool of mercury; so reflective that, below its surface, Wilson's body disappeared.

It was quiet here, so Jim unpacked the lunch Grace had made him—a hardboiled egg, a cold beef and cheese sandwich, a pickle, and a clutch of purple grapes—and ate, as Wilson slept atop the water's surface.

When he was done, a wave of drowsiness overcame him, too. Without another thought, he leaned against the willow behind him and drifted into a peaceful, contented sleep.

* * *

The sun had begun its slow downward arc into night when he awoke.

Stretching, he disentangled himself from several long, thin willow branches that had draped themselves amiably over him, coiled possessively around his shoulders.

Looking down, he saw Wilson sleeping on the banks of the pond. He was completely nude, Jim noticed, and his clothes were scattered around him as if he had been in haste to remove them.

Jim would have turned away then, headed for home before the doctor himself awakened, but for one thing.

The water began to *move*.

Blinking rapidly to clear his eyes, Jim gaped as the silver coin of the pool elongated, seemed to stretch toward Dr. Wilson. As he watched, the water slid beneath the doctor's sleeping form, lifted him from the earth, brought him back into the pond.

Slowly, sensuously, Wilson was enfolded by the water: first his limbs, then his chest, then his face, smiling as the waters received him.

Jim leapt to his feet in alarm, prepared to descend the hill and leap into the water to rescue the doctor. But just as he pushed away from the willow, Wilson broke the surface of the water, rose into the gold afternoon sun, wreathed in a million silver spangles.

And he cried out from a mouth dripping argent sparks.

Jim had heard cries like that before, coming through the thin walls of a whorehouse, floating on the night air from the edges of a cattle drive camp.

Wilson bobbed on the water for several seconds, his face serene and content. Then, with a seemingly mighty effort, he swam ashore, pulled himself out of the water. Grabbing his shirt, he toweled off, dressed languidly in the clothes from his pack.

As he dressed, Jim gathered his debris, silently left the little glade so that he would be sure to get home before the doctor.

* * *

Dr. Wilson's mood heightened daily, and he became a fixture, both at home and in town. He began entertaining, holding dinner parties, inviting Mr. Krieger, his partners and their wives over for coffee. On occasional evenings, he would even play a game or two of rummy with Grace and Jim.

He also began courting a widowed woman, who, coincidentally, ran the town's pharmacy for her dead husband.

As Dr. Wilson seemed to come into himself, his visits to the pond grew infrequent, until they tapered off entirely.

Once he was sure that Dr. Wilson was completely occupied with the new woman in his life, that he wasn't making trips to the pond any longer, Jim made plans to revisit it himself.

The day Jim chose was during the waning of that summer, when the morning starts out teasingly cool before the sun reasserts its dominance, and the air itself seems to melt.

He ate a hurried breakfast, packed himself a light lunch, wandered into the yard. Taking his time, he pushed into the dense undergrowth of the woods, picking the narrow path that had been worn by Dr. Wilson on his previous trips.

Jim felt like a kid again, about to do something that was equal parts fun and forbidden. Impatience bubbled up within him, and he increased his pace.

It was not difficult to find this time. He paused at the base of the hillock, took a deep breath, climbed to its top.

The scene that greeted him was not as he remembered.

The pond had shrunk under the hot caress of the sun, leaving a wide margin of thick, black ooze that faded into a lighter, scabby mud. The water huddled in the middle of this was brackish and thick, clotted with waterweeds and algae.

Bedraggled cattails slumped against one another on the far end, and even the trees seemed to lean away from the remains of the little pool.

Jim nearly gagged on the stench, a hot, rich miasma of decay, as he stood, flabbergasted, on the crest of the hill.

But more than that… he felt something unlike what he had experienced there before. Then, he had felt a seductive atmosphere clinging to the glade: a becalmed, lazy sort of sensuality.

Now, however, all he felt was hurt and betrayal and a lingering, seething layer of resentment. He felt this all in the space of the first few seconds he gazed down at the ruin of the pond.

None of this was directed at him, he knew, good or bad; it was because of Dr. Wilson, or, rather, because of his absence.

Confused by the nonsense of this realization, assaulted by the foreboding feelings, and repelled by the sight and smell of what the pond had become, Jim staggered back down the slope, walked home in numb silence.

* * *

Just as everyone expected, Dr. Wilson announced his engagement to Mrs. Clairine Woods, the widow of the deceased town pharmacist. Many local tongues wagged at the marked change in the doctor's demeanor—and not a few more at the shrewd medical monopoly he was rumored to be creating.

An early fall wedding was scheduled, with a reception to follow on the lawn of Dr. Wilson's estate. Preparations were made for the wedding and the arrival of a new wife.

Summer bled into fall, and Jim spent more time raking leaves and pruning dead branches than mowing or planting. He kept so busy he seldom thought much of his strange experiences with the pond.

Raking leaves one bright, cool, early October morning, he smelled something that penetrated his skull and drew forth a memory. It was the smell of wet, mildewy decay, and it made his stomach twitch.

At first he thought it was nothing more than damp, molding leaves, but it hadn't rained in more than a week.

Following his nose, he walked cautiously around the house to where the path through the woods began. Just on the verge of the trees, the earth was soaked, the grass matted. Here and there along the bottoms of their trunks, the trees were draped with waterweeds and long, dark strands of foul-smelling green algae.

Jim felt his heart begin to accelerate, labor in his chest.

He set his tools on the grass, went back to his cabin to lie down for a spell.

The morning of the wedding arrived, and Jim skipped his usual early breakfast to take one last spin through the grounds. He had planted a profusion of mums around the entrance to the house to give some additional color to the surroundings, and he wanted to check to be sure they were perfect.

He bent down to one plant to snap off a broken stem, when a scream resounded from the house.

Rising so fast that his knees cracked like splitting wood, he dashed up the front steps, stuffing the yellow flower into his pocket. The front door was open, and he slid across the polished tile in his wet boots.

"Grace! What's the matter?"

She appeared at the top of the steps, ashen, her mouth agape and forming silent words.

"Are you okay?" he asked, rushing up the stairs toward her.

His feet squished on the staircase rug; it was soaked.

Alarmed, he pushed past her, turned toward Dr. Wilson's room. The carpeting became wetter as he approached the door, which was half open.

It swung heavily back when he touched it, revealing a nightmare.

The room was in a shambles, furniture tumbled everywhere, lamps overturned and shattered, wet clothing strewn in improbable places.

Everything was stained with green muck. Ropes of algae, thick and mucilaginous, hung from the bed's massive posts, draped from the fireplace mantle, festooned the paintings on the walls. Rank brown-green slime stained clothing, towels, bed sheets, the wallpaper.

The smell of wet rot hung oppressively upon the air, cloying and nauseating in its intensity.

Dr. Wilson lay stretched atop his rumpled bed, dressed in his wedding clothes—a white day jacket, black trousers, a black cravat, shiny black shoes.

The doctor's face—eyes open—wore a look of sublime ecstasy. His skin was a pale shade of blue, and he, of course, was quite dead.

He was soaked to the bone. From the doorway, Jim could see his shriveled blue fingers, curled like flower petals. Around one gleamed his new gold wedding band.

The room, the smell, became too much for Jim, and he lurched to the window, threw it open, and dry heaved into the morning air.

Looking down, he saw green stains along the grass where he had seen them a week earlier. They led to the side of the house, up the siding and across the windowsill that his hands gripped tightly.

Snatching his hands back, he turned them over. His palms were stained a dark, dead green.

* * *

"Death by misadventure," Jim said, lighting up a fresh cigarette. "That's what the coroner wrote in his report. But no one who was in that room believed that."

He exhaled a cloud of smoke, and I took a drink from the warm beer I held.

"Not me. I *knew*. Besides, I was in the room when old Doc Hampton showed. He opened Dr. Wilson's mouth to have a look-see inside, and a gush of water and wet cattail fluff spilled out. Only I knew."

I didn't want to say it, but I felt obligated. "What? That the pond had gotten into the house and drowned the man? That's *crazy*."

Jim turned and gave me a sour look. "I told you I read a lot during my time at Dr. Wilson's. One of the books I read said that a person is made almost completely of water.

Why do you think the oceans hold so much attraction for men? Because water attracts water, calls out to its own.

"Someone once said that the sea is a harsh mistress. But I think that's only half right. *Water* is a harsh mistress—and a jealous one."

I could think of nothing more to say. His story had held me, pinned me at some essential level where I couldn't wriggle away.

"Drain it, I say," he muttered. "Drain that son of a bitch before it loves somebody. Before somebody loves it."

He gave me a funny look, said good night, and vanished into his house.

I stood there a while longer watching the pond out there in the darkness. I heard the calming sound of the wind rustling the reeds of its hair.

And I felt something stirring inside me; the desire to see it up close, to cup my hands in its water, to gaze at my reflection in its mirrored surface.

Rushing back inside, I closed the house against the sight and sound of the pond, went back into our bedroom and woke my wife.

I made love to her then, to keep my thoughts at bay for a while.

* * *

That was about two months ago.

Jim passed away quietly one night in his sleep shortly after telling me his story, his mind relieved of its burden.

The pond, however, is still here.

For the past week, I have awakened in the middle of the night, not sure of where I am, snapped my eyes open onto a vast, black, pin-pricked sky circling above me.

Beside me, like a lover, the pond laps at its banks, curling around me, dampening my skin.

My wife has begun to wonder why my pajamas are wet every morning.

I haven't told her.

I don't think I should tell either of them about the other...

THE CLOSED EYE OF A
DEAD WORLD

They say windows are like eyes.

Even the word *window*, from the Norse *vindauga*, means the eye of the wind.

What they don't say, though, what they *never* say, is if that eye is looking *out*...

Or looking *in*.

* * *

"This is the last listing I have... the very last one."

Martin turned, hearing the tone of mild exasperation, annoyance in her voice. He supposed he'd earned it, earned it over the last two weeks he'd dragged the real estate agent to literally dozens of houses. Each one tramped through from attic to basement; each one ultimately rejected.

This house seemed different, Martin thought, as he peered through the windshield of the car. It was quintessential country: a farmhouse sitting on perhaps an acre or two of land. Trees in the front yard, their limbs blowing gently in a breeze that he imagined smelled of laundry drying on a line, pies cooling on a windowsill.

A porch wrapped around the house, a swing listed desultorily. Whitewashed clapboard siding. Even a picket fence around the front lawn.

It was Norman Rockwell country, *The Waltons* country.

They climbed from the car, and Martin inhaled the clean, light early summer air, filled with the sap of trees and the pollen of flowers and the brown wetness of the river that curled just off the back of the property.

The agent opened her leather portfolio, flipped through dozens of papers, most scrawled with a large red X. "Here it is," she said. "Beautiful farmhouse on 2.3 acres. About 1,600 square feet. Three bedrooms. Two complete baths. Electric and propane. Hardwood floors. Umm... about 90 years old. Foundation in good shape. Roof needs work. Extensive work needed inside. Several outbuildings."

He heard her shuffle papers. "One owner, a Philip Dorset, professor of theoretical physics at the local university. Died intestate, so the county court has been trying to unload it for a while. Probably have it for a song and a dance."

"I think this is it," he muttered, more to himself than to her.

She heard him, blew a little puff of disbelieving breath from her pursed lips.

"It needs a lot of repairs," she warned.

"I can see that."

"It's sat vacant for more than two years."

"Okay."

"It's in a floodplain."

He shrugged.

She gave him a long, measuring look, holding the red pen poised to X through the sheet.

"Do you even want to look inside?"

* * *

Soon, he was signing papers, passing checks, getting keys. A succession of white vans pulled in and out of the gravel driveway, disgorging teams of contractors—carpenters, electricians, plumbers—all of whom noted the house's imperfections, its failings and put various prices on fixing them.

The house seemed to have more than its fair share of oddities, something that Martin attributed to its scholarly—and by all accounts eccentric—former owner. A heavy iron door opened onto a space barely big enough to squeeze into, not even large enough to be considered a closet. At the rear of this antechamber, there was another identical iron door, set into an exterior wall, sealed shut, with no corresponding opening on the outside of the house.

A second electrical box in the attic that seemed to power nothing. A set of switches installed next to it were for motion-control floodlights set on the roof of the house, facing the river.

The strangest thing, though, was the lack of any porch, veranda, or patio on the back of the house, the side that faced the river and offered what was arguably the best view. The wraparound porch stopped on the left and right sides of the house without actually wrapping around the back.

Much to his confusion and initial dismay, there was not one window that opened onto the backyard, either.

He wondered why the good professor wouldn't have wanted to unwind after a hard day of teaching theoretical physics on a deck overlooking such an idyllic scene.

* * *

When Martin had settled into the house, he began to chip away at smaller projects, concentrating first on his bedroom. On the day the siding contractors began replacing the old clapboards, he decided to repair the drywall there.

The largest hole in this room was at the foot of the bed, halfway up the southern wall that faced the river. Since Martin had every intention of putting windows here, there was no reason to fill it. As he moved away, though, he saw a small glint of light within the hole.

He stepped back, bent to look, expecting that it went all the way through to the outside. It was roughly the size of a football, its edges ragged, as if something had broken through. The paper backing along its borders was splayed out, as if whatever it was had punched into the room from outside.

He slowly put his hand to the hole, slipped a finger inside, expecting cobwebs or spiders or any of a number of unpleasant things. Instead, what his finger touched, cool and smooth, was unexpected enough to cause him to jerk it back.

The light again caught something, something just behind the drywall.

Martin smiled, brought his hand to the left edge of the hole and ripped a chunk of drywall out, then a larger chunk. He exposed an area roughly four times larger than the original hole, enough to see what lay beyond.

Outside, Martin found the foreman, a bird-faced man whose white overalls draped his lean form like a bed sheet held up by a pole. He saw Martin coming, and his face fell just a bit.

Taking a deep breath, Martin smiled. "I found a window... in the back... inside the bedroom. Can we take a look?"

At the back of the house, two men were busy removing old siding. Martin indicated where the window should be, and the foreman had the men peel back the clapboard.

Martin watched as the workers stripped the siding, watched as the morning sun caught the glint of glass.

The foreman removed his cap, scratched his bald head. "Well, I'll be," he mused. "Why you'd board over a window, especially one that looks out over the river, is beyond me."

Martin laughed, started back in, when something caught his eye.

The workmen had exposed the entire window now, revealing a hole in the glass about the size of a softball, spiky cracks radiating from it.

He noticed the shards of glass around the hole were pushed *inward*, as if something outside had broken it.

The hole lined up perfectly with the hole he had found in the bedroom drywall.

* * *

That evening, Martin carried a book and a mug of tea into his bedroom.

Feeling all was right with the world, Martin turned down the comforter atop the bed, peeled back the sheet, fluffed a pillow. Standing first on his right foot, then on his left, he peeled his socks off, tossed them into a laundry basket sitting beneath the single item that had made the day complete for him.

A window.

A large, reglazed window that looked out across the back of his property, to the river, to the fields that lay beyond the opposite bank.

The night was cool and breezy, with the tang of growing plants, of mowed grass, of flowers and pollen and damp earth. Smiling again, he raised the sash, opening the window fully.

The window installer had replaced the broken glass, but there was no screen yet. He'd taken its dimensions and promised Martin a new screen in three or four days. But tonight, pleased with his new window and the perfect evening, Martin decided to sleep with the window open. He'd take his chances with any bugs that might wander in during the night.

Taking one last look outside, he crawled into bed, read a few pages of his book before the day caught up with him. When his eyelids began to feel heavy, he replaced his bookmark, set the book on the nightstand, and turned out the light.

* * *

At around 2 a.m., things began to happen... things Martin slept through.

The window, whose tracks were antique and well worn, began to slip in its casement, sliding down inch by inch until it was almost closed.

Outside, there was movement, a shifting, lurching darkness that seemed somehow not part of the landscape the window opened onto, but *superimposed* over it.

It flitted in the distance, an eldritch shade that seemed to have no shape or substance, no color or depth. It flowed over the fields across the river, fell into its furrows, skidded atop its ploughed ridges.

It crept, a dark, suffuse mist, crept until it piled atop the bank of the river, seemed to collect itself, coalesce until it possessed not just color and depth, but mass… and *form*.

Pulling into itself, like a cat preparing to lunge, it shimmered in dire anticipation, shuddered like an animal.

At that moment, the window slipped the final inch or so in its casement, closed with a *click*.

Upstairs, in the attic, there was a brief electrical *snap*, the hum of a circuit being closed, and the floodlights mounted on the roof exploded into light.

To a person standing in Martin's backyard, the halogens lit a perfectly ordinary scene, a backyard at night, trees limned in white, flecked with shadow. Farther, their light fell diffuse and patinate on the riverbanks, an iridescent mist on the fields.

To a person standing in Martin's bedroom, though, to a person looking *through* his new window, the lights fell on a far different scene.

The scene that Martin's window showed was primal and alien, elsewhere… *otherwhere*. Instead of his backyard, there was a dense and impenetrable wall of green foliage, lush as a jungle, damp and rank as a rainforest. Its leaves, of unfamiliar shape and hue, brushed against each other in a wind that smelled vaguely of nutmeg and eucalyptus, whispered warnings in a language that was not of this earth.

Limned in the glow of the floodlights, was a shape, bestial and menacing, vibrating with some suppressed emotion that reeked of anger, of bile, of thwarted intent.

For a moment. And then it flowed back, back through the alien foliage and the alien shadows, back to wherever it had stepped from.

The halogens remained on, though, splashing the scene with crisp, unreal light, forcing the thing, the shape, the shadow to remain hidden within the denser black of its realm, out of the glare of the lights.

But eyes, carious and yellow, peered from the leaves, throbbed in time with the unseen thing's breathing.

The floodlights remained on until dawn.

For a few hours more, Martin slumbered, the window now showing only his backyard, the river, the fields.

* * *

In the morning, Martin lay for a few seconds feeling the deliciously high thread count of his sheets, the weight of his comforter, the warmth of the sun shafting in through the window.

He listened for the sound of birds, the rush of the river, the breeze blowing through the open window.

No sound reached his ears; no air stirred the room.

The window was closed, not open, as he'd left it last night.

Martin threw the covers back, approached the window. He looked through the clean sheet of glass before tentatively raising it, as if it might be jammed or stuck.

The window slid smoothly, and he threw it all the way open. When he did, the breeze slipped in like a cat that had been waiting patiently outside. He caught the scent of honeysuckle, the rich miasma of the river.

As he stood there letting the breeze curl around him, he looked at the casement. The channel the window fit into was old and worn. Martin's eye was caught by a small brass plate, no more than an inch square, embedded into the bottom of the windowsill. He looked to the left and saw another. From each, a thin wire, painted over, ran to the middle of the sill, disappeared into a small hole that had been drilled there.

Wondering what purpose these two contacts might have, he looked up at the bottom of the window frame, pushed the casement up as far as it would go. Sure enough, there were two of these small brass plates embedded there, positioned to contact the two placed in the sill when the window was closed.

Yet another eccentricity from the good professor, he supposed. He wondered what this one did, though as far as he could tell, none of the other little oddities served any conceivable function.

He pulled the window down, closed it, waited for something… a sound, a movement of some kind.

Shrugging, he opened the window, went into the bathroom to start the day's rituals, and promptly, entirely put it out of his mind.

* * *

The next day, Martin was busy inside the house as the contractors finished the new siding. Afterward, he was exhausted. The sun had only just set when he decided he didn't want to eat, didn't want to do anything but go to bed.

A quick, very hot shower later, he pulled back the bedcovers. His freshly scrubbed, still damp skin felt a wisp of air curl from the open window, still screenless. Tonight he would need that air, so he didn't want the window closing in the middle of the night.

Looking around, he saw the supplies he'd left out from the day's work, arranged neatly on a small drop cloth in the corner. A used paint paddle lay across a can of mud. He took the stick of wood, about a foot in length, and propped the window open with it.

Pleased, he almost literally fell in bed, pulled the thin sheet over him, turned off the light.

And slept… for a while.

* * *

A noise awakened him, a noise so unfamiliar, so outside his experience, that he lay there, eyes open, not yet afraid.

It sounded, all at once, mechanical and animal, metallic and organic. It came through the window, outside, nearby, vibrating the glass. But it also seemed distant, not just physically, but in a sense that it seemed to be slightly out of synch with reality. As if it was vibrating through some other dimension to reach his ears.

He lay there motionless, listening to this phantom sound, trying to place it, when it came to him.

It was the roar of some creature.

Cautiously, as if it might attract unwanted attention, he crept to the window, crouched to look outside.

The window was propped open at least a foot and a half by the paint stirrer. Martin looked through this gap, saw his backyard. He saw the sparse trees, the featureless lawn that fell away to the river just a few feet below.

Nothing more.

The sound continued, grated at his nerves. It definitely seemed to be coming from somewhere outside the window, but Martin could not tell from where.

And it seemed to be getting closer.

Again, not just in feet and inches, but in *dimensions*, as if it were dragging itself through realities to get at him. There was a *wrongness* to it, a sense of violation that tinged the air, as if this sound was not meant to be heard in this place.

It's probably a raccoon, he laughed. *A deer in rut or something completely ridiculous.*

That roar was so angry, though, so full of rage, so completely alien, that Martin decided to close the window for the evening... just in case.

Standing, he lifted the window slightly, unwedged the paint stirrer.

As he did, he looked out again, this time, though, through the glass.

It should have been his backyard at night, the sparse trees, the featureless lawn that fell away to the river.

But it wasn't.

The first thing he noticed, through the glass, was the moon... *a* moon. It was halfway up the deep indigo of the sky and large, larger than he'd ever seen. Not the mottled grey he was accustomed to, but a pale, purplish silver, iridescent, like oil on water.

Its violet light fell on a jungle so lush, so aggressively verdant, that it seemed to muscle up against the house. The moon's nacreous light fell on the edges of all kinds of dark leaves, oblong, serrated, thin like the blades of knives, broad and flat and as big as elephant ears.

These dark, silver-tipped leaves smelled of tropical flowers, of citrus and honey. They stirred in a cool, lushly humid breeze redolent of nutmeg, of coriander, of something sharp and medicinal.

Martin didn't—as characters do in a movie—rub his eyes or blink comically. Instead, he frowned at this, then slowly, slowly lowered his head.

He lowered his head until he looked under the sash of the window, through the open area between it and the windowsill.

Sparse trees, the featureless lawn that fell away to the river just a few feet below.

No lush rainforest whose trees whispered one to another in a secret, unearthly tongue.

Swallowing, he raised his head back to the window, to peer through the glass.

And started, lurched backward.

For there, clearly superimposed over the shadowed, swaying jungle, was a dark, amorphous form that blotted out the trees behind it. Its edges were indistinct, blurred.

Its eyes, for there were eyes within its darkness, were a jaundiced yellow, so malevolent that they seemed to drip venom.

Suddenly, the shape moved, detached itself from the greater blackness and heaved itself toward the house.

As it did so, that roar, so oddly natural and artificial at the same time, reverberated through the glass, entered Martin's bedroom like a physical presence. It hurt his eardrums, hurt his mind, the more so because it seemed horribly out of place, not designed to vibrate *this* air, not meant to be detected and processed by *his* senses.

Shivering involuntarily, Martin pushed from the window, fell back against the foot of his bed.

The window, no longer propped open by the paint stirrer, slid closed in its tracks.

As it shut, there was an audible *click*, a buzz of electricity somewhere in the house.

The floodlights mounted on the roof facing the river snapped on.

Where the pale light of that huge moon had been soft and lyrical, the halogens were harsh, clinical. The wall of the dark jungle seemed to lean away from their light, pull its branches back as if attempting to shield itself.

There, cast in stark relief by the halogens, was something so alien, so outside of human experience, that Martin's brain simply could not take it in, could not process it.

It pulsated with some dark energy that crackled from it like lightning. A maw, huge, cavernous, and yet another, different shade of black, opened within the twisting, billowing form, opened and opened and opened.

Its eyes boiled like lava, fixed on Martin.

Martin knew, knew in an instant that the lights—those lights, mounted on the roof—were meant to keep it at bay, keep it from the window.

It was too late for the lights to do any good now.

The thing was too close.

The creature roared again, this time in mingled rage and pain, and it leapt, hurled itself against the house.

Martin fell to the floor, scrabbled to the bedroom door.

His hand reached for the doorknob, and as it closed on it, as he pulled himself up from the floor, there was a violent concussion. The window and part of the wall it was on exploded, sending a blast of broken glass, splintered lathing, and a cloud of powdered plaster into the room.

And it... the thing... the creature.

Martin was shoved against the wall from the force of the explosion, and he felt more than saw the thing billow into his room, like ink blooming in water. Wreckage rained down upon it, but didn't seem to touch it. Nor was the debris absorbed by the creature's dark, formless mass.

Rather, shards of glass, knife-sharp splinters of lathing passed through its body, slowing somewhat, as if they were falling through a thick gel.

The thing pulled itself in through the hole where the window once was, gathered, expanded.

Part of it, little more than a wisp, touched Martin's outstretched bare foot. Where it contacted Martin's flesh, a mouth opened on the tendril, as if by reflex, opened as wide as the maw of a shark. And though Martin could see no teeth within that fathomless opening, he was sure of its purpose.

He tried to jerk his foot back.

Too late.

The mouth closed, and the eyes, those terrible, nightmare yellow eyes, slid through the mass of whatever made up its body, slid down through its form until they hovered right over Martin's outstretched foot.

They locked on Martin's eyes just as its yawning mouth closed.

The pain was immediate, intense, and yet somehow removed. It felt electrical in nature, like touching an exposed nerve or cracking your funny bone, and it caused Martin's entire leg to twitch uncontrollably.

He felt no teeth within that mouth, but something did exert pressure on his skin. There was heat, deep and intense, and it seemed to find his bones, concentrated there until his foot felt as if it were on fire, melting.

"Shit!" Martin shouted to the dark thing, then propped his other foot against the bedrail, propelling himself across the slick, wooden floor into the hallway.

He climbed to his feet, but his left foot, the one that had been in the thing's mouth, was limp, without feeling. Martin had a quick mental image of a stump, cauterized like charcoal yet still oozing blood. But he pushed it away quickly, slammed the bedroom door.

The thing, now that it had a taste of him, roared in anger, and that roar shook the house, made Martin's heart tremble in his chest.

Breathing hard, he looked up and down the hall.

The bedroom door would not hold it. For a moment, he wondered about Philip Dorset, professor of theoretical physics. He wondered what the good professor had been up to in this house... what windows he'd opened onto what other worlds, other dimensions.

Windows that, once opened, he had been unable to fully shut.

This wasn't the first time that something had come through the window that Professor Dorset had opened. Martin knew that with certainty.

So what had he done before?

The room! The small antechamber behind the iron door!

The thing behind the bedroom door stirred. Martin could hear it within the room, moving, tossing his bed aside, pressing itself against the other side of the door.

Martin turned down the hall, raced toward the strange iron door, dragging his dead foot just as the cloud creature let loose another tremendous, agonizing roar of frustration.

He slid to a stop, grabbed the cold iron handle of the strange door. It opened grudgingly, screeched in its own kind of defiance. But Martin yanked at it, and as he did, his bedroom door, just down the hallway, blasted from its hinges, flew into the wall across from it, shattered.

Martin ducked into the small room, cold and smelling of rust and mildew, ducked, and turned to look back once more.

The thing oozed from the bedroom, swelled like a living cloud. It filled the narrow corridor, scraping both sides, dislodging pictures, gouging plaster as it came after him.

With a grunt of effort, Martin pulled the door shut behind him, sealed himself in the small room with a resounding, satisfying *clang!* There, he slumped in the darkness, his back against the cold iron of a second door, at the back of the small chamber... and listened.

* * *

It was outside the little antechamber in seconds, pounding on the door, the iron clanging like a gong. Martin could not see the door in the pitch black, but it surely couldn't weather that kind of punishment indefinitely.

But it wasn't the door he was immediately concerned with. He could feel the frame itself lurching, buckling under the blows. Little blurts of metallic dirt puffed into the air with each of the creature's blows.

If the door didn't give, surely the frame would simply collapse after a while.

Martin realized that he had to do something.

He also realized that if the professor had created this space as a kind of panic room, safe from the creature, he wouldn't have planned it so poorly; he would have taken the doorframe into account.

The thing roared again, and it jangled in Martin's mind... jangled something loose.

The other door... the one behind him.

What did it open onto?

Theoretically, it should open onto the side yard, but Martin knew that there was no opening there on the outside of the house.

So this door, which he had never bothered to even try to open before, must open somewhere.

Some *otherwhere*.

Turning in the cramped confines of the space, he felt along the cold, flat iron, found the door latch.

After who knew how many years of disuse, though, the iron latch refused to budge. Decades of moist, humid air coming off the river had finally rusted it shut.

Martin heaved against it, but the latch didn't move, not an inch.

The other door, under assault from the nightmare creature, jumped and rang under its blows, almost hummed from the vibration of its howling.

It was going to give, Martin knew that, was sure of it.

Once it was down, the thing would float into the room, take Martin whole inside its great, gaping mouth and…

No! Martin screamed in his own mind. *That's not going to happen.*

Back and forth he rocked the iron latch, back and forth and back and forth, and little by little, he felt the thing move, stubbornly.

Back and forth and back and forth, he rocked the iron latch, and he felt the rusted metal flake off under his hands like old skin.

Back and forth and back and forth until, suddenly, it snapped free. With shaking hands, he drew the bolt back and pulled the door open.

There was just enough space to accommodate the door swinging in without Martin having to move.

Instantly, cold air flooded the room, bitterly cold, frigid. It whipped inside, filling every corner, bringing with it a whirling, stinging dust of ice and snow.

Throwing his hand up to ward his face, Martin saw a frozen landscape, white and flat and featureless, under a dim, blue star. A few hillocks on the distant horizon were the only interruption in the absolute flatness. Anything else was either buried under the unrelenting ice or hidden in the shadows cast by the tiny blue sun.

Whatever he was going to do, he had to do it quickly, because the air of this place was sub-arctic. He would freeze to death quickly.

He knew what he was going to do; it just took him a moment to gather the shreds of his courage.

Holding the door open against the wind with his foot, he turned his body, glad that the chamber was so small, that the doors were so close together.

Taking a deep breath, he measured the pounding of the monster against the door, waited, his hand on the latch.

In a heartbeat, he threw the bolt, jerked the door open.

It was dark, and the thing was dark, too, the only illumination coming from the blue light reflected from the frozen landscape beyond.

Its momentum carried it into the room; it passed Martin so close that he felt the pressure of its form against his body, smelled the smoky, nutmeg scent of it.

But its furious momentum was too much, and it shot past Martin, through the open door.

Realizing the danger too late, it grasped at the door frame with tendrils of darkness, tried to pull itself back into the tiny room, to get at the maddening thing that had eluded it.

But the wind frayed its form, yanked it away, dissipated the thing in an instant. Within a second or two, it was smeared across the landscape, just wisps and tatters of gloom. Even its roar was lost, drowned by the greater roar of the cold, dead wind of this cold, dead world.

Martin waited for a second, only a second, then threw his weight against the open door, fought the wind until it was closed, the latch locked.

His breathing heavy, condensed in the air, he slumped against the wall, waited to see if the pounding would resume.

After a while, when it didn't come, he went to the living room, collapsed onto the couch, and slept.

* * *

A few weeks passed, then months.

With the window boarded up again, Martin could finally relax in the house, enjoy the quiet country living for which he had bought it. As a tradeoff for losing the bedroom window, he built a large deck on the back of the house, where he could grill his meals in the spring and summer, drink a beer, and watch the river go by.

He walked with a cane now because of his foot. But he was getting accustomed to it.

Life was good… for a while.

Until late one night in October, when the air was thin but still comfortable, and clouds moved like smoke over the face of the moon.

Until one night when he was awakened from a deep sleep by banging, loud and ringing.

Until one night when the iron door, the second one within that small, useless chamber—the chamber that had saved his life—rang with angry, insistent blows…

…*from the other side.*

Until one night when he remembered that a door is a kind of window, too.

SNAPBACK

From: Serent, Dr. Henry D.
Sent: Aug 14, 2027
To: Project Head
[Sosq.DOD.Proj.LOOKINGGLASS.24-107-89@blops.DOE.gov]
Cc: RESTRICTED
Subject: EYES ONLY REPORT.
Proj. Day 254, Seq. 2, Data Stream 4-08-79XCV
Attachments: SOSQ Report 8/14/27.hexaq.doc.encrypt.key9

Protocol 7 continues with Lab 4 in continuous lockdown. Checklist follows:

Power Grid: Steady for last 187 hours following interruption almost 8 days ago. Fourth back-up generator was delivered 8/10 and brought online at 04.30 on 8/13.

Containment: Magnetic, plasma and ionic fields active, and analysis indicates all containment fields impermeable for 187 hours following power interruption. Residual chronitons detected initially have continued to decrease steadily.

Tau Field Status: The field remains steady and permeable to ingress/egress of all data and bioforms.

Grid Node Report: Stable.

Personnel Report: Two agents are involved in situations where input is necessary. Possible termination of grid access and extraction of agents may be necessary. Highlights below. Detailed report will be filed per Protocol 7 Indices.

Agent 9/56-Q-47-X-LG-24: Grid Node 9, Annum 1567+. Insertion successful. Agent biometric reports are steady and Green. Continuous data downloads have commenced and are available online, per EYES ONLY strictures. No pertinent data yet.

Agent 9/34-G-39-X-LG-12: Grid Node 17, Annum 986-. Limited local contact reported. Language dialect problems continue. Agent reports increasing difficulty in maintaining low profile. Indigenes may present a serious threat to the safety of the agents and the security of this phase of the project. The ingress of three indigenes into the tau field and the subsequent damage done in Lab 4 remains a concern. IT IS RECOMMENDED THAT THIS AGENT BE EXTRACTED AND THIS GRID/ANNUM STUDY BE TERMINATED IMMEDIATELY. Agent reports ready to return ASAP, with all wipe down protocols completed and documented. A quick decision on this grid/annum will allow us to funnel resources into a higher priority grid/annum.

Agent 9/45-J-20-X-LG-56: Grid Node 23, Annum 2457-. Day 189: Still no contact with indigenes. Project has moved into a detailed study of the environment, cataloging local flora and fauna, pollen spores, atmospheric conditions, weather, water sources, and tectonic activity. Agent reports extraction possible in 27 days.

Agent 9/12-B-98-X-LG-17: Grid Node 47, Annum 1789+. Day 487: Project continues smoothly. Total immersion in culture, with indigenes quite accepting of agent. Data and biometrics continue uninterrupted. Agent has requested a back up be inserted as soon as is practical. Back up agent will be assigned to pose as 'spouse' since agent's unmarried status is becoming somewhat of a concern among the indigenes. Given the inadvisability of introducing genetic material from our annum into this grid/annum, a 'mate' from this era has been deemed out of the question. Agent 10-44-G-35-X-LG-55 has accelerated immersion learning and will be ready for insertion, pending directives, in 12 days.

Agent 10/78-D-64-X-LG-89: Grid Node 1, Annum 3190+. Day 10: I continue to maintain my strenuous objection to this experimental grid/annum. The tau field, elsewhere quite stable, is unstable. Agent reports are slow, and drops in the data stream continue to plague our analysis and sometimes even our comprehension of the information. Biometrics are sketchy and what we do have seems... *odd*. Review Day 5, 01:24:05, and Day 7, 10:45:16. See what you think. Agent reports are available online, EYES ONLY. Protocol 7 strictures in place. Input from DOD/SOSQ-89 would be helpful here with regards to the expected duration of this experiment.

From: SOSQ Project Head
Sent: Aug 14, 2027
To: Serent, Dr. Henry D. [h.serent.x-lg-prime@blops.DOE.gov]
Cc: RESTRICTED
Subject: Re: EYES ONLY REPORT.
Proj. Day 254, Seq. 2, Data Stream 4-08-79XCV
Attachments: Lofeed.stuf
CONFIRMATION CODE: RW-POT-78-X/CKLK, DELTA
8/14/27 Report received and filed. All appropriate protocols in place. EYES ONLY in full effect.

Now that that's out of the way, how the hell are ya? Sometimes hard to imagine you there, two miles below the desert. Might as well be in space with the Mars colonists. A metal tube is a metal tube, whether it's in deep space or buried in sand. But I hope you're holding up.

Glad the new generator came and was installed quickly. You should be happy about that, at least. Backups of backups of backups, as you always tell me. Also glad to hear the mess was contained and cleaned up from the ingress of the "indigenes". (Love that word! That single word in your reports is worth—I've calculated—at least $1 million a mention from Congress!) Anyway, must have been quite a thrill to have three of King David's soldiers crash your party. Hope there were kosher meals in the cafeteria that afternoon!

Okay, so I know you're irritated, Hank. I can always tell when your reports revert back to *bureaucratese* instead of your own voice. I've reread your paper on the advisability of aiming Looking Glass forward rather than back. And I've made your views known to those above me. No clear answer yet, so you know what that means in government ops: *proceed*. I see and understand the variables you're experiencing with that grid/annum, and very much appreciate the dangers you've noted. However, you understood the parameters of this project when you came aboard (OK… you were *drafted*). You knew that the backflow research was primarily a field test of the concept of the tau field, prepping the way for the eventual forward-flow studies, which, as I continue to remind you, was the keystone of getting the interest of the military… and their money.

So, continue your reports, continue your admonishments, but stay on this. It's that vital… as you well know. Take a few days off, watch some movies. Have a weekend with that woman in IT you mentioned a few weeks back… Rachael? Renee? I can't remember, but do something to take your mind off of being in that little metal tube buried in the desert. You need it, you've earned it, you deserve it. Local news feed is attached for your reading pleasure.

~Pete

P.S. BTW, this just in. Immediate retraction of agent from Grid Node 17, Annum 986- is authorized. Close it down and seal the stream.

From: Serent, Dr. Henry D.
Sent: Aug 16, 2027
To: Project Head
[Sosq.DOD.Proj.LOOKINGGLASS.24-107-89@blops.DOE.gov]
Cc: RESTRICTED
Subject: EYES ONLY REPORT.
Proj. Day 256, Seq. 7, Data Stream 4-08-81XCV
Attachments: SOSQ Report 8/16/27.hexaq.doc.encrypt.key4

Protocol 5 underway, as Lab 4 is now back in full-time service.
Power Grid: Steady for last 238 hours.
Containment: Magnetic, plasma and ionic fields active and steady 238 hours following power interruption. Residual chronitons, which were initially decreasing, are now increasing steadily. Team 2 assigned to task. Full report expected in 24 hours. See H.S. for details.
Tau Field Status: The field remains steady and permeable to ingress/egress of all data and bioforms.
Grid Node Report: Stable.

Personnel Report: Immediate retraction of agent from Grid Node 17, Annum 986- was completed as authorized. Grid/annum stream was closed and sealed. Agent is debriefing now, and final reports from this grid/annum are available online, per Protocol 5 guidelines. Agent will be transferred to the newly opened stream at Grid 44, Annum 1352+ as soon as he is fully trained (estimate: 3 weeks).
Okay, Pete: yeah, I'm pissed. I mean, why stick me out here on this damn project, pay me this exorbitant salary and entrust me with the biggest blackops program we've got if no one is going to listen to me or my team? Why stick all this brainpower out here if it's just going to be ignored? And don't tell me this is the way the military works. That's bullshit…
But, okay, I'll calm down. No real news to report, though we continue to get some awfully funky readings from Grid 1, Annum 3190+. Funky, I know… I need to be more precise. I've got my best people on it, but the stream appears to be extremely unstable. I can't figure out how to explain what we're seeing. I'm encoding our captured datastream and attaching the link. Maybe your boys up there can make heads or tails out of it.
And for your information, her name is Ranel, and she's the perfect mixture of mind and body. We had dinner just the other night, caught a

screening of a classic '90s movie and... well... a gentleman doesn't divulge details. Needless to say, it took my mind off of a lot of things.

But really, in all seriousness, see if you can get my point across to those-who-shall-remain-nameless above you. The little hairs on the back of my neck are prickling. I just can't shake the feeling that something wicked this way comes.

From: SOSQ Project Head
Sent: Aug 17, 2027
To: Serent, Dr. Henry D. [h.serent.x-lg-prime@blops.DOE.gov]
Cc: RESTRICTED
Subject: Re: EYES ONLY REPORT.
Proj. Day 256, Seq. 7, Data Stream 4-08-81XCV
Attachments: Lofeed.stuf
CONFIRMATION CODE: JT-JTG-43-X/CVBO, SIGMA
8/16/27 Report received and filed. All appropriate protocols in place. EYES ONLY in full effect.

Okay, so it's out in the open—you're pissed, but I'm trying on my end to get someone to at least put their eyes on your recommendations. But, again, think of what you're asking. You're asking them to abandon the very thing they put their money into this for. A look into the past is interesting, sure. Like Jesus on the cross, Michelangelo painting the Sistine Chapel, Napoleon frozen in Russia. But these have no strategic value; they're purely academic. You know that—you knew that coming into this.

But the future... to get a glimpse into the future? That's the ticket. To see who's going to cause problems that we need to prepare for? Who's going to smuggle weapons, develop nukes, arm terrorists? Which country will be spoiling for a fight? That's what the military paid for... a fast dance and a fuck later, not a slow dance and a peck on the cheek.

And... really? *Funky?* What's your PhD in, anyway? You're not old enough to have graduated from Berkeley in the '70s. Be more clear. Stupid bureaucratic layman, remember?

Ranel, huh? Interesting name. Glad you're doing something to take your mind off of the blahs...

From: Serent, Dr. Henry D.
Sent: Aug 19, 2027
To: Project Head
[Sosq.DOD.Proj.LOOKINGGLASS.24-107-89@blops.DOE.gov]
Cc: RESTRICTED
Subject: ALERT!! EYES ONLY REPORT.

Proj. Day 258, Seq. 3, Data Stream 6-90-22DFG
Attachments: SOSQ Report 8/19/27.hexaq.doc.encrypt.key1aprime

PROTOCOL 8 ENACTED. Lockdown in effect. All reports except for those coming from this office have been terminated. The central computer core and the Collider Ring have been powered down and the tau field generator has been narrowed to accept only data from all open grids/annums.

Power Grid: Steady.
Containment: Reporting steady, but chroniton radiation is increasing *exponentially*.
Tau Field Status: Stable, except in 1 grid/annum
Grid Node Report: Stable.

Sorry to cut the normal report short, but you wanted funky, so you got it.
Reports coming in from Agent 10/78-D-64-X-LG-89: Grid Node 1, Annum 3190+, Day 15 are disturbing. Evidently there's something going on in this grid/annum that is *catastrophic*. Agent's biometrics and data streams are in extreme flux, but from what the analysis team can decipher, there are some serious environmental disturbances occurring there... and they aren't isolated to this particular grid. They may be planetary. I say 'may be' because... well... shit... we just can't tell at this point. I'm uploading the telemetry with my normal (hah!) report. Maybe your eggheads can tell mine what's going on.
Not funky enough? Here's the kicker. The causality point we're directing the tau field at to open Grid 1, Annum 3190+ isn't just unstable... it seems to be *moving*.

From: SOSQ Project Head
Sent: Aug 19, 2027
To: Serent, Dr. Henry D. [h.serent.x-lg-prime@blops.DOE.gov]
Cc: RESTRICTED
Subject: Re: ALERT!! EYES ONLY REPORT.
Proj. Day 258, Seq. 3, Data Stream 6-90-22DFG
CONFIRMATION CODE: HM-CJF-32-X/JDSIV, EPSILON
8/16/27 Report received and filed. All appropriate protocols in place. EYES ONLY continues in full effect.

WTF? Protocol 8? We have never put Protocol 8 in place.

I immediately uploaded your latest report to the higher ups, and their egg heads are indeed looking at the data with tremendous concern. Needless to say, you've got everyone's attention on this... finally.

What precisely do you mean by 'the causality point is moving'? That's not possible, Hank. NOT. POSSIBLE.

Get back to me immediately. Lord, I wish phone lines worked down there.

From: Serent, Dr. Henry D.
Sent: Aug 20, 2027
To: Project Head
[Sosq.DOD.Proj.LOOKINGGLASS.24-107-89@blops.DOE.gov]
Cc: RESTRICTED
Subject: ALERT!! EYES ONLY REPORT.
Proj. Day 259, Seq. 9, Data Stream 10-01-98MMT
Attachments:
UPDATED SOSQ Report 8/19/27.hexaq.doc.encrypt.key1aprime

I'm dispensing with the usual reports because, well, they don't mean anything right now.

We've been up all night down here—whatever that means—studying this. We're bleary eyed and our brains hurt, but here's what we know at the moment:

Agent's reports from Grid Node 1, Annum 3190+ have been partially deciphered. There appears to be some planet wide catastrophe, something involving the atmosphere... we don't know. Could be weather related, could be solar, could be a comet/asteroid strike. But we know it's big... we know it's planetary... and we know it's an Omega Event. Pure and simple.

More disturbing? The causality point for Grid 1, Annum 3190+ *is* moving. Repeat: this causality point is moving, despite our theories to the contrary. We're working on it now, but there's no arguing with the telemetry data.

Even more disturbing: it's moving *backwards*... do you understand what I'm saying?

It's moving backwards in time. To keep up with it, we've had to readjust the tau emitter every two hours or so. And then we have to hunt around for it.

Right now, Annum 3190+ is at the causality point for 2844+... and it's still regressing.

This isn't funky anymore... it's *terrifying*.

From: SOSQ Project Head
Sent: Aug 20, 2027

To: Serent, Dr. Henry D. [h.serent.x-lg-prime@blops.DOE.gov]
Cc: RESTRICTED
Subject: Re: ALERT!! EYES ONLY REPORT.
Proj. Day 259, Seq. 9, Data Stream 10-01-98MMT

Okay, slow down... grab some shuteye and a cup of coffee, because you have created a shitstorm up here, and my umbrella is leaking. So you're gonna catch some of it.

The higher up's eggheads are saying that what you laid out is flatly impossible. (That is, except for one ultra egghead from MIT who is saying that it makes perfect sense when looked at from a quantum level. Yeah... whatever. I don't even think my reading glasses see things on the *quantum level!*)

Causality points *don't* move... they *can't* move. So, now we're reanalyzing the stuff you sent up and trying to make sense of it from another angle. I will keep you posted, but make sure I get any updates as fast as you can get them to me. The boys upstairs are practically beating down my door for your response, and I haven't even pressed the damn 'Send' button.

There...

From: Serent, Dr. Henry D.
Sent: Aug 21, 2027
To: Project Head
[Sosq.DOD.Proj.LOOKINGGLASS.24-107-89@blops.DOE.gov]
Cc: RESTRICTED
Subject: ALERT!! EYES ONLY REPORT.
Proj. Day 260, Seq. 1, Data Stream 09-24-93STT
Attachments: SOSQ Report 8/21/27.hexaq.doc.encrypt.key1aprime

Can't sleep... coffee is about all that's keeping me (and everyone else down here!) awake. Well, that's not entirely true... coffee, caffeine tablets... and *fear.*

Do you know what it means when *scientists* are afraid, Pete?

It means there's something you damn well should be afraid of.

The fucking causality point is moving!!! Tell the idiots to review the data without having their heads up their asses. The finest minds on this project are *down here* in this metal tube in the desert, as you put it, and we're all in agreement. You can tell the eggheads for me to shove their candy-ass theories up their... well, their candy asses. There should be plenty of room when they remove their heads.

Review the new telemetry reports. No further biometrics or data are coming in from Agent 10/78-D-64-X-LG-89. Nothing for roughly 18 hours. He's dead, or that *world*—that *annum*—is dead.

And there is no doubt—impress this upon them, Pete—there is no doubt that the causality point is moving... regressing... back flowing, if you will. Latest readings have it at Annum 2713+ and still moving.

I don't know what else to say. I extracted all my agents from all current grid/annums and closed every open portal. The collider is in minimum power mode and the tau field is focused entirely on our moving causality point.

Tell me what to do here, Pete. Tell me something that makes me think we didn't just fuck up on a colossal scale.

From: SOSQ Project Head
Sent: Aug 21, 2027
To: Serent, Dr. Henry D. [h.serent.x-lg-prime@blops.DOE.gov]
Cc: RESTRICTED
Subject: Re: ALERT!! EYES ONLY REPORT.
Proj. Day 260, Seq. 1, Data Stream 09-24-93STT

Everything's gone quiet on my end. Plenty of long faces and closed mouths... you know what that means around here. It means you're right, and they're afraid to acknowledge it.

They don't know what to do, so I sure hope there are enough coffee and caffeine tablets down there with you to keep your guys alert and thinking... because there's nothing left up here.

How could this have happened? How can a causality point fucking *move?*

From: Serent, Dr. Henry D.
Sent: Aug 22, 2027
To: Project Head
[Sosq.DOD.Proj.LOOKINGGLASS.24-107-89@blops.DOE.gov]
Cc: RESTRICTED
Subject: ALERT!! EYES ONLY REPORT.
Proj. Day 261, Seq. 2, Data Stream 06-28-92BHT
Attachments: SOSQ Report 8/22/27.hexaq.doc.encrypt.key1aprime

Fear? Well, there's plenty of that to go around here, too. But it's a great motivator... so far, at least. I just hope that it doesn't cause us to crawl back into our little rooms, curl up in the corner, and cry for our mommies.

How could this have happened? *Do you really want my answer to that, Pete?* Because I think you know what my answer would be... minus a few four-letter words.

How can a causality point move? Well, that's the thing we've been bashing around down here. Here's what we think at present... and I warn you, it isn't comforting on any level.

I used the words *back flow* in my last email. But that's not really a good metaphor. A more apt metaphor for what we're dealing with might be a rubber band. Think of time as a rubber band that's stretching into the future. The past is done, used up, and time is sort of pulling it along. The future, though, is constantly stretching the other end of the rubber band. (I know, I know, but keep with me here). But that stretching doesn't go any more forward than a few brief milliseconds... if that. We don't know why that is yet. Perhaps the future isn't something static, already set like the past. Who knows?

What seems to have happened is that when we fired up the collider and aimed the tau field at a future event, we stretched the 'rubber band' forward, more than it could handle. Now, I don't know if 3190+ was too far or if 2028+ would be too far or if even one second from this very moment would be too far.

But what we did went too far: it taxed the entire physics of time beyond its nature. And now the rubber band is snapping back—for lack of a better, more scientific term. *It's actually bringing whatever was in that annum back to us*... the whole kit and caboodle, hurtling backwards through time. Very probably wiping out whatever was between that annum and ours... whatever that might be... or was... or will be... or... jeez, I hate temporal riddles. (A funny thing for a temporal scientist, don't you think?)

Pete, we still haven't defined exactly what 3190+ is bringing with it, but whatever it is, it's not the second coming of Christ or the Rapture or the Elysian Fields.

And if this analogy... metaphor... whatever holds up, there's every reason to suppose that the snapback will bring it right to our doorstep. Right back to where it started...

The causality point is, at this very moment, skirting the edges of 2413... and *accelerating*. We figure there's about 18 hours before it reaches 2027...

From: SOSQ Project Head
Sent: Aug 22, 2027
To: Serent, Dr. Henry D. [h.serent.x-lg-prime@blops.DOE.gov]
Cc: RESTRICTED
Subject: ALERT!! EYES ONLY REPORT.
Proj. Day 261, Seq. 2, Data Stream 06-28-92BHT

Jesus. I mean... *Jesus*...
Everyone's walking around here with sphincters so tight that if they were to eat charcoal, they'd shit diamonds. People... higher ups... I mean *real*

higher ups... are leaving, going home to be with their families... deserting... *giving up...*

I'm going to hang around. Since Janey died, there's no one to go home to anyway. Maggie's moved away and Josh... well... who knows?

Has it occurred to you that you're sitting in a metal tube thousands of feet below the ground? Has it occurred to you that you're sitting on 15 floors of supplies, with everything from toilet paper and distilled water to MREs and batteries?

Has it occurred to you that your team, all 258 of them, might be all that's left in the end? Might be the only ones to survive this... whatever this is?

Jesus, Hank...

From: Serent, Dr. Henry D.
Sent: Aug 22, 2027
To: Project Head
[Sosq.DOD.Proj.LOOKINGGLASS.24-107-89@blops.DOE.gov]
Cc: RESTRICTED
Subject: ALERT!! EYES ONLY REPORT.
Proj. Day 261, Seq. 4, Data Stream 12-21-63JFT

It's an asteroid, Pete. One about the size of Texas.
It hits New Zealand or the area right around there.
It's a planet killer...
Pete... God protect you... all of you up there...
It's at annum 2302... probably 7 hours or so...

From: SOSQ Project Head
Sent: Aug 22, 2027
To: Serent, Dr. Henry D. [h.serent.x-lg-prime@ blops.DOE.gov]
Cc: RESTRICTED
Subject: The Future... hah...

People are fleeing here like rats out of a... well... you know.

The media's caught wind of something, but no one knows yet. No one knows. I guess they never will. I'm staying right here, my friend. I'm glad, at least, that one of my close friends will live through this.

Stay safe, Hank. Lead a good life. Get with Ranel... marry her... have 10 or 12 children. Tell your staff that the policy of non-fraternization is hereby officially lifted and that, as my last order, I command them to hook up and repopulate the human race... *the entire human race.*

I am weeping right now, but there's no one around in the building to even hear me. I think I will weep until the moment the damn thing hits and the pressure wave or the heat wave or whatever wipes out this annum.

Should have listened to you. Cold comfort now to be told you were right, huh? But there it is: you were... are... will be. Temporal riddles... yeah, they suck.

Good luck... and God bless, my friend.

Say a prayer for the souls of all mankind. You and your people will be the only ones left to remember us... and ask for grace for us. I hope you do both.

From: Serent, Dr. Henry D.
Sent: Aug 22, 2027
To: Project Head
[Sosq.DOD.Proj.LOOKINGGLASS.24-107-89@blops.DOE.gov]
Cc: RESTRICTED
Subject: Re: The Future... hah!

Pete? It's at 2045... moving like a juggernaut.
Take care, dear friend, and save a chair for me wherever you end up. We'll see each other again, I'm sure... I hope...
God forgive us all.

From: MAILER-DAEMON@ 23CFP:GOV.DOD/DOE/LG
Sent: Aug 22, 2027
To: Serent, Dr. Henry D. [h.serent.x-lg-prime@ blops.DOE.gov]

Your e-mail to:
[Sosq.DOD.Proj.LOOKINGGLASS.24-107-89@blops.DOE.gov]
was undeliverable due to the following reasons:
Delivery timed out.
Recipient does not exist.
No known mailbox. No known domain.
System will not resend. Please try again with a live address.

From: Serent, Dr. Henry D.
Sent: Aug 04, 2027
To: Project Head
[Sosq.DOD.Proj.LOOKINGGLASS.24-107-89@blops.DOE.gov]
Cc: RESTRICTED
Subject: EYES ONLY REPORT.

Proj. Day 244, Seq. 5, Data Stream 09-08-63JCF
Attachments: SOSQ Report 8/04/27.hexaq.doc.encrypt.key3

Protocol 3 continues, with all divisions reporting normal. Checklist follows:

Power Grid: All three generators report steady. Collider at full power.

Containment: Magnetic, plasma and ionic fields active and working.

Tau Field Status: The field is steady and permeable to ingress/egress of all data and bioforms.

Grid Node Report: Stable.

Personnel Report: Highlights below. Detailed report will be filed per Protocol 7 indices.

Agent 10/78-D-64-X-LG-89: Agent will be inserted at 09:45 this morning into Grid Node 1, Annum 3190+, despite my ongoing objections to this phase of the project. There is still, in my opinion, not enough data to show us what the results of a forward incursion might be. Protocol 7 strictures for this part of the project are in place. Team reports stream is stable, causality point is targeted and tau field is at full strength. Agent reports ready, as to the medical, insertion and power teams. If no other word is received from SOSQ-DOD by 09:30, insertion will proceed.

From: SOSQ Project Head
Sent: Aug 04, 2027
To: Serent, Dr. Henry D. [h.serent.x-lg-prime@blops.DOE.gov]
Cc: RESTRICTED
Subject: RE: EYES ONLY REPORT.
Proj. Day 244, Seq. 5, Data Stream 09-08-63JCF
CONFIRMATION CODE: HM-HO-43-X/SISU, THETA
8/04/27 Report received and filed. All appropriate protocols in place. EYES ONLY in full effect.

I'm assuming that the insertion went as planned. It's about 09:50 here.

Aww, shit… we just lost power here… backups kicked in… thought that couldn't happen… at least I didn't lose this note… I hate typing in all those frikkin' code letters.

Wait a sec… something's happening … people screaming in the hallways. Something about a bomb or… an asteroid.

Hank, I'll get back to you.

From: Serent, Dr. Henry D.
Sent: Aug 04, 2027
To: Project Head

77

[Sosq.DOD.Proj.LOOKING GLASS.24-107-89@blops.DOE.gov]
Cc: RESTRICTED
Subject: Re: RE: EYES ONLY REPORT.
Proj. Day 244, Seq. 5, Data Stream 09-08-63JCF

Pete? What's going on? Are you okay? The feed lines from outside have all gone dead... even the trunk line... and that should *not* be possible.

Hey, buddy, kind of nervous here, all cut off and everything... get back to me.

From: Serent, Dr. Henry D.
Sent: Aug 04, 2027
To: Project Head
[Sosq.DOD.Proj.LOOKINGGLASS.24-107-89@blops.DOE.gov]
Cc: RESTRICTED
Subject: Re: RE: EYES ONLY REPORT.
Proj. Day 244, Seq. 5, Data Stream 09-08-63JCF

Pete? We're getting a little nervous down here. What's going on up there? The inner and outer blast doors have sealed and the computer has declared Protocol 9.

What the fuck is Protocol 9?

From: MAILER-DAEMON@ 23CFP:GOV.DOD/DOE/LG
Sent: Aug 04, 2027
To: Serent, Dr. Henry D. [h.serent.x-lg-prime@blops.DOE.gov]

Your e-mail to:
[Sosq.DOD.Proj.LOOKINGGLASS.24-107-89@blops.DOE.gov]
was undeliverable due to the following reasons:
Delivery timed out.
Recipient does not exist.
No known mailbox. No known domain.
System will not resend. Please try again with a live address.

THE MIRE OF
HUMAN VEINS

Lisa rubs absently at the iridescent skin of her arm, which powders at her touch.

Dust with the rainbow sheen of oil on water drifts to the placemat set before her at the kitchen table, glittering like tiny fish scales in the wan morning light of the kitchen.

She remembers, long ago, sitting on her father's lap, rubbing at her father's arms, his skin powdering at her touch, glittering on her fingertips.

You are your father's daughter, her mother always tells her.

Lisa holds her cereal spoon limply in one hand, distractedly draws it through the gray milk. She notes in an equally distracted way that several black bits float to the surface in the wake of the spoon.

Flies... dead flies.

They float to the top like plump raisins, and she had willed her mind long ago to accept them as such.

Without missing a beat, she slides a spoonful into her mouth, swallows it.

If you swallow without chewing, it is impossible to know what you're swallowing.

Lisa learned through hard experience that this is preferable to arguing with her mother. She simply swallows everything her mother gives her, everything her mother tells her.

She is her mother's daughter, too, but arguing with her is best avoided.

She can be... *scary.*

As she thinks this thought, as she remembers those occasions when her mother's demeanor quickly shifted from merely spooky to terrifying, she feels a touch on her back, the press of skin against her bare shoulder.

"I'm glad to see you eating breakfast." Her mother's voice is high-pitched, wavering, like an unsure violinist, trying yet unable to hold a perfect note. The squeak of her voice, the touch of her hands against Lisa's skin—*Why do her hands feel so cold, so... bristly?*—sends a shiver through Lisa's body causing an uncontrollable tremble.

Lisa's mother senses this, removes her hands from her daughter, steps back.

Lisa turns in her seat and looks at her mother. "No need to get all mushy, mom. It's just breakfast."

Her mother's hands move in the air, as if wanting to stroke her hair, stroke her cheek. Lisa watches her mother's hands weave incantations of thwarted love in the air, and thinks it makes her look eldritch, insectile.

Unaware of her daughter's thoughts, her mother smiles. Lisa finds that smile the scariest thing about her. It is the overlarge smile of a mouth that is too big to be contained by its head, too small to contain the improbable number of peg-like teeth that it does.

"Well, it makes me feel good," she says, her hands palpating the air between the two. Lisa watches her long, impossibly thin-fingered hands whose shadows creep long-legged up the walls.

She finally lowers them to her sides, as if by sheer force of will. "You have no idea how important it is for a mother to know that her children are well fed."

Lisa smiles again, but inside her, in the depths behind that smile (*and oh, there are depths, oh yes, depths of which her mother has no idea*), its foundation cracks, falters. There is something about what her mother has just said, something about how she said it that makes Lisa feel squirmy and exposed.

Before her crumbling façade can reveal what has been building inside Lisa with great and secret effort over the last year or so, she stands, kisses her mother on a cheek that feels hectic and feverish beneath her dry lips, and grabs her backpack.

"Have a good day at school, honey," her mother's voice calls after her.

Lisa stops at the mirror in the foyer, checks her teeth for flyspecks before leaving.

At school, Lisa sees herself as something apart from the other girls, something special, though she is neither arrogant nor particularly self-possessed. She is merely sure that she is unlike the other girls here, unlike them in a fundamental, unusual way.

Maybe it is because of the changes she is going through, the changes her body is working on unbidden, day and night like a machine left on, left unattended with nothing more than a vague blueprint to work from. These changes are profound, Lisa realizes, yet so unfinished she feels she must be wearing a sign that reads *Under Construction*.

She knows that some of these changes are normal, to be expected… the swelling of breasts, the flaring of hips, the sudden urges and secret fires that seem so important, so desperate.

And then there is the coming of the blood…

Yes, the *promise* of the blood, as her mother calls it.

There are other changes, though.

The shimmering dust on her skin.

The enigmatic nubs on her back that mimic the bumps on her chest, growing from her shoulder blades like insect bites.

The strange, fluttery feeling inside her all the time now, day or night. It makes her feel as if she is bouncing against glass, some flat pane of glass that is just in front of her, hedging her in, keeping her from something so desirable that she finds it necessary to hurl herself against it again and again.

She has no idea why, no idea what the unseen glass is keeping her from.

Whether it is protecting it from her.

Or protecting her from it.

* * *

Lunchtime and Lisa eats alone, not through any conscious choice, though this makes her feel as if the other children, on some level at least, grant her the respect of privacy.

Floral scents drift from the soft, reusable lunch-sack her mother packs for her every day. A sandwich of butter and honey and granulated sugar on soft, pillowy white bread. A thermos of green tea her mother brews special for her, light and floral and achingly sweet.

With each bite, with each sip she feels regal, like some ornate and magnificent butterfly, taking in a sweetness that is hers and hers alone.

That sweetness, redolent of the nectar of some potent and powerful flower, seeps and oozes into the depths inside her, those secret depths that no one but she knows of, drop by golden drop until it becomes a languid, syrupy lake inside her.

For some reason that is still vague to her, that secret, golden pool, dreamy and sweet almost beyond comprehension, always makes her think of her father.

He gave his life for us… for you, her mother tells her.

Lisa, of course, takes this in, as she takes in everything her mother gives her, tells her.

It makes her sad.

That sadness brings a torpid, poignant drowsiness that makes it difficult for her to concentrate during the rest of the day.

* * *

The man is black.

Not African American, but *black*.

His skin is the color of a black crayon, of coal, of darkness, so devoid of luster that the kitchen light seems trapped inside it. He is bald, and the dome of his head is like a night of fallen stars.

The whites of his eyes and his teeth are black, as are the pads of his fingers. The little half-moon lunula of each fingernail is a new moon.

He smiles at her as she sits to dinner, with a smile like the opening of a hole within a hole.

Her mother introduced the strange man casually as Lisa slid her book bag to the floor in the foyer earlier. Her mother had been sitting on the couch in

81

the living room, sitting very close to the man. They hadn't been holding hands, but their hands, resting on their own thighs, touched.

It seemed even more intimate.

There was an atmosphere within the room as Lisa stood there, wondering who this man was. An atmosphere that felt congealed, wiggly like jelly that had been poked and still quivered from this contact.

Her mother introduced the man as *Mr. Ari* or something like that, something that sounded Greek, though he didn't look at all Greek.

At dinner, he sits at the head of the table, the chair both she and her mother always leave vacant for the ghost of her father. He had not been asked to sit there, and this presumption on his part angers Lisa, though she betrays no emotion.

There is something cooking on the stove. The steam from it fills the kitchen with an aroma that is tantalizing, off-putting. It smells of meat and dust, spices, something earthy, musty.

Her mother brings the steaming pot to the table, places it on a trivet and ladles out brown broth first into the man's bowl. Lisa sees the man watch the bowl with something approaching avidity. He nods to her mother when she has finished, his black eyes wide and moist.

Her mother dips the ladle back into the pot, fills Lisa's bowl.

The broth is thin, brackish, rust-colored. As the liquid settles into the bowl, shapes float to the surface like flotsam.

Ants, flies, roaches.

Closer now, the smell is different, rich yet spoiled, like chicken soup that has been left out too long.

Lisa hears the black man slurping.

She closes her eyes for a moment, sighs.

There's going to be a lot of swallowing at this meal.

She opens her eyes, sees her mother thoughtfully pouring her a tall glass of milk.

Lisa sips warm, gummy clots of insects, washed down with mouthfuls of milk. She sees how her mother looks at the black man, how they watch each other over spoonfuls of their soup.

The scene has a resonance, an insistent quality that wants to remind her of times spent around this table long ago, with her mother and her father.

But she resists the demands of that memory, that allusion.

Lisa notices that, though both their hands are clearly occupied *above* the table, they seem to be holding hands *below* the table, just out of sight.

It is an incongruity that hurts Lisa's head, so she concentrates on swallowing her soup instead.

* * *

Later that night, in her bed, Lisa thinks of veins, of the intricate web of veins inside her that flow with her blood.

As she lies there, smothered in blankets, smothered against the moans and soft voices coming through the thin wall that separates her room from that of her mother, she thinks of the blood that pulses through those veins.

It is her blood, yes, but it is also *her* blood.

It is also *his* blood, her father's, so long gone now, so long dead.

So long and so long and so long...

If she lies there very still, if she ignores the cries of her mother, she can hear the sound of that blood working its way through the mire of her veins, the unknown pathways that snake through her body.

Those veins go through places within her that she will never see, never know. In a way, those veins know more of her than she does of herself.

As she thinks these thoughts, these thoughts drowning out the sound of her mother's heavy breathing, the black man's coarse gasping, she feels a tickle on her leg, under the covers.

She rolls over toward the lamp on her nightstand, the lamp that is always on these nights, even when she is sleeping because she cannot be without light, rolls over and peels back the covers.

On her leg, halfway up her thigh, is a spider the size of a peanut. It is black with an interesting yellow design crisscrossing its plump abdomen.

It is paused there atop her skin, as if knowing that its presence has been revealed, as if awaiting some kind of judgment.

Instinctively, Lisa slaps it, crushes it against her thigh. She wipes the mashed and twisted thing off her, off the bed.

As it tumbles to the floor, she hears a keening wail pierce her mother's bedroom wall.

Then silence.

* * *

Saturday and she is preparing to do her chores.

Lisa has a list of chores to keep her occupied on weekends. She knows that it is as much to allow her mother to keep watch over her as it is to keep the house clean.

Sometimes there is a grocery list, oddly scant for two people, often with strange items listed.

1 doz. eggs
1 gal. whole milk
1 loaf bread
1 container mothballs
1 package light bulbs, 100 watt
Dryer sheets

But today, there is no shopping. Instead, Lisa's mother, still behind the closed door of her room, has left a note on the kitchen table. It has two lines on it, written in her tight, crabbed hand.

Eat your breakfast.
Clean the cobwebs.

Lisa reads this note as she stirs the oatmeal left for her in a pan on the stove. She moves the spoon through the gray, curdled stuff, seeing the transparent bits of wings, the segmented legs, the tiny, faceted eyes staring up at her quizzically, as if confused at finding themselves in a breakfast food.

She thinks for a moment that she will skip breakfast, just do her chores.

Her mother, though, will know. She feels that her mother is actually, right then, watching her. She knows that she is, with her eyes, those eyes that are dark and fathomless, those eyes that are only two, but seem like dozens, hundreds.

All focused on her.

Besides, she shrugs, *eating breakfast is No. 1 on her list.*

It is that important, as if feeding Lisa is the only part of their relationship that means anything these days.

So, Lisa eats her breakfast, mostly in swallows, cleans her single dish and spoon, the single pot, and goes to do her chores.

* * *

There are so many cobwebs.

Lisa supposes it is because the house they share is an old one.

That's what her mother tells her, and Lisa has no reason to disbelieve her.

Most weekends, the cobwebs must be swept from the corners of rooms, along the baseboards, from the tops of curtains, the bottoms of bed skirts.

She pauses outside the room next to her mother's. This door is never opened, always locked. Lisa has no idea what is in this room. She has never seen the inside of it, and is forbidden from making the attempt, or even asking about it.

Besides, this room oozes bad odors into the hallway, something that smells strongly base, strongly astringent. Over it, as if to cover it, is the smell of mothballs, the reek of which Lisa finds so foul that she holds her breath, preventing their vapors from entering her body, getting inside her and spoiling something within.

Because of the locked door, because of the mothballs, Lisa doesn't dawdle here. Quickly, she drags the duster along the seams of this door, catching cobwebs that have managed to squirt from inside the room.

When she is done with this, she takes a shower, eager to get their shivery feeling off her body. Cleaning the cobwebs is her least favorite chore, hated out of all proportion to the task. There is something distinctly unsettling about them, how they return despite constant cleanings, how they drape in the dark corners of the house, how they sway in unfelt breezes.

And then there's what they're made for.

To catch prey, to kill things.

To eat them.

The shampoo washes out of her hair and into the tub. It sluices over her, mingles with her skin's powder, turning into a glittering foam as it swirls down the drain.

Out of the shower, she wipes away the film of moisture from the mirror and stares at her face. With her hair wet and slicked back, her face is blank, androgynous. She seeks in her mirror image any sign, anything that will support her feelings of uniqueness, her special place in the order of things, but finds nothing. Nor can she see the web of veins that drapes across her flesh, just below the skin, carrying her blood, *her* blood, *his* blood through all of the secret places of her body.

She notices that her eyebrows are becoming bushy, the blonde hairs lifting, unfurling like delicate fronds.

Her father's eyebrows were like this, even more so. His were almost like antennae, twitching with sensitivity and emotion.

Lisa turns her back to the mirror, looks at the small, conical nubs of flesh arising from her shoulder blades. Two, just like in front, though smaller. She had pointed these out once before, when she had first noticed them, but her mother dismissed them.

Still, Lisa checks them daily, to see if they are... *growing*.

Satisfied that they are, she turns, brushes her teeth, wraps herself in a towel and walks to her bedroom to finish getting dressed.

* * *

She never sees, never hears the black man leave her mother's room, her mother's house that day. She never sees the black man again, and her mother says nothing more of him, offers no explanation.

* * *

A few weeks later she is awakened in the night by something painful that tears through her insides.

Rolling in the bed, she clasps her hands low over her stomach and moans in distress. It is a rippling wave of cramps like nothing she has experienced before.

She remembers dinner, something like chicken and dumplings except it was *not* chicken, and she clutches her spasming stomach even tighter.

Throwing the covers off, she staggers to her feet. Her gut feels tight and hard, but her insides feel disturbingly liquid, roiling like a deeply distressed inner sea. She stands there for a moment, her hands clutching the covers, her fingers splayed on the mattress for support.

Plipplipplipplip.

At her feet, just within the circle of light cast by the lamp, are what she at first thinks are bright copper pennies falling onto the carpet.

One strikes her bare foot, spatters.

Lisa bites her lip, walks quietly down the hallway to the bathroom, leaving a trail of pennies behind her, as if in a fairy tale where she would need them to find her way back.

* * *

"Well, it came last night," Lisa says, eying the glass of orange juice set before her, trying to see if anything is floating in it... anything she would need to know about. "Just be thankful you missed it."

Her mother is turned to the stove, stirring something.

"What's that, dear?"

"You know... what we talked about? The blood. Well, it came last night." Lisa takes a tentative sip of the juice, but it is smooth and free of foreign objects.

Her mother stops stirring, doesn't turn.

"Are you sure?"

"Positive."

Lisa hears a deep, quivering sigh issue from her.

"Why didn't you come get me?"

"I did what you showed me... with the box under the sink."

"Any problems?"

"Nope."

Lisa takes another sip of the juice, thinking she might want to slow down, save it for whatever her mother is cooking.

"Well, that's great," her mother breathes, turning to Lisa and patting her head. "This calls for a celebration."

"It does?"

Her mother smiles her disturbing smile at Lisa. "Absolutely. I'll cook you something special for breakfast. What would you like?"

Lisa looks doubtful. "It's just my period."

"No, it's finally happened, don't you see? It's what your body was made for, what *you* were made for."

"Well, in that case, how about pancakes?"

Her mother's smile, if at all possible, widens.

"How about chocolate chip pancakes?"

Lisa nods, eying her mostly filled glass of juice.

She knows that, despite her mother's strange cheerfulness, there won't be chocolate chips in the pancakes.

She's glad she saved the rest of the juice.

* * *

That night, she is very aware of having the thing jammed up inside her. She finds it hard to believe that something so soft and small can cause such discomfort.

She tells her mother that it's like a fairy tale, that tale of the princess and the pea. Her mother tells her that she won't notice it for long.

But she does, here in her bed.

Thinking of it also makes her think of the blood again, and the veins, the endless web of veins inside her.

She hears noises again this night, the shuffling of feet, grunts and growls, liquid mewlings.

Lisa wonders if the black man has returned to her mother's room.

She falls asleep, carried away by the cold dream of her father at the center of a giant web. But this is no spider web. The web he is trapped in is composed of veins, great throbbing veins.

His extravagant bushy eyebrows twitch and twitter with each pulse of the veins, gather together in concern when he sees her dream self.

As sleep encloses her in the darkness she has come to fear, she sees his mouth moving, speaking, but they are words the English language cannot penetrate. They rise toward her with great momentum, then lose that momentum, fall back to enmire themselves in the web next to him, useless, unheeded.

As dead, as silent as her father.

* * *

Her mother is not awake when Lisa rises, muggy and disoriented from her night of dreams. Lisa dresses, brushes her teeth, goes downstairs.

The kitchen is dark and untouched. There is nothing cooking on the stove, no note on the table. The room has an eerie, spectral quality to it, as if she is still upstairs and only dreaming of being in the kitchen.

She takes an orange, an apple and a banana from the fruit basket on the table, slips these into her book bag and leaves for school.

At the doorway, Lisa pauses, considers calling for her mother.

For some reason, some reason that slides from her grasp as slickly as an eel, she doesn't.

She's not afraid that her mother will answer her, will come downstairs.

She's afraid that she won't.

* * *

After school, the house is dark and silent.

She throws the door open onto an atmosphere that is thick and anticipatory, as if the house has contracted itself, tightened its muscles awaiting... something.

Someone.

It's still early spring, and dusk has already settled on the shoulders of the horizon. The kitchen is various shades of grey when she enters, sees the table set, the note atop her plate.

It's her mother's handwriting, she knows, but only barely. Its slanted, jagged letters are strung together as if under duress.

Eat your dinner. All of it.

Lisa sets the note on the counter and sees a plate wrapped in clear cellophane. She unseals the plate, finds two of her mother's sandwiches; the smell of the honey is thick and cloying.

Glancing at the ceiling to where her mother's room is, she knits her eyebrows together in confusion. She carries the plate to the table, opens the refrigerator.

She takes out a pitcher with a Post-It note stuck to it, as if in Wonderland.

Drink this. All of it.

Lisa shakes her head, brings the pitcher to the table. The pale celery color of the liquid within lets her know it is her mother's special tea.

Appreciating the fact that she doesn't have to swallow great wads of this meal, Lisa starts to eat. Chewing a mouthful of the sandwich, she pours herself a glass of tea, fragrant as a flower garden. It washes away the sticky honey from her mouth, and it is all sweet, sweet.

While she finishes the first sandwich, she hears sounds from upstairs, as if two pieces of fabric are being drawn over each other...or ripped apart. A skittering rustle across the upstairs floor sends a deep and powerful tremor of fear through her. A chorus of small, impatient, voices are all talking at the same time... muttering, whispering.

Her heart begins to beat faster, though she doesn't know why.

The bumps sprouting from her shoulder blades itch maddeningly, and she rubs them against the back of the chair.

Lisa reaches for the second sandwich, notices that her arms are covered with powder, as thick as if she had applied makeup to them. It billows from them with every movement, sends a cloud of multi-colored dust into the air, snowing onto the table.

She might have worried at all this—wants to worry at all this, but there is a deep lethargy growing inside her, a calming fog that rolls through her veins, carrying somnolence to every cell.

She goes on eating, filling her stomach with the second sandwich and glass after glass of the cold, bracingly sweet tea.

When she is done, she rests a hand on her distended belly and burps. It tastes of honey, and sweet, green growing things.

Lisa pushes herself from the table, stands.

Upstairs, there is a susurration that seems to imply many, many things moving; many, many feet.

"Lisa, dear," comes her mother's voice from within that sound. "We need you."

Though her mother's voice sounds cracked and distorted, as if playing from an old-fashioned record album, Lisa obeys.

"Coming, mother."

* * *

The stairwell is dark, but a light from the upstairs hallway bleeds onto the landing, and it calls to Lisa, beckoning her on as much as her mother's voice.

Lisa stumbles up the steps. Each lifting of her foot is laborious and strained, like moving through molasses.

It seems to take minutes to climb the stairs, step after plodding step, but she is at the top now, staring down the hallway.

The light comes from a sconce near the door that is always locked.

She steps toward it, and that light flickers, dies.

It is replaced by a sharp knife of light that slices across the hall floor.

The door is open.

Lisa stops short, places her hand on the wall for support.

There is a vibration, a tickle that runs through the floorboards, the walls.

There is a sound, a rustle like dry leaves in the fall trying to speak.

There is a smell, deeply biological and rank, like venom and nausea.

She places her hand on the open door, pushes…

Inside, it is a nightmare, and it requires Lisa's mind several moments to understand it.

At the far end of the room, wedged into the upper corner, is a bestial shape, molded from darkness. Until it moves, Lisa is unsure what it is.

When it does move, Lisa's heart vibrates in her chest like a trapped animal, shaking with a fear so deep and integral to what she is that she nearly swoons.

Legs. It is the legs of the thing moving that does it.

Legs. Eight of them, long, tapering to hairy points.

Legs. They were tucked into the thing's body, but now they unfold, seem to spread across the entire room.

"Lisa," says a high-pitched, reedy voice from some part of the thing.

"Mother," she breathes in response, and it feels like a breath that has been trapped inside her for years, waiting to find a way out.

89

Lisa opens her mouth to speak again, when she feels a tickle across her foot.

She pulls her eyes away from the thing that is her mother. Her eyes roll in their sockets like orbiting planets, until they are pointed down.

A host of small bodies is racing across her feet, up her legs.

Small, furry, agile.

Like their mother.

She can hear the creaking of their tiny voices.

Lisa steps back, breathing hard, heart pumping.

She turns to the door, but there is no light there any longer. The only light is here in the room, and she feels compelled by it.

"Hush, child," her mother says, unfolding herself from the corner of the ceiling and stepping down, each leg stepping gently, careful not to crush the eggs, enshrouded in a caul of webbing, the hatchlings that teem across the floor. There are so many, so very many that the floor looks like a carpet whose pattern is constantly shifting.

"No," Lisa says, and feels a tremendous pain in her back that nearly brings her to her knees. She holds the doorframe, shudders as she hears the material of her shirt rend.

"It is who you are, dear. Who you were made to be."

"No," says Lisa, feeling something wet and sticky unfold from her back, sees a puff of rainbow powder in the air.

"It is the way of things. Your father gave his life for yours," her mother says, stepping closer, her rank odor now a physical presence in the room. "That you might live to give yours."

More of the spiderlets climb her legs, step through her hair, tangling it. Some dangle from her arms, some dangle from her... *wings?*

She feels the hair of their small bodies, stiff as bristles, poking at her naked belly, her neck. She can feel the quivering of their bloated abdomens, black with a curiously familiar yellow pattern.

Lisa wants to step into the darkened hallway, wants to flee down the darkened stairs, but there is something about the dark, some terrible thing about the dark that keeps her there, despite her terror.

There is something about the light in the room, something about the crazy dark prisms of her mother's clustered eyes that keeps her there, despite her terror.

Her mother leans in a bit more, and she smells of spoiled meat, a sharp, acrid odor that can only be poison.

"You are your father's daughter," she whispers, lifts one long, impossibly thin leg to stroke Lisa's cold, trembling cheek. "And your father knew how important it is to feed his children."

* * *

Lisa rubs absently at the iridescent skin of her arm, which powders at her touch.

Dust with the rainbow sheen of oil on water drifts over the spatters of her blood, glitters like tiny fish scales in the null-light of the nursery.

Her brothers and sisters take it in, take it away...

THE
SCENT

He steps outside, pauses on his front stoop.

William is not an old man, not by today's standards, but he is a hat man. He is not bald or even balding, but he is a man who believes in hats. He believes in the fashion of hats, the safety of hats. What a hat says about its wearer.

In an age when men no longer wear hats, William wears hats.

And not just any hats. Not baseball hats or any of their varieties, to be sure—'gimme hats' with the names of insurance companies or local feed stores, caps emblazoned with the logos of college or professional teams or even caps with rap words on them, meant to be worn bill backwards.

A hat, to William, means a fedora with a crisp crease, perhaps a staid, squat bowler, or a conservative Homburg. Even a cool Panama or a rakish pork pie like those worn by Sinatra or Martin. On occasion, he's even been known to step out in a Stetson.

Today, he wears a tawny suit of tweed topped by an expensive beaver felt fedora; a rare and expensive hat, it makes him feel stylish and gives him a jaunty, nostalgic air.

He fingers its brim as he stands there, azaleas in bloom on either side of his porch. The cherry and dogwood trees are in blossom, too, and their over-sculpted, fuzzy pink and white blossoms give them the look of poodles standing on their hind legs.

As he adjusts the angle of the fedora, he inhales deeply their mingled odors: the fruity, flowery scents, mingled with the musky, almost sexual smell of the Bradford pear trees lining the street, brazenly announcing their availability to every passing bird and bee.

William walks to work, as he does each day, rain or shine. It is why he bought the condo in this marginal neighborhood on the verge of downtown St. Louis. Gutted and rehabbed throughout, William's townhouse is beautiful: all hardwood floors and pristine, white gallery walls, and stainless steel appliances.

Outside, though, the neighborhood is gutted. To either side of his condo are decaying tenements, collapsed warehouses and piles of bricks and debris that once, when whole, might have housed livery companies or taverns or rendering plants.

His neighborhood is marginal, yes, but he has had few troubles. With no car, he's not experienced any of the multiple thefts and break-ins many of his other gentrified neighbors have been subject to. His townhouse is fully outfitted with a state-of-the-art security system, which in the two years he's lived there has only gone off twice, and one of those occurrences had been caused by him. His backyard patio-cum-garden, small though it might be, is enclosed by a solid brick wall 10 feet in height, topped by a "decorative" row of iron spikes.

On his walks to and from work, he has never been mugged or assaulted. He is, though, constantly approached for money by men and women who plead various needs, all jointly understood to be false. The mother who needs an operation. The bus ticket for some vital trip. Money for a meal or to bail a loved one out of jail. William gives money or not depending on his mood and the creativity of the story, bestowing it when he does as much as an award as charity.

Having set the tilt of his fedora to keep the sun from his eyes, he steps down onto the pristine sidewalk that bisects his small, merely ornamental front lawn and sets off. The crisp, level lines of this sidewalk give way quickly to cracked and shattered pavement. In some places, great swaths of it are picked away like scabs, revealing the shocking red of cobblestones beneath; the desiccated, jumbled flesh of an older time; the time, perhaps, of the livery and the rendering plant.

William steps gingerly over these scars, barely noticing them anymore. He crosses Tamm and then Pestalozzi Streets, skeletal buildings lining each side like pallbearers. The trees give way to stunted, sprawling bushes whose flowers are small and stingy. Their odors are sharp, spicy, unpleasant, though they cover, somewhat, the musty, mothball aromas that waft from the abandoned buildings along this stretch of his path.

Here, a structure that once housed a carriage company. Here, a tannery. Here—disturbingly, right next door—a butcher shop. All closed, all gone years ago. Their faded signs, ghostlike on the brick sides of their buildings, give tantalizing clues to what they offered. Igloo Ice and Cold Storage. Renner's Valves and Boilers. The Eston Millinery Co. (William once peeked inside this building, through a hole in a boarded window. He saw nothing but dark emptiness. The intense, acrid smell of urine kept him from exploring further.)

All that is left of these places now are their sagging brick husks and the smell of their decay—dusty and moldy with the generic, loamy odor that all things offer up when they finally return to the earth.

But these were all old and accepted parts of William's world by this time. In the two years of walking back and forth to work, he'd seen all of these, noticed them in their turn as some piece or part of their structures caught his eye. He'd had time to study those things that held his attention, until they drifted again to the background, allowing some other detail or structure to come forward.

But now all is background to him, and he rarely devotes any time these days to thinking about his surroundings.

So, he walks, humming to himself, enjoying the coolness of the air, the shade cast onto his face by his hat.

When he smells it: a scent.

A new scent.

Not the death dust of the buildings, collapsing like shriveled lungs.

Not the chemicals of the ancient factories, still wheezing out their toxins.

Not the jungle aroma of the weeds tangled in the overgrown lots.

No, this is new. At once flowery and bitter, sweet and burning. He inhales, and it leaves his nostrils and throat feeling raw, abraded.

And it is disturbingly, elusively familiar.

He turns completely around, slowly. But there is nothing new here, nothing that could be giving off this increasingly intoxicating scent.

Here is the baby carriage factory, empty and heartbreakingly austere. Across the street, the low, ramshackle remains of the stables for the St. Louis Municipal Police Mounted Patrol, abandoned for nearly a century, still exuding the aroma of dry hay and moist droppings. Further up a bicycle repair shop and the collapsed remains of a fur exchange, whatever that was.

William sniffs the air again deeply, half expecting the smell to have vanished. But, instead, it has grown stronger.

Hints of juniper make him think of gin and tonics taken on his patio, complete with their final acid twist of lemon. But the scent also evokes hyacinth and honeysuckle, and even—briefly, lightly—tea roses.

William has never, in his two years of walking this route, never smelled anything even remotely like this.

But that's not true, he dimly knows, not entirely...

Something vague and shadowed lurches in the lizard part of his brain that processes smell. It fires synapses meant to bring forth memories. But there is a gulf here, a span, an abyss that cannot be bridged. So William's brain twitches with the smell, but cannot identify it, cannot place it in its rightful context.

He breathes it in again, a heady, pleasurable lungful. His eyes roll up into his head like the wheels of a slot machine, slowing to reveal their cherries, lemons, or bars.

What is it? he wonders. Then, tripping on its heels, *I have to know.*

He readjusts his brim with a quick, defiant snap, then lifts his nose into the air, turning and drawing deep breaths in through his nostrils as if he were a champion bloodhound.

It seems stronger behind him, to his right.

He turns, walks back past the boarded and graffitied windows of the Applewaite & Sons Trucking Co. He smells rot and old wood, oil and the phantom vapors of ancient gasoline, and, as everywhere, the flat, soupy tang of urine.

But above it all, rising like an aching high note over a bass choir is the scent: sweet and hinting of foliage and flowers. Cartoonlike, it reaches tenuous, smoky fingers out to him, fairly pulls him along.

A dark, narrow alley runs between the Applewaite & Sons building and its neighbor, Mugler Publishing & Printing. The alley's uneven surface is strewn with broken bottles, an old tire, a rickety stack of warped wood pallets, and the ubiquitous single shoe.

William pauses, momentarily brought to his senses by the instinctive alarm the alley sets off in his urban brain. At its end there is a wedge, a sliver of brilliant light, where the sun shines through to the ground again. To get to that light, though, he must pass through a space that is dark and dank, restrictive, with many potential hiding spots.

But the scent is insistent, overpowering his sharper senses.

He breathes deeply, coating his lungs in it, and steps into the alley.

It is like stepping into another world, another time.

The smells here are stronger, deeper. There is a womblike thickness to the air; liquid and organic with undertones that speak of grit and decay.

William steps forward cautiously, the scent lulling him, urging him on by degrees.

He nears the alley's exit. The wedge of sunlight has become a panel, narrow and tall, that rises above him. It reveals the space between the rear of the buildings, with the gaping, toothless mouths of their dark loading bays. Doors dot the brick structures here and there, some wooden and warped like badly set bones, others metal and rusting like oozing sores.

He puts a foot forward, out of the dark and into the light of this industrial courtyard, when he hears it... *them.*

Sounds.

Voices, muffled and constrained.

He freezes, dark, rainbow-sheened water soaking into his loafers

The voices are not speaking.

What he hears are not words, not conversation.

But there is a definite sense of command and protest, of compulsion and repulsion.

Of desire and fear.

He hugs the edge of the rusted and sagging remains of a fire escape, peers slowly around the corner of the building.

The elusive, ephemeral scent that has led him here takes on a forceful physical presence; it goes from ghost to revenant with shocking rapidity, striding from the shadows, the dappled sunlight and striking not just his nose, but his entire body.

William recoils from this blow. But his eyes do not close, nor do his nostrils stop bringing the scent inside of him; he takes it in gulps as if it, and not the air it is carried on, is what his lungs, his body, his mind craves.

It is flowers now, the scent: strongly, assertively floral. But there are so many colors to it, so many tones. Sharp lime and pine. A crisp, astringent soapiness. And underneath, barely perceptible but pervasive, a sweet reek of rot.

Still, he takes it in as his eyes take in movement in the mottled shadows. A figure, tall, heavy, masculine, looms over another, smaller, thin, feminine.

Their heads incline toward one another, their lips almost touching.

The man is all shade and outline. The woman, wearing a tight, bone-colored dress, reveals him beside her more as an absence, something missing. One of her hands, long, tapered nails painted eggplant, is flat against his chest. The other is not visible. One of his hands is cupping her chin, lifting her face to his.

Shaking his own head dully, William realizes what he's stumbled onto. Lovers or whatever passes for lovers in this rundown, scabrous neighborhood. A village Romeo and Juliet meeting in the ruins for sex. If he stays, William knows that afterward, in addition to the crude sex, he's likely to see an exchange of money or drugs… or both.

Slinking back around the corner of the building, he frowns, the power of the scent broken. It was only cheap perfume, after all, something to cover the other less pleasant odors of her addictions—the unwashed body of her customer, the meth-rotted teeth, dirty hair that reeks of sour sweat and cigarette smoke.

He takes a deep breath and exhales sharply. How could he have found the odor pleasurable, much less intoxicating? The scent is oily, cloying. It seems to ooze on the air, cover his skin in a sticky layer of scum. He feels it at the back of his throat now, coagulated there like blood.

He turns to head back down the alley, disgusted and disappointed.

A gurgle, liquid and strained.

He stops moving.

The blood within him stops, too—hesitates.

Suddenly, he is horribly sure that what he has just seen is not a prelude to sex…

Slowly, he advances to the corner again, edges around it.

The hand that William had thought rested lightly on the man's chest now looks stiff and clenched, its muscles taut with the effort to repel.

The hand that William had thought lifted her chin delicately now grasps her neck, squeezes tightly.

Another bubble of air escapes her lips.

The man's other hand appears now, arcing over his head like a dark wing unfurling.

A shiny talon at the tip of that wing descends powerfully.

Raises. Lowers.

Again.

Again.

Something that sounds like drops of rain patters to the ground, pools in the shadows at their feet.

Then, the man, the shadow, the shape turns toward William, fixes him with his eyes.

Instead of recoiling, reeling from the man's glare, William freezes.

The man's eyes glow from beneath the brim of his hat. They are hot, laval, and they roil in their orbits like balls of incandescent gas.

Hat...?

William notices, for the first time, the hat worn by the shadow.

Unconscious of what he's doing, his hand moves to the brim of his own hat, strokes it as if to reassure himself that it still sits atop his head.

The shadow smiles at him, his fiery orange eyes flashing, his teeth a white and even arc within the dark of his face.

He turns, fades away, and is gone, lost within the denseness of the worn buildings.

William remains still for a time. The shape of the woman is abstract against the relentless pattern of the cobblestones. She is all curves and spirals and glistening pools of red and cream. She is a painting now; he has reduced her to a kind of art.

He takes a single, tentative step forward, stops.

Two things come to him immediately, like sudden electric bolts.

There is the smell of blood: metallic, and as intimate as the change in his pocket. It floats on the air, recrimination and guilt, and it envelops him in a cloud.

Then there is the scent again, above, below, inside him.

It is bitter now, like old limes: sharp and too sweet, with a powdery tang like the taste of aspirin crushed between dry teeth.

And it is him, he realizes.

Me. My scent.

But William wears no cologne.

What he smelled today, noticed for the first time, is not the city around him, not the scent of its life and decay. Rather it is the scent of *him*: his shampoo, his soap, his shaving cream.

More, it the essential smell of him, his skin, his sweat, the whiskers that push up from beneath, and the blood that pulses through him. It is the smell of his failures and successes, his faith and fear, his affectations and the true self that lies quivering at his center.

It floats from him, wicked from his pores, surrounds him in an aura of his own making.

Another realization sweeps through him, impatient, yet seemingly content to wait for these first two to have their effect.

It is *his* scent, too.

His knees give, and he falls forward like a penitent, vomits onto the cold, slick ground.

His head bows forward until he feels the cool grit of the cobblestones pressing his forehead.

That's why it was so strong here... so overpowering.

I never smelled it before, but he wore it like a cape, like the shadows he shrouded himself in.

He wore it as if he knew it.

And he smiled at me because he recognized it.

Recognized me.

Weakly, he pulls himself to his feet, absently wipes his mouth.

He backs away from the woman's body, down the alley, back onto the street.

It is raining now, lightly, and it is as if a gauzy curtain has been draped over the city, softening its rougher features.

The sights, smells are familiar once again, but he draws none of them in any longer.

His own smell fills his nostrils now, plugging them against all else.

With a hesitant look in the direction he'd set out in this morning, toward his office, he turns back to his home, sets out through the rain that way instead.

When he arrives, he enters, locks the door behind him, goes to his closet.

On the patio in his backyard, within the 10-foot walls with their iron spikes, he burns all of his hats one by one, watching their dark smoke drift up into the misty, impersonal grey of the sky and fade, fade, fade...

CHILD OF DIRT

A child?

But how?

His wife had never slept with another man, he knew that, took it as an article of faith.

Primarily because he trusted her, loved her still.

But also because—and he didn't want to be cruel, not even here, in his secret heart—he knew that there would be few other men who'd want her.

She was plain and obese, not a hand you can bluff your way out of. Her hair was lank and brown, not the sparkling brown of the models on TV commercials for shampoo, just *brown*. The color of... well, other brown things. Her eyes were too close together, too deeply set; like raisins pressed into a cookie-dough face by a fumbling child.

But he loved her—perhaps not deeply and madly, but honestly and truly, nonetheless. Things had never been wildly romantic between them, but they'd been good. She adored him, and cold is the person who can't be swayed by another's adoration.

Hers was a gentle, uncomplicated soul, and the thought that her lavish affections were falling into an increasingly bottomless well, never to be acknowledged, never to be returned in kind, would have horrified her, perhaps even killed that small part of her that his love clung to so dearly.

Until her announcement...

* * *

She awoke one morning, earlier, bouncier than usual.

She'd awakened him, a rarity since she usually worked nights, and he found himself being kissed lasciviously.

"Hey, whoa! Slow down, slow down!" he yelped, amused, aroused, confused.

"That's not what you wanted last night," she said, kissing him deeply, in a way that she hadn't kissed him in ages, that he hadn't *allowed* himself to be kissed in ages.

"What are you talking about?" he asked, her face so close that she breathed in his question.

"Last night, you were... *incredible!* I mean, at first I was tired, but well... *wow!*"

She shot a hand under the covers that at first lingered, then became provocative. Just as he was about to let her continue, she pulled free, patted his chest.

"Now, I think you deserve a nice breakfast before you go to work."

He lay there as she left the room, trying to figure out exactly what had happened, then threw the covers back. As he turned to roll out of bed, he noticed the sheets on her side were soiled, dark splotches on the butter yellow cotton.

He drew a finger across one. It smelled of earth, and stagnant, brackish water, and he frowned, wiped his finger on the already soiled sheet.

* * *

After breakfast, he started upstairs to grab his suit coat. He went to the staircase, his hand on the newel post, when he saw something on the runner: an indistinct, dark smear. It went all the way to the top, a meandering line that marred the clean beige carpet. He wiped a hand across it, came away with a smudge of dry mud. His eyes drifted from the hallway to the family room.

He followed the trail to the sliding glass doors that opened onto the deck. He pressed his nose to the glass, saw the mud cross the deck, disappear down the half dozen or so steps that led to their backyard. His gaze wandered to where the property dropped off, behind a thin screen of birches and scraggly forsythias, to a storm drain behind the house.

And he saw—thought he saw—branches between two of the forsythias that looked broken, pushed inward... as if someone... *something* had...

* * *

A few weeks later, he woke early, the sun barely over the horizon and the sky deepest, darkest blue. Light seeped from beneath the bathroom door. As he closed his eyes, he heard the door open, heard the scuff of it against the carpet. Vaguely, he waited for her weight to settle on the bed.

"Honey? You need to wake up and hear this. *Honey?*"

"Mmmm, okay," he groaned, rolling over.

She stood silhouetted in the doorway still in her sleep clothes, a tattered Ramones t-shirt from a concert years earlier.

She was holding something, a little white plastic stick she twirled in her right hand.

"I'm pregnant," she cried; then she cried literally, tears spilling down her plump cheeks, onto Joey Ramone's faded face.

She leapt into bed, the box springs groaning. She covered his face with sloppy, tearsmeared kisses. She blurted words at him at a dizzying speed, and he was unable to sort them out. "... baby... parents will be freaked! ... the room... doctor... vitamins... names... girl... boy..."

Without lifting his head from her shoulders, he muttered, "Were we trying?"

"You can get pregnant even if you're not trying," she said, then kissed his earlobe as if forgiving his question.

"But we haven't... ummm... even... I mean, when's the last time we even made love?"

She pulled from him, looked at him carefully.

"Remember, a few weeks ago, after I got home from the late shift?" she asked, wiping tears on the corner of her t-shirt. "You came into the shower with me?"

While they did do various exciting and pleasurable things, he was sure—*absolutely* sure—that nothing they had done could possibly have resulted in a pregnancy.

But he simply nodded, kissed her.

Her chubby face lit up in a way that didn't just tug at his heart, but tore at it.

"Our baby," she said, the tears coming again. "Our baby."

Our baby, he thought. *Our baby.*

"Here, here," she said, hands fluttering over her expanded stomach. "He's kicking. Give me your hand... *your hand!*"

He felt the hard, gourd-like arc of her belly through her maternity top, felt the rise and fall of her breathing, could even feel her heartbeat, faint and tremulous. But no flutter, no twitch, no greeting from whatever floated within.

"Nothing."

"Well," she huffed. "He was doing the mambo a minute ago." Grabbing his hand and hiking her blouse up, she placed it onto her taut, bare skin. His hand splayed across it, as if palming a basketball, one finger resting on the nub of her belly button.

"Talk to him. Let him hear your voice."

Feeling ridiculous, he lowered his head until his lips grazed her skin. "Ummm, hi, baby. It's daddy..."

He barely got that word out when the tight skin of her belly stretched like a drumhead, something moving across it like the wake of a boat on water. It stretched and rippled, took on a shape...

... the shape of a small face.

It strained against the skin of her abdomen, lunged at him like a snapping dog. Her skin draped over its blunt, blindly searching features like a wet sheet, filled the tilted hollows of its eyes, stretched across the small open 'O' of its mouth.

"Jesus Christ!" he screamed, sprawling off the couch, banging his head on the corner of the coffee table.

"Teeth," was all he could say before he passed out.

* * *

Three months, fifteen days later.

They race to the hospital, he driving, she in the passenger seat, huffing and puffing. He lets her hold his hand, but doesn't allow her to place it on her belly. Too caught up in the throes of her labor, she doesn't notice.

She is on a bed, mostly nude, with sheets draped over her. Her thick, columnar legs are splayed, raised slightly, and she is screaming—screaming and sweating, sweating and cursing.

The thing slips from her, slides out of her curtained womb on a gush of amniotic fluids, screaming, screaming.

And then the thing he *thought* was his son, the empty, shriveled thing attached to the cord, comes out like a deflated balloon.

The doctors say it is the placenta, must be the placenta.

But he sees their faces, those of the nurses, sees the horror there, the confusion.

It *isn't* the placenta.

It is his son, his *real* son.

This thing, this hideous thing is the son of another...

He is confused.

Why don't they see this?

The doctor holds the thing aloft, and he sees, thinks he sees a look of vague concern cross the man's face, a little frisson of discomfort.

"Would you like to cut the cord, dad?"

As if entranced, he steps closer, numbly takes the clunky pair of hospital scissors a nurse gives him, reaches out to place the rubbery, braided thing between its two blades.

But its cries increase in volume, rise in pitch as he approaches. Its dark eyes fix on him, and it sees him, he knows it sees him and doesn't want him anywhere near.

Its mouth stretches open, open wide enough for him to see those teeth, those teeth he'd seen months earlier pressed against the skin of his wife's belly.

His hand shaking uncontrollably, he drops the scissors.

They clatter to the floor, barely before of him.

* * *

Home.

He cannot be brought to touch it, and when he even comes near, it cries, wails as if his very presence is an affront.

She gives him moist, sorrowful glances, but can offer no explanation, no comfort.

He can't get back to work quickly enough, and she knows this. At the front door, he barely pauses to peck at her upturned cheek.

It is pressed to her, wrapped in blankets. He glances at it, sees that its eyes are tracking him as he leans in to her, as if measuring the distance to his throat.

He pulls away, turns, and leaves the house.

* * *

Crying in the night.

She doesn't stir, doesn't act as if she hears it at all. *Perhaps this is a test*, he thinks, propped on one elbow and watching her. She is testing him to see if he will be a father and go see what is wrong.

Then, it strikes him that he is *crazy, insane* to think the things that he does.

How can he hold himself separate from her... *from him*... any longer?

And how can he possibly think that the child is anything other than what he appears to be?

His child.

The crying, the teeth... all in his head... in his head, made up by him to avoid the responsibility, the love, the tie to him, to her.

Sometime during the course of his thoughts, the crying has stopped, and the house is silent.

He stands in the hall and listens, hears only his own heartbeat, his own breathing.

The nursery door is ajar and he sees the yellow glow of the Winnie-the-Pooh nightlight she'd installed so that he wouldn't be there alone, in the dark. The light throws lengthy shadows of the mobile that hangs above the bed: strange, spidery shapes that creep up the walls, straddle the ceiling.

And he hears him in there, in his crib, cooing, cooing like a real baby.

He pauses in the partially open doorway, listening to that sound, and it reaches into him and finds a soft, unguarded place that brings tears to his eyes.

My son, my boy!

He pushes the door open, and the baby's cooing stops as if cut off by a knife.

And that awful certainty comes back.

How could it know it was him?

He tiptoes to the crib's side, peers in.

The baby, in a plain white onesie, lays on its back, glares at him with malice and hatred so fervid that the air around the crib seems hot, infected.

But that could not be.

And then it moves; shockingly, unexpectedly, moves, rolls over and pulls itself upright, its chubby little hands grasping the crib's slats, hoisting it up until it stands, stands on its two wobbling little legs.

Eyes, laval and hot with rage, steam at him, and the little mouth works: open and shut, open and shut, snapping impossible teeth at him, impossible and sharp.

He takes a step away, falters, his heart freezing like a cowed animal in the den of his chest.

It shrieks then, shrieks with a terrible, maddened, high-pitched tone that echoes in the small nursery.

Instantly she is there.

She reaches into the crib and picks it up, gently cradles it to her.

"Shhh," she coos, the shrieks still hanging in the room. "Mama's here, mama's here."

Though quiet, it glares at him, its eyes still roiling with rage.

And he looks away, lowers his eyes to the carpet in front of the crib.

There he sees something that makes his bladder feel loose.

A patch of dirt at the side of the crib, as if... as if someone, *something* had stood there, had come there in response to the child's cries, to comfort it.

Numbly, he turns, sees that the dirt is connected to a rough, wavering line that leads across the carpet, from the side of the crib back to the door behind him.

Distantly, as if in a dream, he hears—thinks he hears—the whisper of the sliding glass door downstairs closing.

He does not, not even once, entertain the thought of going downstairs to see what it is.

* * *

Nothing left but to leave.

He moves out the next morning.

There are tears, lots of them, some of them even his.

But he is determined and will not be swayed.

"I've done everything for you," she says, and he agrees, knowing that this is true. "I've given you a son... a beautiful son!"

"No," he says, simply shaking his head. *"No."*

"No?"

"No. Not mine. That is not mine." And he points at it... yes, *it* again... and shudders when it turns to him, follows him with eyes that shouldn't know what they know.

"Not yours?" Her mouth moves silently around these words.

"It *hates* me. How can you not see that?"

"He's just a baby. It's just a phase. He's yours; of course he's yours. Who else's would he be?"

He takes the handles of the two suitcases he's packed. "I don't know. I don't want to know."

"This is crazy," she wails at him as he opens the front door. "He's our baby... *your* baby."

"It may be a baby. It may be your baby. But it isn't mine. I know it... and it does, too."

* * *

It's not crazy if you think it is.

That's what he tells himself, what he repeats in his mind as he drives out to pick it up, to take it with him for the day.

She smiles, not nervous, not concerned, but gratefully, lovingly, as she hands it over strapped in its pumpkin seat, a bag stuffed with diapers and ointments, with bottles and powders and wipes and toys.

It, though, does not smile.

It, in fact, looks worried, begins shrieking as soon as the handle is passed from her to him.

But he coos down at it... at *him*... coos and shushes it gently, but does not reach to touch it, to comfort it.

He knows that she watches from the window as he straps the pumpkin seat into the car, closes the door.

She blows him a kiss.

And he returns it because he loves her, and for the first time he is sure, absolutely sure of that single emotion, that emotion which had been so unfaithful to him in the past, so apathetic.

He waves to her again, a smile spread across his face, sees his face reflected in the rearview mirror, ghastly, stretched taut.

He remembers *its* face pressing through the skin of her abdomen, *stretching*.

* * *

Down the hill, not too steep.

It has grown silent, its screaming has ceased. It watches him with careful, intense eyes as he undoes the buckle, lifts the seat from the car.

He is two blocks behind his own house, which he sees at the top of the hill, behind the birches and forsythias where the land falls off. He manages the descent while carefully holding the pumpkin seat at his side.

Reaching the bottom of the little valley, he looks around. A thin stream snakes from the mouth of a storm drain. There is a wedge-shaped concrete apron that juts from the bottom lip of the storm drain as it emerges from the side of the hill. Dirty, scummy water trickles from it, choked with weeds and debris.

He sets the pumpkin seat onto the concrete apron, peers into the dark recesses of the storm drain.

Six, ten feet in, it swallows the light, and he sees no farther. Nothing but the circular concrete walls of the pipe and the thin ribbon of dirty water that trickles down its center.

It contemplates his every move, sitting there in the pumpkin seat, wearing its little Oshkosh bib overalls and its little fake tennis shoes. Its eyes follow him, wondering what he is going to do next.

He reaches out; it starts, its eyes widening, and it hisses, catlike, venomous.

But he grasps the harness that holds it, releases it, removes the straps.

It remains motionless for a time, then shrugs off the harness, lifts itself from the seat...

... *stands.*

Stands on two tiny legs that neither shake nor falter as they bear its weight.

It moves with a speed, a fierceness that takes him by surprise. He feels those tiny, sharp teeth close on his arm, and there is a hot, needlelike pain, the warmth of blood spilling. He feels its tiny tongue lapping, lapping at the blood.

He grabs it with all his strength, pulls it from him, hurls it away.

The tiny body flies through the air, strikes the edge of the concrete apron, flops to the wet ground, lying there stunned.

Dear God, what have I done? What have I done?

Unafraid now, he takes it... *him...* in his arms, lifts him from the muck, clasps him.

What was I thinking? What have I done? I can't have... can't have...

He stumbles, his back to the storm drain, still holding him tightly clasped, smelling the downy hair on his head, feeling the sticky wetness on his face and hoping, praying that it is mostly mud.

After a moment, when his anxiety subsides, he lifts him to get a good look at the boy, at his son. There is some blood, not a lot, a bump on his forehead that is turning black and purple.

But that isn't it, isn't it at all.

The boy smiles at him, at his father, smiles like a baby boy, like a child is supposed to. Color suffuses his cheeks and his eyes twinkle merrily. Then he laughs, and it is like clean water, the laughter of a baby, innocent and full of pure delight.

And his heart leaps to see it, to hear it, to know that it isn't too late, that he hasn't done anything yet that he can't take back.

Of course this is his child.

But then he notices that he... *it*... isn't looking at him, isn't laughing for him, smiling at him.

It is looking *behind* him, into the darkness of the storm drain.

He doesn't turn, doesn't want to know.

But he hears it behind him, slithering behind him in the mud and brackish water of the drainpipe.

Hears it hiss gently, not at him, but at the child... *its* child.

Feels its breath, cold and spoiled on the back of his neck.

Last of all, he hears the child say its first word as it throws its arms wide for an embrace.

"Da-da."

ORIFICE

She told me on the way home, "When you make a hole in something—*anything*—something else will want to get in through it... or *out*."

She had flounced away after that—flounced, with her sparkling brown hair bouncing and shimmering in the sunlight, dancing across the freckles on her bare shoulders. I remember how her hair had smelled then, sunny and clean and vitally alive. I can inhale even now and draw in the ghost of its presence, haunting in its intoxication.

And she had smiled. I saw a glance of it before she turned to walk away, bright and sharp enough to cut and cauterize in one swipe.

Or out, she had said.

Christ...

As she turned, her midriff top hiked up a bit—just a bit—to expose her taut, early summer belly, the smooth curve of her abdomen as it swept up to her breasts.

And her tattoo.

It was supposed to be a rose, red and black with touches of green here and there. Its stem began at her diaphragm, with the petals of the flower unfolding within the valley of her breasts.

A flower. That's what she had wanted.

To me, it never looked like a flower.

But this is now, and that was…

… before…

"You want a what?" I asked as we sat shoulder to shoulder at a coffee bar in one of the more Bohemian parts of town she preferred.

"A tattoo," she said, as if it were the most natural of desires. "Don't tell me that you, of all people, have a problem with that?"

She giggled over her double latte, and that sound irritated something deep inside me, something whose existence, up to that point, I had been unaware of.

Jesse moved in a strange circle, filled with slackers and hackers, New Agers and Xers, post-hippies and post-yuppies, headbangers and rappers, white supremacists and black Muslims, and I moved with her—albeit mostly in her wake.

Her friends were into wild music, strong liquor, stronger drugs, wilder sex, everything. As Jesse succumbed to the varying gravitational influences of these friends, I tried all of it with her, without prejudging the experiences, without carrying away a lot of baggage afterwards.

Most of the things we did with her friends I had never even considered before meeting her—and frankly, some of the things I'd never do again. But Jesse seemed to enjoy our relationship like that, and I happened to, also, so what the hell, you know?

In fact, I think that's what angered me most—my own response to her *wanting* a tattoo.

I tried not to screw my face up too much as I formulated my answer.

"A tattoo," I repeated, giving myself time to think of something more meaningful to say. "That's… umm… *interesting.*"

I hid my face behind the steaming mug of herbal tea that sat mainly untouched before me. I hated the stuff, but Jesse thought I looked pale and said it would help.

"You're serious. You really don't want me to get a tattoo," she said, setting her own cup down and peering intently at me.

"It's not that…" I stammered, trying desperately to think of what it was. "It's just that… I don't… Okay, I don't want you to get a tattoo."

"Why not?" she pressed, her look turning to one of baffled wonderment.

"I don't know. It's just that… I think they look… cheap." I whispered the last word, turned my eyes away. "Besides, why now? I mean, I guess I'm kind of surprised you don't already have a few."

"Mikey! You're so sweet. Dopey, but sweet."

She kissed me, and it was strawberries and cherry licorice, sweet and sticky, and I remember it so vividly that it hurts me even now.

"Of course they're cheap. That's why I want one," she said, flashing me a wicked leer and raising her eyebrows. "And I want one now because… well… because I'm ready for one."

"Uh-huh… where?"

"You're not jealous, are you? Of Mutt?" And her voice rose an octave, as it did whenever she thought some miraculous insight had been visited upon her.

Mutt.

I hadn't even thought of him. He worked in a tattoo shop down on 72nd. He was one of the crazy satellites Jesse still held in an erratic orbit; a past lover of hers who came to more of our parties than I might have preferred, and who still, I thought then and know now, had some sort of hold on her.

Jealous? Yes, sir. Guilty as charged. Sign me up. Book 'em, Dano.

"No," I responded. "And I meant where on your body, not where in the city."

"Oh," she said, as if destroying that particular insight meant little to her. "I was thinking of something on my chest or stomach."

"I like your chest the way it is."

"You didn't mind me getting my nipple pierced."

"You can take that out. Tattoos are just… I don't know, Jesse. I've gone along with nearly everything you've wanted. Christ, I even wore that male skirt you bought me—and for an entire weekend. But this… it's so *permanent.*"

When I turned back to her, I saw a face I didn't see often. It was not exactly cross, but crossed: full of silent measuring and analysis.

"Mikey, *you* decided to wear the skirt, which, by the way, I still think you looked really hot in. But this is *my* body, *my* decision."

She was right. This was the first time I had ever tried to impose my feelings on something she wanted to do to herself. I never told her how to dress or how to wear her hair, never even thought about it.

"You're right," I admitted. "But you asked me, and I told you."

"Fair enough," she said, her mood shifting back to playful. "You'll come with me and hold my hand, won't you? At least to make sure Mutt doesn't make a pass at me."

"I'll come," I growled.

* * *

The needle touched skin, vibrated with the small hum of a person in deep concentration.

A smell—electrical, full of ozone with metallic undertones—crackled from everything in the cramped little backroom of the tattoo parlor.

There was a brief moment of contact, full of excitement and anticipation.

Jesse grasped my hand, squeezed it tightly.

Then, the needle broke the skin, punched through.

A dot of color, a bright, iridescent green, lay side by side with a perfectly circular dot of blood that had been coaxed to the surface by the tattooist's instrument.

Jesse's skin flinched, relaxed.

The needle approached again, penetrated.

With casual impatience, Mutt wiped a cloth across Jesse's quivering belly, brushed his long, braided, white-boy Rastafarian hair out of his eyes and over his shoulders with a great clacking of wooden beads and a smell not too dissimilar from that of a wet dog.

Mutt was just that: a shaggy, brooding dog of a man. He leaned over Jesse, shirtless, his skin a dirty, greasy olive in color, with numerous piercings and tattoos covering his well-muscled, yet slight form.

I didn't really find him repugnant, merely mildly disgusting. Yet, I could see it was these very same qualities that had attracted Jesse to him originally. I could see, despite myself, how they had been together, how his careless hygiene and rumpled demeanor might have appealed to her.

As I thought these things, Jesse was stretched out topless upon a battered barber's chair of dubious lineage, Mutt straddled over her. His hands moved on her, bracing himself, roving here and there over her, stretching her skin, wiping at it.

It was impersonal enough, but she writhed under his touch, seemingly as excited by him and the constant pricking of his needle as pained by it. Her compact, rose-colored nipples were stiff and achingly erect, her breasts a mass of goosebumps. Light shone from the single gold ring that looped through the areola of her left nipple.

I began to feel distinctly uncomfortable, voyeuristic in a jealous, envious way that I had not experienced before with Jesse.

This is what they had looked like together when they made love long ago.

This touching, as professional as it appeared, grabbed that part of me that had shambled into the light earlier when she had first mentioned the tattoo, and shook it fiercely, like a dog worrying an old shoe.

And that part of me was becoming angry.

A rapier-thin moan hissed from between her lips drew me back. When I looked down again, a bright green line snaked from just above and to the right of her navel all the way to the midpoint between her breasts.

One of Mutt's hands, large and flat like the blade of a shovel, clenched Jesse's right breast, held it away from the area he was working on. A single, dirty-nailed finger rested casually, familiarly atop her nipple.

"Hey," I muttered. "Watch it."

Mutt looked at me through the veil of his hair and smiled the smile of a cur, toothy and nervously courageous.

He slowly, conspicuously removed his finger from Jesse's breast, moved his hand so only the heel of his palm held its weight aside.

Jesse didn't notice—or chose to ignore—this exchange, and Mutt, too, quickly forgot it, and me.

It took nearly two hours to complete this particular piece of 'body art,' as Mutt called it. Jesse lay exhausted when he finished, but I still held her limp hand, patted it.

Mutt told us in diffident tones that the area around the tattoo would hurt a little for a while. Maybe a couple of days. To shore up this statement, he shrugged, then helped me put Jesse's shirt back on. Her bra I wadded up, crammed into my pocket.

I paid Mutt myself, with my own money.

It was as good a way to make up to Jesse for my earlier disapproval as any I might be likely to come up with later.

As I forked over a rather large amount of money to Mutt, I asked what it was he had permanently affixed to Jesse's chest.

Mutt folded the cash into a thick, dirty bundle and pushed it into the front pocket of his long, baggy shorts.

"It's a flower, man," he smiled again, this time disarming in its brutal, blunt dislike of me. "A fuckin' flower."

He shook his head, laughed roughly, then disappeared into the recesses of the filthy little tattoo parlor.

He took my question as an insult.

But I truly couldn't tell what it was.

* * *

We stumbled home after it was done, her and I.

Jesse seemed overly tired and sluggish for so simple a procedure, but who was I to know? I had no tattoos; certainly no other friends or lovers of mine sported them.

Like so many things that Jesse dragged me into, I was not experienced in this.

So, I half-walked, half-carried her back to our apartment in some cheap industrial space on the north side of town. We talked a little on the way, before she became so tired that I had to carry her.

"When you make a hole in something—*anything*—something else will want to get in through it. *Or out*," she'd laughed, describing her personal philosophy of tattoos.

I laughed, too. She could make you feel giddy even when you were mad at her.

Two buses, seven blocks of walking and countless wondering stares later, I got her home and closed the door behind us. My arm was numb from holding her up, but I gathered her to me nonetheless and carried her through our open, minimalist living space to bed.

Jesse didn't stir much as I removed her Doc Martens, unsnapped and then slid her jeans down and off. She wore no panties, and her bra was still a ball in my pocket.

I hesitated at removing her shirt when I saw that virulent green line oozing up her belly in the darkness underneath. I thought of her rolling over in the night, pressing her naked body to mine, pressing that thing to me... and I shivered.

I left her shirt on, stripped myself and crawled into bed with her.

She smelled like the tattoo shop, like Mutt, like blood.

I fell asleep facing away from her.

Late that night, I awoke.

The wind stirred the sheer curtains covering the huge, open windows that were one entire side of our apartment.

I heard the ghostly huff and rumble of a train in the distance, near the river.

Industrial dusk-to-dawns spilled pools of orange-sherbet-colored light onto the floor.

Something moved next to me, rubbed against me with urgency.

"Mikey?" I heard her breathe into my ear. "Are you awake?"

Suddenly, I was. *Very.*

"Umm," she purred, her hand reaching around me, grasping me. "You are."

I turned over and found her face, kissed it.

Her lips were as cool as the night air, moist.

Her skin, though, was hot and sticky. For a moment, I thought she might be delirious, feverish from an infection due to her damned tattoo.

But her hands and lips left me little time to think.

So, I didn't.

As we embraced, I noticed that, at some time during the night, she had removed her shirt.

Jesse seemed frantic in her lovemaking, nipping and rubbing and pulling me to her until the sheets and pillows were kicked away, leaving just us, tangled, sweating and breathing heavily.

She lay back, relatively docile, as I trailed kisses across her breasts, down her belly.

As my head pushed lower, my hand reached up for purchase in the darkness, slid across flesh.

Something wet and accommodating engulfed my index finger, drew it in, sucked it.

My excitement neared crescendo. I became more frantic, my kisses more fervent, lingering as I descended.

Her mouth scoured my finger, released it, drew in the next.

I can't begin to describe how intense this experience was, how it overwhelmed my senses.

Until she spoke.

"Come up here."

Aside from panting, her voice was certainly unaffected by any of my fingers.

I instantly broke the surface of my desire, and with chilling clarity moved the hand that was being sucked on.

It swept up the curve of a breast.

In one motion, I uncorked my finger from whatever held it and lifted myself to see what it was.

My finger came free with a sound not unlike that of pulling a wet sneaker from a puddle of thick mud.

"Here," Jesse pleaded, still writhing beneath me as I hovered over her on unsteady arms.

I looked down, and those arms nearly gave out.

The ridiculous orange light oozed across Jesse's body, falling full on the tattoo that lay between her breasts.

Where the bud of the rose should have been, though, there was a dark hole in her flesh. It gaped like a glistening wound, and its edges opened and closed wetly, making little slurping, kissing sounds.

I closed my eyes. Opened them.

My fingers had been there, *in* there.

With force that was more spasm than coherent movement, I pushed myself away from her, tumbled over the edge of the bed and thwacked my head on the cold, concrete floor.

Not too hard, but it stunned me for a moment.

It took some time for Jesse to realize I was not there anymore.

"Mikey?" I heard her voice above me. It sounded normal now.

"Here," I grunted, pulling myself up and rubbing the back of my head.

"Where did you go?" she asked, moving across the bed toward me.

I saw a slim, white hand, hesitated, took it.

"What happened?" she asked again, helping me to a sitting position next to her on the bed.

"I don't know..." I hesitated, hoping she would think it was the blow to my head, and not the terrified beating of my heart, that had me rattled. "My arms just gave out, I guess."

From within the orange-tinted darkness, I saw the gleam of her smile.

"Dopey. You're probably still exhausted from carrying me home. Just lie here with me."

Even that, frankly, was more than I was capable of at that point.

She drew me near, and I stiffened, resisted a bit, put my hand out... to ward her off?

... to see if it was still there?

It wasn't.

My hand encountered smooth, unbroken flesh that arced gently upward in either direction.

No ragged, slurping hole.

"Hey!" she giggled, pulling my groping hands away. "Don't start something you can't finish. Just lie back and relax now. Fall asleep."

Jesse pulled me to her again, and my head fell toward her breast.

But I couldn't relax, couldn't nuzzle my head to her... not there, anyway.

"I need a drink," I said, pulling away perhaps a bit too brusquely.

"Sure, okay. Whatever."

"I'm gonna get a glass of juice. Want some?"

"Nope. I'm going back to sleep. Hurry back," she yawned, gathering the sheets and pillows and nesting them around her.

I padded across the floor to the kitchen area, drew open the refrigerator door. Light exploded from it, and I reached in, dazzled, and grabbed for the juice container.

The acidic orange juice, drank straight from the container, cut through the dust and mucus that filled my mouth, cleared my aching, swirling head.

I didn't hurry back to bed.

Don't know how long I stood there watching her as she fell quickly back into sleep, as if the past fifteen minutes had been no more than a dream.

Must have been a while. The orange juice container slipping from my grasp roused me. Rather than open the fridge again and let the light out, I drained the rest of the juice, left the empty container on the counter.

I fell asleep on the couch near the windows, feeling the breeze and the edges of the curtains tickle my skin.

And watched the pale crescent of Jesse's body wax under the approaching light of dawn.

* * *

When I arose late in the morning, she was gone.

It was already becoming hot as the sun climbed the blue hill of the sky. A thin, lazy wind curled into the apartment without disturbing the curtains.

The heat also brought with it more of the industrial smells of our neighborhood—tar and asphalt; unknown, probably caustic, and most certainly carcinogenic, chemicals; burning diesel and oil from the hundreds of tractor trailers that swarmed around the area, all topped by the rich, rotten miasma of the nearby river.

As my head cleared, I remembered the day, the night before.

The tattoo.

And Jesse was gone.

For some unfathomable reason, this alarmed me.

Angered me.

Understand, if you don't already, that Jesse and I were what are charitably called 'free spirits.' Or as my father called us, 'deadbeats.' We had no schedules, no constant source of employment. Nowhere we had to be at any given time.

And it certainly was in keeping for Jesse to leave without telling me where she'd be. I never worried about this, because she always turned up none the worse for wear.

I told myself this as I scrambled into my clothes, laced my boots.

I told myself she was okay.

I told myself she wasn't with Mutt.

That she wasn't at the tattoo parlor.

* * *

She was, of course. I knew it immediately.

But why?

Was she getting another tattoo?

Was Mutt finishing the flower he had begun yesterday?

Or was it something else?

The word *affair* went through my mind then, derailing my thoughts.

What a dumb, antiquated word it is. Not a word for the Pepsi/MTV generation—a word suited more for the nine-to-five middle manager screwing his secretary or the bored suburban housewife seducing the paperboy.

Not for me. Not for Jesse.

I mean, Christ, we were living together; we weren't married.

As I considered all this, the dark, hulking thing within me that had flexed its muscles while Mutt shimmied atop Jesse the day before was growing stronger.

It had quietly fought my conscience; it had won my heart.

And had I been listening, I could have heard the sound of it coming now for my brain, screaming like an enraged juggernaut.

Maybe I could have gotten out of its way.

Maybe I would have wanted to.

* * *

By the time I reached the tattoo parlor, it was late afternoon. The waning sun already threw shadows into the canyons between the buildings, and everything looked uniformly grey.

Of course, there was a closed sign in the yellowed, barred window of the shop. But lights were on, and I could hear music from within, vibrating the glass: Korn or Tool… something.

Of course, the door was locked.

I was prepared for these eventualities.

Slipping around the corner, I made my way down a narrow, littered alley to the back of the building.

A battered metal door was embedded in the building here, rusting like a raw sore. Blocking it was a municipal trash dumpster filled with garbage.

It was on wheels, and a few hard pushes got it moving easily.

Mutt must have been depending on the dumpster to block access to the door, because it was unlocked.

The knob turned easily, quietly, and I found myself in a storeroom filled with darkness, stacks of boxes, and garbage from lunches past. But mostly, darkness.

Another door, half open, led into the backroom where, yesterday, Mutt had made holes in Jesse's skin.

Something will want to get in...

I closed the back door behind me. It creaked loudly on its ancient hinges, but the music was so loud in there I didn't worry.

I stepped cautiously into the wedge of light that pushed through the open door.

Even as I peered around the doorjamb, some part of me—some part that had not been thoroughly cowed by my anger—did not expect to see Jesse there.

That part of me understood that I was about to make a fool of myself.

It was pretty damned surprised, then, when I saw Mutt and Jesse locked naked together on the battered and spotted reclining chair.

His mouth and hands were all over her body, and her response was much the same as it had been with me the night before: feral and unthinking. Her hips pumped, ground into his lean body as he worked her into a frenzy.

One of his spatulate hands stroked the area between her breasts...

... the tattoo.

As I watched in anger and anticipatory horror, the tattoo rippled, as if his hand had passed across the surface of a pool of water.

Suddenly, it took on depth, became three-dimensional.

It was a hole again; the hole that had sucked at my fingers last night.

It was oozy-shiny, raw and wet, coral pink at the edges.

As Mutt's fingers toyed with this orifice, he pushed himself up along Jesse's body, positioned himself above her.

I saw his erection bob into view, and I was horribly sure where he meant to put it.

Something will want to get in...

With a flash of insight Jesse would have been proud of, I realized what he was doing.

He loved her—that much was evident. He hadn't broken up with her a year ago; she'd broken up with him. Or, as was more likely, she simply drifted away from him, like an errant moon breaking orbit.

Sometime after that, Mutt must have come to realize why he had lost her. It was for the same reason that I knew, standing there watching this, that I, too, would eventually lose her.

I will put it to you bluntly.

You could fuck Jesse, but you could never touch her heart.

Mutt had tried, and she had ended up stealing away from him as a prisoner escapes from jail.

She had stayed with me for so long because I had never tried.

Never cared enough to bother.

Mutt, though, had waited—waited until he had finally seen his chance.

He had tattooed a hole, an entrance to Jesse's heart, not a flower.

Something will want to get in...

Now, he was going to touch her heart in the only way he knew how... in the only way she knew how to let him.

His back arched, his buttocks tensed.

The curve of his back, so pronounced now that his knobby spine threatened to pop through the taut, shiny skin, flattened, drove down.

The tattoo above Jesse's heart accepted him.

He pressed down to her chest, shuddered deeply, like a dog shaking off water.

I could not watch any longer...

Nearly falling into the room, I caught myself, stopped at the side of the chair as the two heaved and groaned near me.

When I looked down, tears squeezed from Jesse's closed eyes.

Mutt turned his head sideways, grinned ravenously at me through his lank braids, grunted.

In anger, I reached out, closed my hand around the first thing it touched.

It glistened in the light, cold in my hand.

With another move from me, it began vibrating in my hand, oddly comforting.

Arcing it over my head, I brought it down hard onto that straining, undulating wall of muscle.

Mutt screamed.

It skipped over his skin like the needle of a kid's cheap phonograph, leaving a meandering trail of red that looked like...

... *like I had drawn a ragged cut, a wound onto the unbroken flesh of his back.*

And it became one.

Mutt wailed, his arms flailing behind him in an attempt to grasp the needle from my hand.

But it was too late.

Blood—or was it red dye?—gurgled from the wound, pooled across the ridges and scarps of his back, ran down Jesse's sides and the cracked, autumn-gold vinyl of the reclining chair.

Jesse screamed then, I think.

116

At least, I hear her scream when I have my nightmare...
I remember bringing the needle up again.
The music was very loud.
Mutt's body flopped to the ground, didn't move.
Red dye, red tattoo dye was everywhere...
I brought the needle down to Jesse.
"I love you."
I said it. Or she said it.
It doesn't matter now.
I remember her eyes then, wide and vacant, trying to stare up at the red blotch I had made on her forehead.

* * *

Now...
That was a year and many states ago.
I don't even know the name of the city I'm staying in... one of those California names, 'San' something.
I'm in a one-room apartment in a part of the city that's so seedy it's nearly fashionable.
Jesse would have liked it.
I often stand naked here at night, as I'm doing right now, with the lights of the bars and tattoo parlors winking at me reflecting off my body.
I look in the mirror that hangs on the door in my room.
And I remember what Jesse told me.
When you make a hole in something—anything—something else will want to get in through it.
Or out.
I have tried, you see, to let it out...
But so far, nothing.
I am afraid that I am empty, devoid of love.
Every square inch of my body is tattooed.
I have shaved all of my hair, replaced it with tattoos.
I have forgotten what color I was—black, white, yellow?
It doesn't matter.
I have pierced every limb or appendage my body has to offer—my ears and nipples first, but then my eyebrows, nose, cheeks, navel, penis, scrotum, the webbing between my fingers.
Last week, I had my tongue pierced and could not talk for three days.
They did it by hammering a nail through it.
And then I realized...
It was so simple, really, when it came to me.
Jesse would be proud.
The holes were too *small*.

Too small for my love to get out.

It took me a little while to save up the money to buy it.

The tired, disinterested clerk at the gun and liquor store told me that bullets—'dum-dums,' he called them, I think—made the biggest holes.

"That," I smiled, "Is what I need, then."

When I saw myself smiling in the two-way mirror behind the man, I saw Mutt.

I think this will work.

I'm ready.

I just hope that I will see Jesse when my love finally gets out.

Because I will tell her that I love her…

HELPING HANDS

We shook hands the first time we met.

How strange, now that I look back upon it.

"Good afternoon, doctor," he said, coming up from his seat in the parlor and rising to his full, towering height.

I shook his hand, firm and strong, and there was seemingly nothing untoward, at this point, about Mr. Benjamin Craddock.

Or his hands.

Our first meeting was conducted just as his hideous malady had struck, and only days before his death.

Are you sure you won't join me in a scotch or brandy before we go on, doctor?

No? I believe I will, however.

We went together into my office, closed the door.

"Please," I said, "Have a seat on the couch or a chair, whichever you prefer."

"I prefer to be comfortable," he said, avoiding the couch as if it were a ravenous beast, and sitting, topcoat and all, straight-backed in the nearby chair.

"Your coat?"

He dismissed me with a wave of his hand. "I think I'll keep it for now. Maybe later, when you understand."

I thought little of it at that point. Though having been involved with alienism for only a very short time, I've learned to note, but pay little heed to, the specific obsessions or neuroses of my patients at this early stage.

As I moved to my desk to get the wax cylinder for the recording machine—I record each of my sessions, have I told you? Marvelous machine. You really should look into one, keep up with the times and all that—I took the opportunity to observe Mr. Craddock.

He looked about 45 years old, with a head of blonde hair and a weathered face, tanned and lined. He was tall, as I noted before, well over six feet, with broad shoulders and a massive, almost immobile neck.

Mr. Craddock exhibited no interest in either his surroundings or what I was doing—unusual in that most first-time patients are very interested in both, signs of their discomfort.

Taking the now clichéd seat at the head of the couch, opposite Craddock's own—I opened my notebook and placed the cylinder into the machine, which occupied a small table between us.

"You do understand that I record all of my sessions...?"

At this, he leapt up, his dark coat flapping about him like wings. "No, I do not, god damn you, sir! I'll not be made a spectacle of between you and your infernal machine! You'll not share my woes with your doctor friends!"

"Really," I said, attempting to calm him. "If you had so little opinion of me and my services, Mr. Craddock, why did you come here? The recordings are as private as my files. No one other than me has access to them. I can assure you—on my word as a gentleman, sir—complete confidentiality."

He stared at me for a moment, face flushed, hands wringing. "Under normal circumstances, I wouldn't have come for your services, *doctor*," he said, the last word dripping venom. "So, don't let my presence here serve as proof of your sterling reputation. But I suppose the machine is acceptable... for now."

He subsided uneasily, took his seat.

The entire exchange had, of course, been recorded. You've heard it, no doubt?

I thought so.

"I realize that this is uncomfortable for you, Mr. Craddock. But I can help only if you relax."

"All right," he replied, still looking very tense.

"Now, why don't you tell me the problem?"

This, rather unexpectedly, produced another strong response from my rather unwilling patient.

"What?" he snapped, turning toward me. "No background? Nothing about my childhood? How can you possibly help me without first putting it into perspective?"

In an instant, I realized that there was more to his reaction than discomfort or embarrassment over visiting someone in my profession.

It was *fear*.

"I'd rather hear about your problem first. Then we'll get to your mother," I said, hoping to inject a little levity to the conversation, but it was lost on him.

Craddock twisted on the couch, and I noticed that his hands left dark, wet smears on the front of his coat.

"My problem… yes. It has always been my problem, hasn't it? That's what my wife told me before I left. What my children said. My friends, when I had any. It's kind of ironic, really."

This seemed more a rhetorical soliloquy, so I bade him continue.

"Well, I see no way around this or to temper its effect on you. And I am paying you quite handsomely to listen to me babble. I suppose I'd best show you," he said, rising again.

"Show me…?" I began, but stopped when Craddock doffed the topcoat. He was dressed in a dark waistcoat, dark trousers, a plain white shirt and a dark blue cravat.

He removed the waistcoat, pulled at the cravat.

His shirt was loose and blousy on him, not at all the fashion these days.

To my astonishment, though, something *moved* beneath it.

Craddock didn't look at me as he undid the buttons on his shirt quickly, savagely. He wore no undergarment beneath it to further cover what grew from the center of his chest.

It was a hand.

A perfectly formed, five-fingered adult hand.

It hung limp from perhaps an inch of wrist that protruded from where Craddock's sternum should have been, palm down, as if someone had reached through him.

Fascinated, but trying not to appear overly so, I rose and stepped toward him.

As if this did not astonish enough, the hand was a *woman's*, pale, smooth and delicate, with a slender wrist and thin fingers, perfectly manicured. Although it grew from him, it seemed untouched by his ruddy skin coloring and his rather prodigious body hair.

I poked at the hand with a pen, and it twitched, grabbed the pen, held it for a moment as if contemplating it, hurled it across the room in a spray of indigo ink.

Startled, I stepped away, asked him to clothe himself, which he did eagerly.

"I don't see what you want me to help you with, Mr. Craddock," I said, reseating myself and stopping the recording device. "You need the services of skilled medical doctor, not an alienist."

120

"The hell you say," he spat, head still down as he buttoned his shirt. I watched, fascinated, as he wrestled the supernumerary appendage back inside the shirt. It fought his movements, poked through a gap between the buttons. He negligently swatted it back in, closed the material around it.

"I know what I need. And I need an alienist, sir, not a surgeon."

He drew his waistcoat about him, then his topcoat, stood ramrod stiff next to the chair.

"I don't see what you expect me to do. You need to have that examined…"

"*Amputated?*" he answered, staring coldly. "Is that what you were going to say?"

I did not answer, but flushed guiltily.

Indeed, that is exactly what I meant to say.

Perhaps if he had listened, seen a surgeon, had it removed, it may have prevented what I will recount shortly.

He moved toward the door as I struggled for something to say.

"You're just like the rest, sir. You don't understand. I can no more cut it off than I could my own hands.

"You see," he said, drawing open the door, turning back toward me, and touching his chest where the extra limb spasmed beneath his clothing. "I can finally feel her."

He left me sitting there, and I shuddered at his last words.

* * *

Your brandy is excellent, doctor, and is proving most efficacious in relaxing me. No, that is not necessary, I feel most able to continue this tale without a rest. We must press on, lest the details overwhelm me prematurely.

As one can imagine, the meeting stunned me, and I was quite unable to receive any more patients that day. I recall one of them was a gentleman of some import, a Mr. Richard Waddoes, who shortly thereafter killed himself.

But, I digress.

* * *

The next I heard of Mr. Craddock was in the papers, of all things.

I had been walking near Hyde Park after a meeting with my solicitor and had stopped to purchase the *Times* from a street vendor. It was an unusually balmy afternoon for October, so I decided to sit for a while, enjoy the weather, and read the paper.

Imagine my shock when, upon snapping open the paper, I was confronted by a rather lurid engraving of Mr. Craddock accompanying an equally lurid story telling how he was the prime suspect in the murders of his wife and children. The bodies were discovered only recently, so the paper said, in Craddock's estate in Aylesbury outside of London, he being a man of some wealth.

Craddock was actively being sought by the local authorities and Scotland Yard for questioning, for he had not been seen since.

Except, of course, by me.

Evidence, so the paper said, indicated that the family had been strangled, the children so violently that their necks had been broken.

I let the paper flutter away, was peripherally aware of a young urchin chasing after the pages, gathering them up no doubt to sell again.

On the long walk home, all I could think of was that hand, slender and feminine and delicate, thrust out of the center of Craddock's burly chest.

Warm though the weather was, I took to my bed with a chill immediately upon my arrival home, and was forced to cancel my appointments for several days, referring them to a colleague, Dr. L_____.

* * *

Did I, at that time, ingest laudanum?

Yes, but your unspoken accusation that I am or was a laudanum addict is quite preposterous. I have seen the terrible price paid by some of my less temperate colleagues, and have always been rather conservative when it comes to the substance.

No, if there is anything I imbibe too much, I'm afraid it is merely spirits, and forgive my having yet another glass. We are coming to the heart of the tale, and I fear to share the details that have brought me to these lamentable straits.

You're sure that you can't loosen...?

No? Well, I quite understand. Excuse my having asked again.

* * *

When I had recovered fully from my shock, I recalled my secretary and began scheduling appointments again and receiving patients. I had, at that time, made up my mind to alert the authorities to Craddock's presence here in our city, and had sent a messenger to Scotland Yard requesting that an officer visit.

A message returned, on a Tuesday morning I believe, informing me that a certain Inspector Lester from the Yard would pay me a call that afternoon.

You find that hard to believe? No? You should. The very answer to my life's calling right before me, shining like the sun, and me to blind to see it.

I spent the morning with two of my most recalcitrant cases—frustrating, frustrating—and was about to leave for dinner at my club, when I heard an altercation in the parlor.

Drawing on my coat, I was fully prepared to leave by the back door, so as not to be forced into accepting another unscheduled patient and miss my meal, when the front door burst open and a large figure dashed into the room.

Craddock!

My heart froze within me, my mouth very likely dangled open.

Miss Delft, my dear secretary—whom, incidentally, I was forced to let go in the aftermath of these events. (Poor dear! How I do hope she is getting along well!)—had no idea who this man was, and was telling him in the most strident tone that he was not to bother me without an appointment.

Craddock lurched to a halt, his dirty and tattered topcoat swaying around him, and pinned me with his burning eyes.

He had the look of an animal, his features disheveled, ashen, drained of all human intelligence, primal instinct alone remaining.

And pure, unreasoning fear.

A thin line of spittle fell from his lips to the expensive Persian carpet, which elicited a gasp of disapproval from Miss Delft.

"It is all right, Miss Delft," I said, when I could find my faculties. "I will see the gentleman. You may leave for the day."

She gave me a most unbelieving look, as if I taken leave of my senses, but acceded and closed the door as she left, leaving me alone with a murderer.

I had been alone with many lunatics before—men who fancied themselves Napoleon or Christ, men who fancied themselves women, men afraid of ordinary things, men afraid of supernatural things—but never a man who had actually *killed.*

What to do with such a man in such a situation?

He, fortunately, took the lead, or I fear we'd be standing there yet today.

His coat opened like the panels of a religious triptych, fell to the floor, revealing a horror that will live inside my mind forever. For even the darkness—or the madness, which you can well attest—could not blot it out.

Hands, dozens of them, a hundred of them, covered his nude body, erupted from every filthy square inch of exposed skin. They writhed along his form, each seemingly possessed of an individual will.

Some caressed him—a rather dainty one, I'm somewhat embarrassed to say, stroked his indifferent genitals. Others tortured him, pinching, pulling, slapping, poking his flesh.

And they were as different as the original extraneous limb had been to his own. There were feminine hands, children's hands, male hands, old hands, dark, light, small and large hands.

His own two were held outstretched to me, beseeching.

"Help me," he wept, large tears rolling down his face, falling like rain upon the waving, upturned fingertips.

"I can *feel. I can feel them all.*"

With newfound strength, I raced behind my desk, opened a locked drawer and withdrew a small box containing a syringe and three vials of morphine, which I keep on hand for my more excitable patients.

Nervously, I filled the syringe, cautiously approached Craddock, horrible and beautiful, I now realized, like a strange male Medusa.

He watched me with cowering, pitiable eyes as I came near—the eyes of a wounded beast.

Unable to find a suitable injection site amidst the undulating appendages, I stabbed it directly into his bare, corded neck.

Craddock screamed, thrust me away, fell to the floor as if pole axed.

Horribly, when he hit the ground, there was a series of loud reports, cracking and crunching.

Broken fingers, you see.

* * *

Yes, I did, at that juncture, administer a tincture of morphine to myself, to calm my own jumpy nerves. Yes, just a brief kiss of the grey lady.

I dragged him—Judas Priest, he was heavy!—across the rug to the couch, trying desperately to ignore the sound of all of those fingers raking along the carpet, snapping and crackling under his weight.

I didn't notice until I had him lying atop the couch, but the hands still moved, as if untouched by the flow of morphine in his blood, as if they took their substance from another source.

Or partook not of blood altogether.

Even under the pall of the drug, Craddock's delirium animated his body, his head thrashing on the pillows, his arms and legs twitching.

I knelt there for a moment, pitying the murderer. Poor wretch! Observe his trials, his torments!

And then a thought came into my mind.

Here is someone who could benefit from my ministrations.

My head began to clear at that thought, when the front bell rang.

I immediately remembered the visitor from Scotland Yard.

What to do? What to do?

* * *

You find that question so hard to fathom?

Are not we both men of science? Are we not trained to seek out the questions and problems that vex life, to answer them, to solve them?

Would you not have done the same in my circumstances?

... *No?*

Ah, well, you are younger than I. You have time to court the mysteries, to seduce the answers from them. I am getting older and am forced, by my age, to abduct them, wring the truth from them.

That is why I lied to Inspector Lester.

Craddock was my captured mystery, and I decided then, unconsciously perhaps, to study him, to learn his terrible, secret truth.

Oh yes, most cunningly, I straightened my clothing, brushed my hair, pinched my cheeks here and there to bring the color back.

How I beguiled the poor man. Oh, it was a brilliant performance.

"Please step in and warm yourself," I said. "Would you care for a cup of tea? Oh yes, I saw him, stood right here, he did. Murderous, he looked," I said. "No, sir, I didn't take him on as a patient. Something about him didn't feel right. Oh, well then I saw the story in the *Times*. That's why I sent for you," I said. "If there is anything else I can do, please let me know. I hope you catch the man. Lord, what a ghastly crime!" I said.

And all the time hating the officer, wishing he would leave. Thinking of Craddock there behind the closed door to my office, lying naked with a hundred hands waving like Sargasso floating atop a deep, dead sea.

A sea of dark truth.

Leave he eventually did, with my kind thanks and another invitation to have a cup of tea, thankfully declined.

I dashed back to my office, locking the front door and my office door behind me.

Craddock, indeed, still lay there, unmoving, save for the waving hands.

Suddenly inspired, I grabbed a pen and a piece of paper, took them to the couch.

I pressed the pen into the palm of one of the swaying hands, and it clenched around it.

I guided it to the paper, and after a moment, it moved instinctively, as if guessing my intent.

He feels me.

It scrawled the words on the sheet in huge letters, passed the pen to a neighboring hand, which took it up, and it, too, wrote upon the sheet. *He feels me.*

And so on, like a ship tossed on great waves, the pen passed from hand to hand, each writing the same three words.

Shaking, I snatched the pen away, and the hands returned to their aimless, rhythmic motion.

I suddenly remembered an article about mesmerism that I had read in a professional journal.

Ah, you read it, too?

I would have guessed you to have dismissed it. But I did not. No, I knew how to proceed then with Mr. Craddock.

But first, I had to let the morphine subside within him.

* * *

That evening, after a meager dinner of cold ham and cheese, a heel of stale bread, and a cup of tea, I revisited Mr. Craddock.

He was awake now, groggy, but entirely aware of his situation.

I was spared, for the moment, the distracting movement of the hands, for while he was under sedation, I had strapped him into a straitjacket.

Yes, very much like the one I'm wearing now, though I don't think I tightened the buckles quite as painfully as you have.

He didn't talk to me at all as I moved about the office gathering what I needed.

But this time, his eyes followed me with interest as they had not done during his prior visit.

I lit a candle and extinguished the gas lamps in the room. We were immediately plunged into darkness.

Guided by the candle's sputtering light, I made my way to the seat nearest the couch.

Though it was my first attempt at Dr. Mesmer's therapy, Craddock was hypnotized within minutes, as he followed my soft, repeated instructions and the bobbing candle flame.

"Mr. Craddock, you will answer all of my questions honestly and accurately. Do you understand?"

"Yes," he answered, and his voice was distant and small.

"Return now to the moment when you made the decision to kill your family. Why did you decide to do it?"

Silence for a moment, and the candle lit his grimacing face.

"Unloving. Incapable of the tender emotions. Love. Accused by my parents, my children, my own wife…" Here, he sobbed.

"… and they were right. *I could not feel them.* They were not real. Just things. Just things," he wailed.

"And now? After you have murdered them?"

"I feel them. All of them. Every feeling, every emotion. Everything I was unable to feel when they lived. They are with me constantly. And I am mad."

"The hands? They are a manifestation of this?" I asked, too eagerly, I must admit, for he noticed the slight change of tone in my voice.

"Yes. They are my hearts."

"Your wife's, your children's, yes. But the others?"

"They have killed since."

I was aghast. "*They?* The hands have killed?"

"Yes. They want me to *feel* more. To fully understand what I could not before."

"But if you feel now, then you are whole. You have what you were missing before."

The fool! I thought. He should have seen a medical doctor. Craddock had been on the right track with the murders, but couldn't see how to proceed afterwards.

It was all so clear to me.

The hands!

Yes, the hands were the cure *and* the disease.

They had to come off.

To cure Craddock, I had to remove them.

Of course I was capable. I was trained primarily as a medical doctor, though my skills in surgery were a trifle off from years of disuse.

They should suffice, though, for simple amputations.

I possessed the instruments, the ether.

I could help Craddock, return the gift he had given me.

For it was then that I saw my life stretch before me like a shining path.

And I was about to set my first step upon it.

* * *

It was 2 a.m. when I made the first cut.

Craddock was, as I said, abominably large and required strenuous effort on my part to get him into the cellar, where I had set up a crude operating theatre. As it was, his legs hung over the end of my wholly inadequate table.

I had laid out my instruments on a small tea table I dragged down the steps, arranged the various other surgical accoutrements to be close at hand when needed, since I would be performing alone.

When everything was finally in place, Craddock was strapped to the table with strong leather belts, anesthetized thoroughly with ether. I drew on an apron and picked up my scalpel.

I selected a hand at random, the dainty female one sprouting from the center of his chest, more intimate than a lover's, and brought the knife to bear.

Oh, what a scene followed. I know not how I kept my sanity intact.

The dainty thing spasmed as the knife scored the flesh of its wrist, flailed in an attempt to grab the instrument, pluck it from my grasp.

There, too, was a hideous scream that burst from the mouth of the unconscious man, though it was not his own. It was high and feminine, echoing in the confines of the cellar.

I nearly lost all resolve upon hearing it.

There was a splash of blood as the knife bit deep, encountering no bone on its way.

Imagine! No bone supporting the horrifying thing.

With a bit of force and a twist of the blade, it separated from the man, dropped to the ground where it continued to twitch and claw for several minutes.

The other hands were suddenly manic, as if they understood my awful purpose. They grabbed at my apron, at my sleeves, pawed at me.

Something snapped within me then. Yes, snapped with an audible sound.

I became furious, lopping off hands with broad, arcing swipes of the scalpel. The cellar became a charnel house, an abattoir as blood and tissue flew in all directions, spattered the gas lamps so thickly that the light took on a deep rose color.

And still I cut and hacked, turning Craddock this way and that as screams of all kinds poured from his mouth. Children and men and women all screamed through Craddock's mouth.

I must admit that I don't know how long I stood there, dripping with gore, slicing at the body of poor Mr. Craddock, a heap of amputated flesh flopping at my feet.

I don't remember when the screams stopped; certainly it was before I excised the last of the hands.

By then, of course, Craddock was quite dead.

While exhausted, I was elated, as you can no doubt imagine.

I had succeeded.

If only Craddock had taken my advice, done this earlier when there were fewer hands, he might have survived the procedure.

I consoled myself with the fact that while Craddock had left this life, he left it able to *feel*.

Fortifying myself with a draught of brandy from a bottle I'd brought down earlier, I went about the task of cleaning the place.

I felt energized, electric. I finally saw how to help, how to make a difference for my other patients. Suddenly, it became so clear that I harbored hope even for the most stubbornly regressive of them.

The cellar was thoroughly cleaned, and Craddock was dissected into small pieces, fed slowly into the boiler so as not to arouse the suspicious sniffs of my neighbors.

Not that the authorities would be searching here for Craddock!

Why, they had no reason to suspect the connection in the first place.

* * *

I grow weary, and the spirits burn in my brain, doctor.

The rest you know, I assume, from speaking with the inspectors.

I was never violent, you understand, never brutal. Always with a cup of poisoned tea or an overdose of morphine. Always quiet and civil and gentle as I helped them solve their problems. Always a proper burial in the garden behind the house.

And afterward, it was as if a new window opened within me, and I was able to see, to finally understand each one.

To feel them.

Unlike Craddock, I understood the curse inherent in the gift.

I removed each eruption as it appeared, a simple operation.

Everything was going so well. I had helped so many people.

Now, I am unable to help anyone.

Even myself.

I help you, doctor?

By Jove, that is true insanity! I don't *feel* you!

And you can't help me, either.

Do you know how I feel?

Do you know how anyone in this asylum *feels*?

I think not.

How can you hope to help me if you don't understand?

You have been kind, I'll grant.

No, I have quite forgotten the straitjacket, but you are kind to inquire as to my comfort.

You could, however, loosen the bandages around my forehead, they are a bit tight.

There...

Ah, better.

But why do you blanch, sir? Why so pale?

The wound has gotten worse, has it?

Bumps?

Five of them, you say?

IN MEN,
BLACK

The dark suit in the plastic dry cleaner bag arrived on a Wednesday, and Travis absently removed the hanger from the doorknob of his apartment.

Using his other hand, he jiggled out his keys, fitted one into the lock, swung the door open onto emptiness, blackness.

He flipped the leaning floor lamp on, slung the dry cleaning bag over the one piece of furniture in the place—a sagging, beaten futon—and went to the refrigerator. It had been a long, hard day at the office, with real estate sales being what they were—or *weren't* these days—and Travis wanted something to clear the dust and sourness from his mouth, something to numb his brain.

He removed a can, popped the top, and drained half before the door shut. Weighing the remainder of the can's contents against how he felt, he reached in just before the door closed and grabbed another.

He set the beers onto the arm of the futon, yanked his tie off, stepped from his pants. Sniffing at the shirt's armpits, he judged it wearable for at least one more day, slid it around a hanger.

In the bathroom's cramped confines, he shed his underwear and stepped into the shower. He let the scalding water steam the day from his skin; steam the thoughts from his head.

When he felt enough of the day had swirled down the drain, he toweled off, stepped into a pair of shorts, and slid on a t-shirt. He flopped onto the futon, and, just like that, the day he had hoped had been washed down the shower drain came back.

Swallowing the rest of the second beer, he flipped the can into a corner and stretched out atop the disarrayed covers on the futon.

Soon, he was asleep.

* * *

When he awoke, he felt muzzy, disoriented. Against the pull of lethargy, he shuffled to the bathroom to void the suddenly insistent beers from last night.

Twenty minutes later, he padded to the closet in his underwear, noticed the dry cleaner bag, still draped over the arm of the futon.

The suit inside was dark, and there was also a white shirt and a tie. The suit and tie were black… flat, midnight black. It had no pattern, no stripes, no sheen. It was as dark and featureless as if it had been spun from charcoal.

Travis knew he didn't own a black suit, had *never* owned a black suit, but he put it on anyway. This one fit his body intimately, as if it had been made for him.

Absently, he reached into the pockets. His left hand closed around a pink message slip, strangely addressed to him.

Pharmacist called. Your prescription is ready.

Travis stood there wearing a suit that wasn't his, looking at a message about a prescription that wasn't his, either.

A short car ride later, Travis found himself standing in line behind an elderly woman in the too-bright neighborhood drugstore. He waited patiently as the woman finished her business, stepped to the counter.

"The pharmacist would like to speak with you at the window marked 'Consultation'," the cashier told him.

Up the aisle a little, he stepped between two dividers that gave the window some measure of privacy. The pharmacist appeared, and Travis stepped back, feeling a scream push at the constriction of his throat.

The man's face was round and bland and white… not just the white of too many hours spent indoors, not even the white of anemia. This was a pallor so deep it appeared almost like makeup. His lips were thin, almost to the point of nonexistence, colorless.

He had no eyebrows.

"I am the Alchemist. I see you received the suit. Good. Your prescription."

The white-faced man placed the bag on the narrow counter between them, kept a thin, ashen hand atop it.

"You remember how to take these?"

In truth, there was something deeply, deeply familiar about all this.

"Take two a day: one in the morning, one in the evening," the Alchemist said, tapping his finger on the paper bag. "And take one whenever you begin to feel… *disassociated*. Not yourself. And always with plenty of water."

Travis nodded, afraid to open his mouth and give release to whatever was waiting on his tongue.

"You're lucky," the Alchemist said, pushing the bag forward and lifting his pallid hand from it. "You get to try to save them this time."

* * *

Back on the main road, Travis dumped the bag onto the passenger seat. The prescription bottle was plain, labeled only with the store's name and his.

Inside, there was a large amount of pills, small stars with eight tiny points, oddly colored.

White, but not the powdery white of aspirin. These were shimmery, opalescent as the light struck them.

He knocked one into his palm, uncapped the water, swallowed the pill.

* * *

At home that night, Travis removed the suit, put it gently onto its hanger. He placed it into the closet, where it merged with the shadows there, congealed into the greater darkness.

The prescription bottle, though, he carried into the kitchen. He threw one of the strange, star-shaped pills into his mouth and downed a glass of water, panting and gasping as he finished it. Before he'd even caught his breath, he refilled the tumbler, drank that, too.

Stumbling into the main room, he bumped into the edge of the couch, his hand finding the cell phone that he'd set onto its arm. He fumbled with the phone, disabled the feature that sent his number out.

Travis, wobbling now from a kind of exhaustion he had never experienced, opened his mouth—dry, despite the water he'd just drank—collapsed onto the bed, his head only grazing the pillow.

And he was fast asleep, gone away...

... *somewhere else.*

* * *

Around 3 a.m., Travis stirred. As if sleepwalking, he lurched to the kitchen, filled the tumbler with water. When he'd downed four glasses, he made his way back to the futon.

Scooping the phone from the dark sea of the carpet, he flipped it open.

For 15 minutes, he pecked at the phone, dialing 39 numbers in all.

When each was answered—and they were *all* answered—Travis emitted a series of strange sounds, staccato buzzes and clicks, mechanical, electrical in nature: pops and sizzles that sounded like shorted wires.

Each number listened for a few moments, there in the dead of night, hung up.

* * *

When he awoke, the sun was just coming through the windows. He ran his hand through his hair, scratched his head.

His heart froze, and his hand began to shake uncontrollably.

There was no hair on his head; it was bald, *smooth*, without even the roughness of stubble.

Looking at the bed, he saw his hair, strands of it, entire clumps of his scalp, whole sheets of his skin with hair still attached, strewn about the bed.

He raced to the bathroom, snapped the light on.

What he saw in the mirror made him brace his shivering arms against the small sink.

Not only was he completely bald, his skin had gone a disturbing, unnatural grey, his eye sockets, his temples, the hollows of his cheeks gaunt and spectral.

He gasped, noticing that he had lost his eyebrows, too, giving him the stricken look of a cancer patient. The hair on his chest and his arms was also gone.

Laughing nervously, he pulled the waistband of his underwear away from his belly and watched a puff of dark hair tumble down his legs.

Still giggling, he went into the kitchen, drank five glasses of water, each filled to the brim, and took the strange pill. Afterward, he showered, dressed in the black suit, and left his apartment, the pill bottle rattling in his pocket.

Travis climbed into his car, having no idea of where he was going other than that he was not going into the office today—probably never again, at least not looking like this.

There was a large white box, plain and unlabeled, on the passenger seat. Inside, nestled in tissue paper, was a hat: a plain black fedora with a plain black band around its crown.

It slid over the smooth skin of his newly bald head, settled low over his eyes.

Beneath the tissue, there was a sheet of paper with names and addresses.

* * *

He steered the car, making turns as if he knew where he was going. On an older residential street, he pulled to a stop in front of a brick bungalow, snug and well maintained. Travis removed the piece of paper, compared the address to the one on the mailbox.

Outside, the air felt too thick, the sun too bright. The front door stood open behind a glass storm door, revealing a tidy, well-appointed house, hardwood floors gleaming, motes of dust swirling in the early morning light.

An older woman appeared in the hallway. She wore a pair of capri-length jeans and the kind of overly floral blouse favored by women of a certain age. Her feet, veiny and calloused, were slid into a pair of scuffed, pink flip-flops.

"Mrs. Hearn?" Travis asked, then halted, his eyes bulging. Instead of his own voice, he heard something flat and monotone, high-pitched, as if someone had sped up his real voice. It sounded distinctly tinny and mechanical.

"Excuse me?"

"Are you Mrs. Gail Hearn?"

"And who are you?"

"My name is Mr. Tesla," he replied, letting the words fall from his mouth without thinking about them. "I am from the government. May I come inside?"

"This about those UFOs?" She still hadn't opened the door more than a crack. "Mrs. Rostenkowski said that a few of you... *people* were down talking to her a couple days ago."

Travis said nothing. He knew those she was referring to, the Annunciators, knew their functions, what they were doing... for, he suddenly realized, he was one, too.

They were like him, doing what has doing, wearing black suits, taking star-shaped pills, drinking glass after glass of water.

"May I come in?"

Mrs. Hearn looked up and down the street as she opened the door.

Travis followed her into a small sitting room. She motioned him to a recliner, while she sat on a couch facing him. The couch was draped with crocheted blankets in a bewildering variety of autumn colors and flanked by end tables sporting clean ashtrays and small dishes of hard candy.

"Mrs. Hearn," he began. "In addition to the UFOs, you saw a creature?"

Travis was unconcerned with the UFOs. He knew what those were, too, the Watchers, knew they had already fulfilled their function in what was transpiring.

Mrs. Hearn narrowed her eyes. "I only told a few neighbors and my family…"

"We are aware."

"Well, I can tell you it wasn't no person or bear or other damn thing," she said, warming to the subject. "My backyard butts up to the park along the riverfront. Lots of trees back there.

"It was about 11 p.m.; I went outside to take the trash out. I caught something out the corner of my eye, about 30 feet away."

Travis already knew what she had seen, the Harbinger, knew what it was, what its purpose was, but let her go on.

"It was about 10 or 12 feet tall, thin with spindly legs and arms. Its head was odd, no more than a bump on its shoulders, no neck or nothing. An enormous set of wings came from its back. Huge wings. They were sparkly, like…"

"Like a moth's wings," Travis finished.

"Exactly," she chuckled nervously. "Then, two little glowing red lights flashed from where I suppose its face was, and it leapt into the sky, flapping those weird wings. Headed over toward the bridge.

"Well, I ran inside, locked the doors, and turned off the light. And that was it. Mrs. Rostenkowski said she's seen it on some TV program. Called it a 'mothman.' Hah!"

"You are familiar with the bridge, Mrs. Hearn?"

"What does that have to do with the price of tea in China?"

"Your husband worked on the bridge."

Now, her frown became angry. "Well, yes, he did, but he died earlier this year. I don't know why you'd be interested in that. Say, what branch of the…?"

"Might I trouble you for a glass of water?" he interrupted. "I must take a pill. My energy is running low."

This somewhat odd statement elicited sympathy from her. At her age, she was well acquainted with the necessity of taking medicines at precise times.

"Of course," she said, departing the room and returning with a tall glass of water. He popped the star-shaped pill into his mouth, drained the glass in a single, long drink.

"I will leave now," he said, handing the glass to her. "It would be wise not to discuss any of this. It could be dangerous for you."

"Is it a matter of national security?"

"A matter of national security," he nodded.

Her eyes widened. "Well, I know a lot of people don't take that seriously, but I do."

Travis stepped toward the door, paused. "And about the bridge. Avoid it if you can. Something terrible will happen."

Travis got back into his car and drove away.

He repeated this visit 38 times that day with the other names on his list before returning home.

And another 39 times the next day, with names taken from a brand new list that he found on the passenger seat of his car.

* * *

Sunday.

He dressed quickly in the black suit, exited the apartment. Over the last few days, Travis had let his mind slip away more and more often, calmly, not fighting the feeling that came over him. He simply let his conscious self float along, tugged by some great, dark current that pulled him from the shores of what he knew, who he was.

For he found that when he did, he knew where to go, who to see, what strange things to say. They were like lines in a script that he had memorized and discarded.

When the compulsion, the *geas* that constrained him loosened, he returned to the little apartment that increasingly felt alien to him, carefully hung up the suit, made a series of phone calls, then collapsed into a sleep so profound that neither reality nor dreams could penetrate it.

The Alchemist had told him to take a pill whenever he felt *disassociated.* Travis had assumed, at the time, this meant feeling *less* like himself.

Now, he knew the man... *man?...* had meant when he felt *more* like himself.

It wasn't important that he be *Travis...* it was important, vital, that he be a *conduit.*

A conduit from what to what, he didn't entirely understand, but he knew that it was important.

Not to him.

But to *them*, the deeper part of that current, the part that pushed him aside, carried him away, the consciousness that eclipsed him.

Oh, to *them* it was important.

To *them*, it was vital.

And behind it all, suffusing everything he did, was the bridge.

Because it wasn't *just* a bridge, not just a structure to bring people from one side of the Meramec River to the other to eat McDonald's and shop at the Super Wal-Mart.

No, the bridge represented something, embodied something more than the ordinary span of iron and concrete and steel arching over a river.

Not here, not in *this* reality…

But in *their* reality, the reality that lay close to ours, separated by the thinnest of membranes?

Oh, in *their* reality it embodied so much more.

In *their* reality, it was a doorway, a thing spanning *our* here to *their* here.

In *their* reality, it was a thing of dread, a thing of fear.

A thing to be destroyed…

* * *

The diner was steamy inside, and the warm, moist air rolled over Travis as he tugged at the door, a little bell tinkling over his head.

Travis stood in his dark suit, his dark hat, stood and surveyed the room. Most seats were filled; the counter was crowded elbow to elbow. Pink-uniformed waitresses wove between tables, bearing trays of food. The clatter of forks and knives and plates made a strange symphony on air smudged with grease, edged with coffee, softened by the warm smell of toast.

"Grab a seat anywhere, hon," said one waitress. "Be with you in a sec."

Travis heard her words as sounds, nothing intelligible. He stepped forward, moved as if in a trance, sat in a booth near the window. His hands, ashen, unreal looking, clasped atop the greasy Formica. He didn't look at the menu or take notice of anything, anyone.

A waitress stood suddenly by his elbow. "What can I get you?"

"I would like five glasses of water, please," he said, the droning, mechanical edge to his voice no longer a concern to him.

"*Five?*"

"And… toast." Travis uttered the last word as if unsure whether he wanted it and unsure he knew what it was any longer.

"White, wheat, or…?"

"May I have a newspaper?" he interrupted.

"Sure, there's a machine right outside the door."

Travis reached into his jacket and pulled out a twenty-dollar bill, held it to her pinched between two fingers.

"I am… not from around here. I am unfamiliar," he struggled with the words.

The waitress took the money uncertainly, touching the part of the bill farthest from his fingers. She scurried away, first to speak in hushed tones with the other waitresses, then to duck outside.

When she returned, she set five glasses of water on the table, along with a small plate of buttered white toast, a copy of the local paper folded in half, and his change.

Travis placed a pill into his mouth. Then, in rapid succession, he drained the contents of each of the five glasses of water.

The Masonville Courier-Gazette's headline was about some local scandal involving a school board member. But there, at the bottom, was the beginning of the story he knew he had been waiting for.

UFOS? MOTHMAN? MEN IN BLACK?

Locals Report Strange Encounters, Warnings about Bridge.

He scanned it, the words entering his brain and completing a complex equation left there by *them*. The equation ran inside him, in the organic circuits that they had begun to understand more fully... *and fear*.

The program set into motion by these words raced through Travis, causing his body to spasm with such force that he shook the table, rattled the glasses.

Heads turned toward him, eyes widened.

Travis stood, upsetting the table. Several glasses rolled from the table, shattered.

His aspect had come upon him now, finally fully activated.

He lurched toward the door, every eye upon him, every face tight with fear.

"Avoid the bridge," he said.

With that, he left, drove to his final destination.

* * *

The bridge arced some 100 feet over the dappled silk of the river below. Its steel span, its thin, gracile cables were painted white—pure, blinding white—in the glare of the sun. From a distance, the bridge looked like a weaver's loom. The weft and warp of its threads held up the flat deck of the bridge as if it were a piece of fabric already woven.

In a way, that was exactly what it was. Well, not *here*... but *there*, the stuff of the bridge had woven a doorway, a doorway that, had they known how to access it, to open it, the people of this reality could have simply walked through to the reality of the others.

And that, *they* could not allow.

So, they sent their Alchemist, their Watchers, their Harbinger, their Annunciators.

Each one of them—the Watchers, the Harbinger, the Annunciators— expressed a profound message, a meaning that apparently didn't translate through the ether separating them from us.

Perhaps that meaning was: *Don't build these structures.*

Perhaps it was: *We come in peace, but don't think you do.*

Perhaps something simpler, perhaps more complicated.

Whatever it was, in all the time they'd felt they had to do this, the message never got through, not in the way it was intended.

Because of that, because of fear, because of incomprehension, the final avatar that was sent, the final avatar that was always sent, was the Plectrum.

Travis, standing there on the deck of the bridge, looking down into the water, cars whizzing past him, realized that he was not, as he had thought, an Annunciator.

He was the Plectrum.

You're lucky. You get to try to save them this time.

The Alchemist hadn't meant 'them'... at least not the 'them' that Travis had thought. He had meant *them*, those entities beyond the barrier, deep in the current that had carried away his mind, his will. It was an honor to be selected as the Plectrum, at least to them.

He drew a deep breath, reached over the railing and touched one of the thick cables. This close, he could see that it was actually formed from 20 or more thinner cables woven together. In turn, those cables were formed from even thinner ones.

The Plectrum—for that was what he was now—touched the cable with Travis's pale fingers, as white as the clouds overhead. He was somehow able to insinuate his fingers between the cables in a way that should have been impossible.

Looping fingers around three of the thinner cables, he flexed his hand, plucked the cables as he might the strings of a huge harp.

A low tremor vibrated the concrete, thrummed through the supports and down the other cables until the whole structure quivered. The tone it produced was so low that it was felt rather than heard, and it momentarily disoriented Travis.

Brief though his bewilderment was, it was deep. So deep, it was as if, his job now done, they had pushed an internal reset button in him.

* * *

He came to in his car, driving. Twitching the steering wheel in surprise, he blinked his eyes, steadied the car.

He was on a busy eight-lane highway with a broad, grassy median. Twilight had settled in, and the cloudless sky was dappled blue and violet and peach. His window was open, and the air outside was comfortably warm, comfortably humid. It smelled of something primal, just beyond his perception. Salt, perhaps...

He looked at himself in the rearview mirror. His face was stretched, gaunt, his skin looked like paper. He felt queasy, shaky.

On the passenger seat was a map of Florida, its shape instantly familiar. He saw a city circled on it... Fort Myers. Rolling atop the map was a prescription bottle and a bottle of water. He reached over, grabbed the medicine.

Take for nausea as needed.

There was a doctor's name from Masonville, Missouri.

That city brought a low, nagging memory from the recesses of his mind. And that brought more, thin, evanescent ones that evaporated in the light of morning.

He'd been sick. He'd quit his job, found another in Florida. He was moving there now. He remembered this, but it didn't seem real, didn't seem to hold the weight of a real memory... of reality.

He popped the top of the prescription bottle, tilted a pill out, took it with a mouthful of water.

On a whim, he got off at the next exit, found a restaurant. Before he went in, he opened the trunk. His possessions... all of them, he guessed. He didn't have much. A few cardboard boxes here, but mostly clothing. He flipped through them, vaguely looking for something, but not clearly knowing what.

Didn't I have a black suit?

But he couldn't find it, and he was hungry, so he let it go.

He closed the trunk, walked across the grit of the darkening lot to the restaurant.

Pausing at a newspaper machine, he read the headline on the copy of *USA Today* showing through the small window.

Massive Bridge Collapse in Missouri

Death Toll Now at 48

He shrugged, walked inside the place wanting, more than anything, a plate of chicken-fried steak and to be left alone for a while.

DARKNESS
UPON THE VOID

The first one squeezed through the soft, smooth skin of his forearm and dropped with a little *plip!* onto the card table as he ate his dinner. It was a plump, featureless white, slightly glossy, and Ed didn't notice it immediately.

And then it moved...

... squirmed.

Calmly, he looked at the arm nearest where the maggot wriggled. There was a small dot of blood there, a thin line snaking from it to the table.

Calmly, he set the fork down and peered at the white thing writhing beside his dinner. The silky taste of pork fat spoiled on his tongue. An image came into his mind, unbidden; chewed clumps of green meat, tinged with rot, with...

Calmly, as if this happened all the time, he leaned forward and vomited. Everything that had been on the plate before returned in a hot, liquid glurt, barely digested.

He pushed back from the table, pushed back and stumbled toward the bathroom.

Dropping to his knees like a penitent, he slapped the toilet lid up and expelled a double-cheekful of his dinner, closed his eyes and spat out saliva, flecks of food that swam in his mouth.

Calmly, he lowered his head against the cool, battered rim of the toilet, and vomited again.

After he had brushed his teeth and rinsed his mouth thoroughly, he sat on the couch before his blank television and licked his lips. He wanted to make sure that he had removed all traces of pork grease, because even its hint made his stomach lurch.

As he sat there on the swayback couch, he tried to think where a maggot might have come from—the single maggot that now moved down the sewer lines enshrouded in a wad of toilet paper.

Rubbing absently at his forearm, his fingers tripping lightly over a bump, a small bubo raised slightly over the surrounding skin, dimpled at its center. He had forgotten about it, forgotten about the blood.

There were quite a few other bumps up and down—not only that arm— but his other as well. Each seemed tight and hot, infected. Whatever was beneath them felt loose and unconnected.

Scratching, he returned to the bathroom, the smell of vomit exorcised by the good folks at Clorox, and he removed a tube of salve from the medicine cabinet. Absently, he applied a dab of it onto each bump, capped the tube, replaced it within the rows of similar medicaments and tinctures, and prepared for bed by brushing his teeth once more.

Before he climbed into bed, he knelt at its side as he had learned as a child, old knees creaking as they touched the floor.

He knelt and tried to pray, but the words wouldn't come.

His prayers had backed up, kept within by some essential clog.

The voices.

He knew it was the voices.

Instead, he tried to visualize something, *anything...* world peace, an end to hunger, an end to suffering. But images disappeared beneath the incessant babble as easily as words.

Sighing, he pulled himself up, slid between the stiff, threadbare sheets and tried for sleep.

* * *

The voice of God had once filled Ed's heart and head. It was as clear and as resonant as a choir in a small church.

The voice of God had been big enough to fill all the spaces within Ed.

And he needed nothing else.

Now God no longer spoke or even whispered to him.

Now his head was filled with *them*, the voices, leaving no room even for his own.

They had crowded out his God, and he had lost Him. Because of this, he lost his church, his flock, his sense of self—all gone, gone not as in *disappeared*, but rather as in *smothered*, drowned out by the rest, lost in a chorus so dense, so overwhelming that he could no longer find himself within it.

Often, he wondered if Ed Martinez really existed anymore as a separate being, an individual. Or if he was a walking polity, the whole of a million voices packed inside, struggling to be heard.

Struggling to get out.

* * *

Ed's spare apartment over the closed butcher shop suited him. After his church had been forced into bankruptcy, he needed a place to live. He received a small severance from the church, a pitiable amount for 20 years of devotion to the congregation, to God. He'd been able to stretch that for 10 months now, getting this apartment, paying the utilities. Food stamps covered his groceries, which weren't much.

That money, though, was running out. Each week, he walked to the bank and checked his balance. Even though not much went out, the balance got smaller and smaller each week.

Ed volunteered a few days a month at the homeless shelter a few blocks over, doing laundry, making sandwiches, ladling soup into bowls, occasionally leading a service in the chapel. Sometimes, he ate meals there, sometimes they even let him take a shirt or a pair of pants.

He took it all, the clothing, the food, the welfare. But what he really appreciated was the opportunity to preach, to speak to people.

Because it was getting harder and harder to do this.

Sometimes, during a service, he lost his train of thought, stumbled over words, forgot passages of the Bible committed to memory long ago.

It wasn't age or infirmity. The din of the voices made it hard for him to hear his own words in his head.

The staff at the shelter had noticed, began finding ways to cut his hours back. They thought he was drinking or tweaking or huffing or smoking or just plain going nuts.

A dim part of Ed knew this, understood it, felt bad about it. He was embarrassed and deeply worried about becoming one of those vagrant street preachers, men with dirty clothing, dirty beards and eyes like a mad prophet's, hurling imprecations at pedestrians.

The staff at the shelter were to be forgiven because they simply couldn't know what was wrong, how difficult it was for him to hold things together these days.

He felt he was disassociating, coming apart like limestone ground into thousands, millions of grains of fine sand, each with its own voice.

They all wanted to come out, to spill out of him.

If they did, *when* they did, they'd take everything with them.

Ed was frightened that, God already having deserted him, the voices would leave him, too, leave him alone inside himself with nothing.

Like an empty church.

* * *

He rose early, his dreams still echoing in his mind. The voices didn't let up in sleep; they were cacophonous, insistent, though he never knew why or what they wanted.

Wearily, he rolled over to the simple alarm clock alone on the TV tray that served as his nightstand. The little radium-illuminated hands glowed a dreary blue-green *5:15*. Outside, dawn shone grey and pink through the smeary glass of his bedroom window.

Ed threw the covers back, and the cold assaulted him physically. Autumn was here, and the nighttime temperatures were plunging into the low 40s. Ed couldn't afford to turn the furnace on just yet, perhaps not at all, so he just kept adding covers to the bed.

Stepping lively, he went to the bathroom, closed the door on the tiny space. Reaching into the shower, he turned the hot water on full blast, let steam fill the room.

He stepped out of the sweat pants he slept in, kicked them aside with his boxers. A quick look in the mirror—old, grizzled, droopy, with the rheumy eyes of his father—then he sat heavily on the toilet.

Feeling the constriction of his bowels loosen, Ed leaned forward, closed his eyes. The hot water was doing the trick, filling the bathroom with clouds of wet, rolling steam, deliciously warm.

As Ed waited there on the toilet, a terrific cramp sliced through his gut, so unexpected, so painful that he bent his head forward until it touched his knees. His stomach bore down, clenched around something inside that wanted release, yet couldn't accommodate to the size of its exit.

Sweat broke out on his forehead as if pressed from his pores by the force of his exertion. He grimaced, gritted his teeth, pushed with all the fervor of a woman giving birth.

Something came out, much to his relief. He could feel it slip from him, feel it touch the cold water in the bowl.

Yet, it was still inside him, too, dangling from him.

And it moved.

Barely restraining a scream, Ed pushed to his feet. The pressure from this was enough to dislodge whatever it was. He felt it slip from his rectum, inch after surprising inch, curl into the toilet with enough force to splash water on his bare bum.

His feet tangled in the pile of his pants and boxers, stumbling as he turned to see what it was that he had expelled.

He expected blood, some extravagant bowel movement curled around itself like a great brown snake.

There was blood, to be sure, spatters and sloshes of it beading against the inner walls of the bowl.

Looped within this bloody water, though, was not a bowel movement but a *snake… an actual, living snake,* black with a rusty crisscross pattern along its thick, muscular length.

It wound within the white porcelain, easily a yard long. Its head, angular and viperish, lifted from the water, apprised him with deep amber eyes and a flicking tongue.

"Ed."

Its voice was a breathy whisper, clearly audible in the echo chamber of the bathroom.

Ed's eyes widened, his heart faltered, and he slapped at the toilet lid, brought it down with a ringing *clunk!* There was wet thrashing from beneath, and he reached out cautiously, flushed.

The toilet went through its cycle, and he flushed it again… again… and again.

Still sweating, still pantless, still breathing as if he'd run up the steep steps that led to his apartment, he lifted the lid cautiously, prepared to drop it and flush again.

But the water was empty, clear, placid.

As free of snakes as Ireland after St. Patrick.

He stood there for a moment, blood trickling between his cheeks, down his thighs, stood there leaning against the toilet tank, trying to get his heart to slow, his breathing to steady.

Had it really spoken his name?

* * *

Ed cleaned up, returned to the rumpled bed, his sheets dirty, smelling of Fritos and unwashed body. He buried himself in the bedclothes, wrapped a thin pillow around his head, rocked back and forth, back and forth to steady his teetering mind.

In his gut, he felt thrashing now, as if the snake he had just passed, that had just slithered out of his body, had not been alone.

He wondered, wondered as he lay there, his mind racing, his body rolling across the bed, wondered what else was inside him.

As that thought crossed his mind, floated atop the rush of voices that swirled in his head, Ed wept.

He thought of Christ on the cross, harassed, tortured, *empty*.

Eloi, Eloi, lama sabachthani?

* * *

Thursday was his one day to volunteer at the shelter, and he would not miss it.

He took an uneventful shower, dressed in his black pants and his black shirt with the collar, which he seldom wore these days. He had a cup of instant coffee and a Pop-Tart over the cluttered kitchen sink.

Locking the door, he made his way down the steep stairwell of his building. At the bottom were two doors. There was a sign on the one to the left, a notice that the landlord had locked out the tenant, the closed butcher shop. A battered lockbox was clamped over the doorknob.

Ed pushed through the grimy glass door and out onto the street.

It was cold that morning, and the grey steam of the walking people rose into the grey sky that closed over the city like a lid. His breath mingled with this respiratory cloud, floated like ectoplasm tethered to his mouth, unable to detach completely.

His feet shuffled the few blocks to the shelter. He nodded to the fat security guard at the front door, made his way into the kitchen. It was already a hive of activity. A few of the workers serving breakfast greeted Ed.

A few twists and turns along the bland, institutional corridors and Ed found himself in the bland, institutional room that was the shelter's chapel. The walls were the same pale green cinderblock. The windows were barred. The floor was the same scuffed linoleum that lined miles of floor within the building. Only the small crucifix on the wall, crooked, gave any clue that this room was different.

Folding chairs filled about three quarters of the space. At the front was a simple podium, small and battered. Ed spent a few moments tidying, straightening chairs that were already straight.

By nine o'clock, there were about 20 people in the room—mostly men, three or four women. All looked blasted. Their eyes had the faraway stare of people who had lost sight of hope so completely it wasn't even worth looking for anymore.

Ed cleared his throat, stepped behind the podium and began the service.

At first, he was surprised at how fluidly, how easily the words came to him. As he gained confidence, he became more animated, feeling the strength of the words as he once had.

He got through most of the service without incident, and he was feeling better, revived somewhat. So much so that he opened his Bible to a random passage and began reading.

"From Ezekiel 36:25, 'I will sprinkle clean water on you, and you will be clean; I will cleanse you from all your impurities and from all your idols. I will give you a new heart and put a new spirit in you...'"

There was pain in his mouth, sharp, stinging.

Something dark caught his eyes, scurried down his arm onto the podium.

The words filled his mouth, slowed, faltered, and he scanned the verse again, tried to find his place.

"Ehh... 'I will remove from you... your...'"

He felt sweat bead on his upper lip, his forehead. Lifting his arm to wipe his brow, he felt something tickle across his lower lip, fall down his chest.

His breath locked inside, he looked down.

A cockroach scuttled along the podium, climbed atop his Bible.

He slammed the book shut on it. There was crunch, a splat of thick, yellow fluid from between the pages.

"... ummm 'I will save you from all your uncleanness. Then you will remember your evil ways and wicked deeds...' "

He realized his hand was still raised, ready to mop sweat from his brow. He felt hot and cold, faint, his legs wobbled.

As he opened his mouth again, he felt a spill of things fall from his lips, bugs of all kinds, small moving legs, flittering wings, hard, chitinous bodies. They were making a curious, crowd sound, like a plague of locusts or a chorus of small, vibrato voices.

They pushed from his mouth, tumbled down his black shirt, piled atop the podium with a sound like potato chips emptied from a bag.

Ed looked aghast, felt the last two or three insects crawl from his open mouth, fall onto the mass that swarmed atop the podium, and over his Bible.

He heard curses from the congregation, gasps, a few women cried out.

Backing from the podium, he stumbled against the wall, his back sliding down it until his butt thumped the linoleum.

A few men jumped to help him, and Ed was glad for that.

He touched his mouth to wipe away any remaining bugs. There was pain, cuts within his mouth, across his lips.

His hands came back smeared with red.

* * *

The administrator of the shelter, a stern, iron-haired black woman who towered over Ed, brought him into her office, sat him on her couch, gave him some water. The staff physician looked at him, peered into his mouth, cleaned him up.

When he was steadier, they gave him coffee, asked him to empty his pockets. They poked through the jumble of stuff he brought forth, surreptitiously removed what looked like a flat package of razor blades, a small folding penknife.

They didn't ask him how he felt or what had happened.

Ed offered no explanation, for there was none that he thought suitable. Besides, his tongue hurt, and his mouth was raw and tasted of blood.

In the end, after things had calmed and several hours had passed, they asked him, gently, not to come back to the shelter. They no longer needed his services.

The administrator urged him to go to the clinic, but he refused. Still, she pressed a card into his hand, along with his blood-spattered Bible, urged him to call and take advantage of the service.

Ed bundled up for the walk back to his apartment. When he was outside, he unclenched his hand, looked at the card the woman had given him.

It was for free mental health counseling.

He laughed, tossed the card into the first trashcan he passed.

There was no need to see a hospital or a shrink.

Because he felt great.

The voices in his head had grown quieter.

He was sure, if more of them could get out, he would feel even better.

He would feel like himself again.

Just maybe, with most or all of the voices gone, there would be room again.

He would come back.

God would fill up the empty space inside him again.

He smiled as he walked home, delighted that people smiled back.

* * *

Ed pulled open the creaky metal door of his apartment building, closed it behind him. If it was possible, it felt even colder in the stairwell.

He looked up, saw the landing outside his door, and sighed.

He wanted to go upstairs, take a hot shower, drink something warm to soothe his aching mouth.

But he was impatient to put his plan into action.

Staring at the lockbox on the doorknob to the shuttered butcher shop, he licked his lips, tasting blood.

The lockbox seemed solid. He hefted it, tugged against the doorknob.

Then he saw screws on the doorknob plate, and knew he'd found a way in.

146

Upstairs in a drawer, he found an old butter knife with a thin, worn tip. He grabbed it, went back down and fumbled the tip against the head of one of the screws. It slid in, gripped, and Ed was able to turn it after a stubborn moment.

Within a minute, one of the screws lay in the palm of his hand. A few more, and the doorknob, lockbox and all, clattered to the floor of the vestibule.

Breathing heavily, Ed drew the door open, went inside.

The voices in his skull roared to life, as if guessing or even knowing what he planned to do. They were shrill, loud, so overwhelming they made his teeth chatter.

One step inside, and he had to stop, put his hands to his skull and press... *hard*... feeling as if his hands were the only thing keeping his head intact.

He faltered, almost fell to his knees.

For a time, he wasn't sure how long, he lost his place in the universe. His mind went black, subsumed within the pool of voices.

Then he saw the blood running down his wrists.

Shaking, he unbuttoned his shirt cuffs, rolled up his sleeves.

His arms were a mass of bumps, slippery with blood.

From each of these bumps, a squirming, twisting thing, dead white in the wan light of the butcher shop, pushed through his skin, swayed to and fro.

Disgusted, he slapped at one arm, then the other, dislodging as many maggots as he could, brushing them to the floor, spraying blood across the dusty tile floor.

Staggering to the back room, his hands slipped across the tile wall. He found the light switch, prayed a silent, almost unintelligible prayer that the landlord hadn't shut the power off yet.

The fluorescent lights flickered, hummed to life.

There it was, across the room in a corner on a stainless steel table.

He went to it, holding onto tables and empty meat cases along the way, leaving a trail of blood and smudged, red handprints as he went.

The meat-slicer gleamed atop its work station; its blade clean and ready.

He'd start with his hand, one hand.

Finding the toggle switch, he turned the slicer on. It growled smoothly to life, a tinny swirl of metallic sound filling the room.

Ed swallowed, placed his left hand, palm down, onto the little platform that went back and forth across the blade, pushed forward.

He expected pain, but was pleasantly surprised when none came.

From the other end of the machine, a thin, ghostlike thing fluttered out, draped onto the table.

Ed pulled his hand away, picked the thing up.

It was a thin flap of skin, hand-shaped, looking like it had been cut from wet tissue paper.

Ed's palm appeared raw, abraded, with a few pinpricks of blood oozing from it.

He replaced it on the platform, pushed again, again.

On the third time, the whirring blade whined, threw out a thin fan of red droplets that sprayed across the stainless steel table.

Ed yanked his hand back, slinging gouts of blood across the room.

The machine had cut away the skin from the flat part of his palm, his fingers.

But instead of blood and bone and meat underneath, he saw that his hand was packed with bugs. Worms frothed to the surface, spilled out. Small beetles, larger roaches, silverfish, ants, weevils, things with wings.

He picked at them with his undamaged hand, scooped them out of the shell of his palm, pried them from the hollow sticks of his fingers.

The voices, which had reached a perfect apoplexy of gibbering, fell silent.

Elated now, Ed went back to the machine, lay his forearm onto the platform, dialed a thicker cut, and pushed his arm through the moving blade.

The whine was rougher, the blade slowed. Blood flew in ribbons across the room, and Ed wept.

Not in pain, but in *relief*, in *release*, in *respite*.

The room was an abattoir; blood dappled the walls, pooled on the floor. Blood dripped from the light fixtures and the water-stained ceiling.

Ed, transported now, moved to the large Hobart saw used to cut steaks and roasts from larger sides of beef. It creaked to life, like a demonic sewing machine, the blade bobbing up and down, slowly at first, then gaining speed.

Eager to evict the inhabitants inside him, eager to make room, eager to prepare a place for his Lord, Ed slung one leg onto the saw's table, pushed forward...

In the end, there was space, emptiness.

In the end, there was a light that rushed forward to fill that space.

In the end, darkness collapsed around him, around that light.

And he, and only he, filled it.

* * *

Detective Broget stepped carefully through the mess inside the now brightly lit butcher shop.

The place was crowded with people, the crime scene specialists, a few uniforms, the medical examiner, EMTs. Near the front door was the landlord, pale as a gallon of milk, gesticulating wildly to one of the uniforms.

Broget thought he heard the landlord complain about *how was he going to lease the place out now?*

The stocky detective stepped as carefully as he could through the puddles, the pools of drying, tacky blood, but it proved impossible. The place was covered in it. He decided to stop trying, but still held onto tables as he passed, to keep from slipping. One of the uniforms skidded in the blood earlier, got covered with it, had to go outside to vomit.

His partner stood near what looked to be a pile of red, soaked rags on the floor near the meat saw. One of the EMTs held a body bag at ready, waiting for the ME to stand out of the way.

"So, what's it look like?" Broget asked.

"A fucking nightmare, that's what," his partner responded, his face tight, pinched. Broget knew why. It wasn't the blood everywhere or the carved up body; it was the smell. The entire place stank like a bank vault filled with dirty copper pennies.

The ME snapped off his gloves, tossed them in a nearby trashcan.

"Looks like it happened about six to eight hours ago. Basically cut and sawed to death, little by little, legs, arms, hands. Bled out, died from shock."

"Mob murder?"

"Nah, looks self-inflicted." He turned to a case on a nearby table, snapped it closed, picked it up.

"You shitting me?" Broget's partner sputtered, spreading his hand to encompass the scene.

"Nope, I do not shit… leastways not about this. Read all about it in my report tomorrow."

The ME gestured to the EMTs, who zipped up the body bag, lifted it, sloshing wetly, onto a gurney, wheeled it to the waiting ambulance.

Broget watched them go, sighed. "Landlord said Martinez volunteered at the New Life Shelter a few blocks over. Served meals, said grace, the usual. I rousted the head lady, and she said they let him go yesterday. He'd been acting strangely for months. Came to a head yesterday when he put some razor blades in his mouth during a service, cut himself up pretty bad, spat blood everywhere, freaked out a bunch of our more refined homeless."

His partner shook his head. "Jeez, let's get the hell out of here. I need to clean my shoes."

They started through the mess back toward the door, when a small, dark shape skittered from under a table, darted across the blood-specked floor.

Broget stomped down hard, twisted his shoe back and forth.

When he lifted it, there was a crushed shell, splayed legs, a splat of yellow.

"Damn roaches."

SHARP EDGES

Monday: Revelation
Ouch, she says, *it's sharp*.
And it is.
So sharp, so very, very sharp.
Thrusting. Shrieks. Warm gushes.
I cry!
I cut!
And the wound hugs my knife, strokes it with its own warm, wet flesh; tries to prevent the blade from entering, but once in, tries to keep it from leaving.
But it enters, and it leaves, reluctantly each time.
Again and again.
Then, it's done.
The warmth fades, the wound dries.
In the morning, I awaken from this dream, disoriented, stiff.
There is a spot, just a spot of blood on the clean, white sheets.
A strange thought runs through my head.
I bleed for them.
I wonder...
Will they bleed for me?
What does this mean?

* * *

Tuesday: Worship
I'm still disoriented today... feel a little strange... like there's missing time... my memory doesn't seem to be what it once was.
I spend the morning loafing around the apartment, doing nothing, really.
I looked again for the key to that locked door, but can't find it.
Imagine having a locked door in your own apartment!
What could be in there?
Something told me to relax... go to the park, take a walk.
Though I seldom go there, the voice in my head is insistent.

The park is beautiful on this fall day: cool, crisp and brown and comfortable. There are others here, forgettable; lost faces, meaningless voices, dim eyes.

But She is among them.

That must be why I'm here, because I don't even remember wanting to come to the park today.

Her hair is radiant, Her eyes luminous.

She is real.

But they surround Her, jostle Her, move about Her as if they were the real ones, not Her.

But I know.

I know.

I hear the irritating voice of the wind in the trees. It thinks I'm not listening, but I am. I choose to ignore it.

As I walk the concrete path that twists through the park like a broken spine, I hear the birds and ducks twitter amongst themselves: meaningless prattle.

They're nervous.

For me.

For Her.

They can't make me nervous.

She walks so confidently among them, so carefree and secure.

The bells begin to bother me, though. Why are they so loud today, so insistent?

She is gracious, laughing occasionally, talking with the others sometimes as they pass by in their grey, sluggish mass.

I wonder why She bothers with them.

I don't. They part around me, give me a wide berth.

I like it this way.

She prefers to wade in among them.

Lovely, so lovely.

I can feel it begin to stir within its sheath.

My knife.

I stroke it through my rough clothing, comfort it.

Soon, soon...

The grey ones stare at me, jealous of it.

Jealous of me for being real.

I move on more quickly. I don't want to lose sight of Her.

The others thin, their numbers dwindling.

She continues through the park, and I am with Her for a moment, beside Her.

Her eyes see me as I pass Her.

Bright, so bright!

I cannot bear them; I turn away.

They burn! They burn!
I move on, managing a smile.
Wounded.
The knife is sheathed; its blade is limp.
She is so strong, so strong.
I am not Her equal.
I move on ahead…
Those damn bells! Where are they?
They are crashing in my head!
I stumble on the path, head into the deep, covering woods to the left, where it is darker but the colors are somehow brighter.
Ahh!
The bells pound in my head as she passes by, doesn't see me.
I press my head into the damp mat of leaves, and it is cool, cool on my hot forehead. I can smell the earth, the things moving beneath it, dying beneath it.
They are a comfort.
When I look up, I see She has gone far down the path away from me, Her light a bobbing will-'o-the-wisp in the evening park.
Suddenly, from Her left, something detaches itself from the undergrowth, moves toward her.
I can see him, smell him, hear his heart race.
He grabs at Her purse, yanks.
The bells!
The strap breaks, and he spins in one motion, darts back into the woods.
He dares!
And She did nothing?
It's a test.
Mine.
I move through the dense woods, crouched low.
I hear his footfalls on the earth, dim and insubstantial, but I can follow them.
He is near a group of large rocks, throwing things out of the purse pell-mell.
His smell is thick with fear and joy, his blood races through him.
I am behind him, knife drawn.
He doesn't notice me.
We go down heavily, the purse and the rest of its contents flying.
His breath bursts from him when we hit the hard, stony earth, me on top.
Can he hear the bells?
No. He is not real.
He hears nothing.
I press down on him with my full weight, and he wriggles to throw me.
But he is small, young, no match.

I cut away his pants.

He twists, sees my knife, becomes frantic.

His wound repulses me. It is hairy, dark, and smells of him, but he must pay.

Pay for what he's done to Her.

I thrust in savagely, to the hilt.

Blood spurts out around my knife, gurgles at the edges of the blade.

I stab into him again and again.

He grunts underneath me, before his breath becomes bubbly and liquid.

Before it stops.

He is still.

I stand and wipe the blade on his shirttail over and over until all trace of him is gone. Then, I sheath my knife.

Dirty, dirty. I feel so dirty.

It takes me a while to collect all of the items from Her purse, but they all get wiped off neatly, put back inside.

I leave it on Her doorstep.

The test is completed.

I pass.

* * *

Wednesday: Remembrance

I was a messy baby, my mother always told me.

"If the other mothers' babies used five diapers a day," she would whine as she picked up my belongings when I got older, "you used 10. What a mess you were. And you never grew out of it."

But I did.

I've gotten neater. If only she were alive to appreciate this fact.

I know I've gotten neater.

Because I've counted.

I keep track of everything I consume.

It's a lovely word, isn't it? *Consume.*

Make the '*u*' long in the second syllable, and the word sounds elegant.

For example, since my adolescence I've used only 24 pairs of jeans, 43 shirts, 67 pairs of underwear, 105 pairs of socks, and 22 pairs of shoes.

Since I'm almost 24 now, I think that these numbers are admirable.

I keep everything washed and folded in my dresser, my shoes neatly arranged, socks balled and in their own drawer.

Order is important, wouldn't you agree?

In an orderly system, everything lasts longer.

Things aren't wasted.

You don't have to consume as much.

You understand.

I think I like you. You appreciate my sensibility in this, unlike...

Unlike the grey ones... th—

Shit!

Four thousand, two hundred and sixteen.

I had to get a new pencil. They always seem to wear out so fast.

Mother always told me that I bore down too hard.

Everything, it seems, is destined to be difficult for me.

Nineteen thousand, four hundred and seventy two.

Tissues, that is.

I have a lot of sinus problems, and I tend to sweat a lot.

Tissues come in handy for a lot of things, like cleaning up unexpected messes.

Four hundred and sixteen.

That's how many boxes of tissues are in the spare bedroom.

I'm ready.

There have only been eight women, you know.

Only eight during my whole life.

That's not bad, I think.

Plenty of men use more than I.

I try not to use more than one a month.

I know. I haven't been at it long.

But what I lack in experience, I make up for in enthusiasm.

I have collected six bras, seven pairs of panties, two skirts, a sweater, five blouses, four pairs of jeans, two pairs of shorts, two t-shirts, five pairs of tennis shoes, three pairs of dress shoes, four pairs of nylons, an odd number of socks, 14 rings, 8 purses, 19 earrings.

Inside the purses were 17 tubes of lipstick, nine compacts, six wallets, three eyelash curlers, a collapsible umbrella, four address books, 132 photos (102 color, 30 in black and white), seven sets of keys, $657.23, 34 credit cards, nine packages of chewing gum, 7 packages of condoms.

I have kept all this, kept it in separate containers in a locked room, each marked with the girl's number: *1* through *8*.

Everything is orderly. Everything is neat.

It should last a lifetime.

I can unlock the door, take down a box and go through the items in it anytime.

And remember.

How Girl 3 was so hard to follow.

The way Girl 6 looked underneath her clothes.

Where the greater portion of Girl 5's body was left.

The way they all looked when I took out my knife.

Through it all, though, just one knife.

I have not used it up yet or broken it, oh no.

I don't have to get another.

Mother would be so pr—
Damn!
Four thousand, two hundred and seventeen.

* * *

Thursday: Penance
My mother always told me not to do this... not to touch it.
You'll wake it up. And it will want to do evil things.
But she was wrong... about so many things, I see now.
Sorry, mother.
It's sharp though, and it hurts me to touch it. It cuts me, eager to drink my blood if I will give it no other.
Sometimes when I touch it, it wakes for just a while, and the world is white, all white, glorious, cleansing white.
It floods through me, scours me out.
Just when it seems as if it might awaken... that it might want to... *do evil things...* it slumps back, returns to its deep slumber.
And I am anointed with its blood and mine, in equal parts, covering my stomach and chest.
Disgusted, I go to the bathroom, and mop myself off with a wad of toilet tissue—just ten sheets, be sure to count them as they roll off—then drop this clotted, pinkish clump into the toilet.
Then, I must bind my hand, for the cut throbs with my pulse and stings something awful.
Tomorrow, it will be healed.
Alleluia.

* * *

Friday: Annunciation
She is in the park today, late.
But Her light is like a beacon, drawing me in.
I toy with Her, passing Her again and again as She walks, waiting to see if there is the barest glimmer of recognition, suspicion, wariness.
But there is none, and thankfully Her eyes do not touch me with their fire.
And I know She is the one.
She is the one.
The true sacrifice never recognizes the nature of divinity.
Until it is thrust upon Her.

* * *

Saturday: Transfiguration

In the end, it happens so fast.

The way it always ends... so fast.

It was twilight when I found Her in the park, running. Always running.

And from what? Not from me, surely.

I shivered at that... what if She knew?

That had never happened before.

But, She was the real one... She never knew.

She took the blade eagerly, gratefully.

I embraced Her, felt Her hot, firm flesh turn to liquid as I thrust in and out.

She leaned her head onto my shoulder, gurgled something appreciative.

But then, the light built... bright, hot, white light, and it was over.

So fast.

I kissed Her when it was done, took Her clothes and other belongings, walked quietly in the moonlight to the old penny fountain, nearly overgrown with weeds and bushes, bathed there.

The grey water turned black as I slid in, scrubbed the blood from my body.

Later, I found my own clothes, dressed, and came home.

I felt cleansed, renewed.

A whole new person.

* * *

Sunday: Rest

I woke early on Sunday, feeling ill.

By that afternoon, I still didn't know why.

In the shower, I found dried blood matted in my pubic hair, flaking in the folds and wrinkles of my penis... *from me?*

I'd better tell the doctor about this.

Maybe tomorrow... I feel so tired, so disassociated...

* * *

Monday: Revelation

Man, I hate Mondays.

I nearly threw the alarm clock from its perch on my nightstand.

It was the same dream... every Monday... why would I dream like that?

And the blood... just a speck or two on my pillow, the bed sheets?

Shit... it's like... I don't know... so... fucking insistent.

I can't stay here in this apartment today, with all its voices and echoes and locked doors.

I think... I think I'll take a walk in the park... I don't usually do that.

Sounds kind of nice this time of year, with the autumn leaves turning.

Who knows, maybe I'll even see a girl.
Just what I need to take the edge off…

THE
LACQUERED BOX

Stephen Becker ended in death where he had spent a great deal of time in life.

In a box.

But this was not quite the type of box that Stephen was accustomed to. This box had neither lock nor chains. Only the weight of its enameled aluminum lid kept it closed.

This box had no sliding panels, no false bottoms, no mirrors. It would be closed, with no great fanfare and by no beautiful assistant. And chances were that if it were opened later, Stephen Becker would still be there.

* * *

Warm autumn sunlight reflected dully off the brass key Vivian thrust into the door's lock. She turned the key, expecting resistance, meeting none. Gin from the glass she held fell in a spray: silver in the sunlight, dark stains on the hallway carpet.

Vivian took no notice of this as she pulled the door open onto darkness, thick and secretive. She took a cautious step into the room, her hand fumbling for the light switch.

The room filled with slow, heavy fluorescent light. It spilled from the ceiling, crept along the floor like ether. Where it oozed into the hall, the sunlight seemed to retreat.

Vivian took the last of the gin in a pinched swallow and set the empty glass onto a small table near the door.

Trunks, cabinets, boxes of all kinds. Swords, crystal balls, colored silks. They filled every corner of the room, all neatly arranged. The walls were covered with lurid playbills depicting magicians such as Houdini, Thurston, Blackstone, Chin-Ling-Soo and others Vivian had never heard of.

One of the playbills hung alone on a wall, framed, as if valuable. It proclaimed:

THE GREATEST MAGICIAN

LIVING, DEAD, OR BOTH!

THE AMAZING
* S * U * R * A * Z * A * L * I *

WILL BE

BURIED ALIVE!!

AT THE ORPHEUM THEATRE

SATURDAY EVENING, MARCH 3, 1888

8:00 P.M.

Above this was a picture of a man Vivian supposed was Surazali, reposing corpse-like in a beautifully lacquered Chinese box, hands clasped tightly over his breast, eyes wide and glassy.

Vivian's eyes lingered there for a moment, turned to the profusion of items in the room. These things held no memories for Vivian, and certainly no magic.

When Stephen first began to practice magic, she had been mildly interested. She wanted to know how things worked, how Stephen was able to fool her, deceive her into seeing things that weren't actually there, weren't actually happening. This was useful information, for once she knew, he would never be able to do that to her again.

But Stephen wouldn't tell her. He would shake his head and say, "It's magic, honey."

Vivian didn't see it that way. It wasn't *magic*. Stephen was keeping a secret from her.

She kept no secrets from him, for, in truth, she had none to keep.

No, it wasn't magic. There was no room in Vivian's life for that. Magic paid no bills. It cooked no meals. It drove no one to work. It simply occupied a space in her home and in Stephen's heart, neither of which she would ever be able to enter.

Now that he was gone, it, too, would simply have to go.

Vivian emptied the room quickly into one of three large traveling trunks. Every type of object, every imaginable color found its way into these trunks. Minutes became hours, measured in swallows of gin, as the room emptied itself of its secrets.

At times, Vivian would pause, holding a particular prop Stephen had deceived her with long ago. She would not put it down until she had figured out how it worked. And each time, she would curse herself when its simple answer became apparent.

Eventually, the three trunks were filled and pushed out into the front hall, near the door. Only the closet remained to be cleared. Its unadorned door swung easily on its hinges, and the aroma of cedar drifted out.

The incandescent bulb spat light onto the contents of the closet, filling it with sharp colors and harsh shadows. In contrast to the main room, the closet was surprisingly bare. The makings of a black tuxedo, crisp and recently pressed, hung in a plastic bag from one of the clothing rods. She had denied her husband's request to be buried in it. So it hung here, like the skin of some dead animal, limp and docile.

Several pairs of white gloves, a pair of highly polished black shoes, a silver-capped cane, and a silk top hat sat on a small shelf above the hanging clothes, all neatly arranged.

At the rear of the closet, there was a large object covered with a heavy, padded quilt. Vivian assumed it to be another false-bottomed or mirrored trunk.

She tugged at the thick quilt, and it slid off as easily as if it were resting on ice.

A large, black box with brightly colored designs, heavily lacquered, gleamed in the bright light. It looked Oriental, and it was perfectly beautiful. Not a scratch, not a smear, not a fingerprint marred the black, glassy finish.

Vivian, in unwanted admiration, drew her hand along its smooth, ebony surface.

A look of revulsion twisted her face, and she quickly snatched her hand back, rubbing it against the legs of her pants.

The box felt slick, cold, and wet.

It must be another of Stephen's stupid tricks, she thought. And not one she was particularly interested in unraveling.

It would go to the garbage with the rest of it.

The box was empty, so she pulled the tuxedo carelessly from its hanger, tossed it inside. The gloves, hat, cane, and shoes followed without ceremony. Using the quilt like an oven mitt, she closed the lid of the box and pushed it out of the closet.

As she closed the door, her eyes fell on the playbill depicting the reposing Surazali, to the box he rested in.

It was the same lacquered box.

Angrily, she covered the box again and pushed it into the hallway with the other three trunks. Minutes later, all four boxes sat outside, in the place usually left for trashcans.

And though the body of Stephen Becker had been buried three weeks before, Vivian laid to rest more of him in those boxes now waiting with the garbage than what was contained in the aluminum casket wrapped snugly in six feet of cold earth.

More, that is, of who he was. More than she could know.

Vivian Becker went back inside of her house, a house now empty now of Stephen, of magic and of secrets, and slept a kind of sleep.

And for a while, at least, she was at peace.

* * *

Halloween. The setting sun had faded to a dull orange on the horizon, a pumpkin pie burnt at the edges. Now, the moon, bright enough to fool people into thinking it was completely full, appeared over the horizon. Its yellowed-white light gave the evening sky a muted, silver patina.

The crowds of kids, costumed, laden with bags of candy, were home now, the streets abandoned, dark, quiet. Leaves, driven by the chill autumn breeze, whispered momentarily, were silenced.

"Get down, you dork," hissed a shadow moving along the lawn of the house next door to the Becker's.

"What if she's still awake?"

"She's not awake. She never answered her door all night. An' even if she is, she's half-crocked by now. Anyway, whaddaya think, she's gonna be out guarding her garbage? She threw the stuff away."

"I guess, but..."

"Why d'ya think she did it?"

The dark shapes on the lawn inched closer to the Becker property, pausing at the driveway. The flickering streetlight reflected four sets of eyes, cast four silhouettes.

"She never liked him."

"We'd better not let her see us in the yard," said the older-sounding voice.

"I told you guys..."

"Aww, Glen, if you're chicken, go home."

With a rustle, two of the three remaining shapes stood and walked slowly, cautiously into the circle of light.

From the darkness behind them, the fourth voice whispered, "Isn't this stealin'?"

Mike, the older boy, glared back. "You can't steal *garbage*, numbnuts."

Confronted by the logic of this, Glen slowly rose to his feet, though he kept well outside the glare of the streetlight. His eyes busily scanned the streets for police or a neighbor.

The first boy onto the Becker's lawn, Eddie, had opened one of the trunks and was pulling treasures out of its depths, unimaginable treasures. Mike and Scott hunched side-by-side, digging through one of the other trunks. A pile of discarded items grew at their feet.

"Can you believe this?" asked Mike.

"I'd die if my mom threw out all my stuff," said Scott, sniffling in the cold wind and drawing the denim arm of his jacket across his nose. "And my stuff isn't half as neat as this junk."

Eddie moved to the trunk covered with the heavy quilt. His hand lightly brushed the quilt, and it slid to the ground. The lemon yellow of the gaslight flickered on the trunk as if it were trapped inside its obsidian finish.

"Wow, Eddie, I've never seen *that* box before," said Scott.

"Neither have I," said Eddie, gazing into the trunk's depths.

"What's in it?" asked Mike, lifting himself from the trunk he was pillaging. He spoke with the authority of one who knew that if anything really neat was found, he could—and would—take it.

"I dunno. Wait... *yuck*! It's all wet in here." Eddie pulled out a single black shoe with a crumpled white glove tucked inside.

"Just a shoe," said Mike as he turned back to his trunk.

"Everything's wet an' sticky." Eddie pulled out a black jacket, a pair of trousers, the other shoe.

"Wow, she even threw away his clothes," he said. He groped around, then smiled suddenly and pulled out a top hat.

"Is there anything in it?" asked Scott.

"Like what, stupid? A rabbit?" came Mike's reply.

"No, nothing," answered Eddie. The hat felt smooth and warm and lighter than he had thought. He started to lift it to his head, when Mike grabbed it.

"I know what we can do," he said, his voice dropping to a whisper.

Glen groaned, "What now?"

"Well, we've got all these clothes, and I'm sure we could find a plastic milk jug in someone's trash. We've got everything we need to make a traffic victim," finished Mike.

"Cool," said Scott.

"No," echoed Eddie and Glen, surprised to be in agreement.

"If you want to play victim, let's go home and get other clothes. Not Mr. Becker's stuff," said Eddie.

"Why not?" Mike laughed. "He's not gonna need 'em."

"It's not right," said Eddie. "He was our friend."

Mike turned to Scott. "You in?"

"You bet!"

"Guess I don't even have to ask you, huh, Glen?"

Glen dropped his head to look at the debris scattered across the lawn. "C'mon, Mike," he pleaded. "The last time, I was grounded for a month."

"Figured," snorted Mike. He faced Eddie. "So?"

Eddie hesitated. "Yeah," he sighed. "I'm in."

"Great. You hit some of the other houses and find a milk jug in someone's trash. Scott, gather up some of those handkerchiefs and that rope."

"Guess I'll be goin'," mumbled Glen.

"Say goodnight to your mommy for me," called Mike after him.

Glen shoved his hands into the pockets of his coat. "Shithead," he muttered to himself.

* * *

When all the stuffing was done, when all the strings were tied, the three boys had a pretty good approximation of a body. A tuxedo-clad scarecrow stuffed with silk and tied together with handkerchiefs and the white rope magicians cut into pieces and then mysteriously restore.

The milk jug, which Eddie had found and quietly filled with water from the faucet outside his home, was handed to Mike. He tied it securely to the dummy. It flopped forward on the dummy's rope neck to rest against its silk-stuffed chest. Mike lifted it, crowned it with the black top hat. A section of rope looped through the hatband held it tightly to the milk jug.

"Sorta looks like Frosty the Snowman," said Scott, sniffing against the back of his hand. "Except for Halloween, instead of Christmas."

They set out for the huge field that bordered an entire side of the subdivision. In the summer and early fall, this field was dense with corn. Now, after the harvest, the field was a series of deep furrows that stretched far into the distance.

Across the bare field lay a narrow, two-lane country feeder that was used mainly by farmers moving their equipment from field to field. It also, however, served as a shortcut for locals seeking a quick way to get to the main highway.

They paused at the base of a gentle, three-foot rise that sloped up from the edge of the field to the road. Its entire length ran above fields on both sides, and local tow trucks made a killing pulling all sorts of vehicles out of these fields.

Mike uncoiled the rope he carried and made a long loop around the scarecrow's midsection. He knotted this several times and gave it a strong tug.

"There, now all we have to do is wait."

* * *

The car banked and swerved as the road humped, like a bronco attempting to unseat its rider.

"Throw it now!"

Scott and Eddie heaved the scarecrow out in a high arc. The white rope reflected the oncoming lights like a phantom umbilical cord.

Silken guts crumpled without a sound against the car's front fender. It rolled forward on the hood, its milk-jug head thumping on the windshield—loudly enough to be heard over the car's squealing brakes.

As the dummy rolled over the car's top, bounced off the trunk and onto the pavement, Mike pulled the rope he held and reeled it back. It slithered over the road as the car fishtailed to a stop. Illuminated in red by the car's brake lights, it tumbled down the small incline and out of sight.

"You goddamned kids!" yelled the driver. He ran to the other side of the car, peering into the darkness.

"If I find out who you kids are, I'm callin' your parents. Hell, I'm callin' the police!" He made one last sweep of the darkness, but could see nothing.

"And I mean it!"

He climbed into the car, slammed the door and squealed the tires.

As the door closed, barely suppressed laughter exploded from the side of the road.

"I told you guys that it'd be the best," said Mike. He coiled up the rope, and Scott and Eddie went to where the dummy lay.

Scott bent to grasp the limp legs, and Eddie did the same with the arms.

"Yuck," said Eddie. "This tux is wet and slimy. I wonder what Mrs. Becker did to it."

"Jeez, it feels like this thing's gettin' heavier," said Mike. "Another car's comin'."

* * *

The second car, whose driver was obviously a veteran of this joke, screamed to a stop, and then honked her horn and peeled out.

Mike grunted this time as he tried to pull the rope in. "It must be hooked on something. Scott, hop up and untangle it."

"Okay."

There was a pause as he hunted for the black shape of the dummy against the night and the asphalt road.

"It's not connected to nothing."

Mike hauled on the rope again. The dummy slid down to the field.

"Just bring it over here so I can wind the rope." Scott and Eddie bent to their task with some difficulty.

It was much heavier. And it felt warm and mushy, like a bag full of oatmeal.

They walked it bent-kneed over to Mike, busily coiling the rope for the next launch. "Take it up the hill," Mike said. "I'm ready."

Scott moaned, but Eddie let his end slide to the ground, disturbed at how real it suddenly felt. "Uhh... maybe we should stop. It's gettin' late," he said.

"What's with you tonight?"

"I'm just gettin' a bad feeling about this. Like..."

"Like what? Like Mr. Becker's gonna come back for his clothes? He's dead! He's not coming back for anything, not even on Halloween! So, what's the difference whether we're using the clothes for this or whether they're rotting in some garbage dump?"

"Like," Eddie continued as if he had not heard Mike, "this might be the night when someone calls the police."

"Fine," said Mike. "Just one more, and we go home. That okay with you?"

Eddie didn't answer. He picked up his end of the dummy, waited for Scott to do the same, then trudged up the hill.

They waited in silence for several minutes until another car came into view. As it rounded the last turn, they began to swing the dummy. It was so heavy, though, that they released it a moment too late.

The car blurred past in a rush of wind, and the dummy rolled across the road behind it. As it tumbled into the bushes on the other side, the rope snapped and a portion of it recoiled back to Mike.

"Missed!" spat Scott.

"Missed?" Mike asked. He put his face up to Eddie's. "You missed on purpose!"

"No," answered Eddie. "It's just heavy."

"I suppose I'll have to go get it since you two are such weenies."

Mike walked across the road, kicking a crushed soda can in anger. "Did you two see where it landed? Or were you too busy playing with..."

A dark shape rose from the brush on the other side of the road, blotting out the sky, the moonlight and the stars. It made no sound, and no features could be seen on its dark face, but Eddie knew what it was.

Who it was.

Mike looked up in time to see it standing on the road directly before him. He was close enough to see the tatters of the tuxedo's tails fluttering in the evening breeze, the rips in the white cotton gloves that showed nothing underneath, the crushed top hat that sat atop something that no longer resembled a milk jug.

One of the gloved hands lashed out, caught Mike across his jaw, rocking his head violently to the right. Across the road, the other two boys heard what sounded like celery snapping.

Mike's body spun in a tight circle, as if captured in a ballet move, careened down the hill on the other side of the road.

Eddie took two steps backwards, forgetting that he, too, was very near the edge of the slope. His right foot flailed for purchase, found none. As he fell, he saw the shape stride purposefully toward Scott.

The stars pin wheeled over his head. The air exploded from him painfully. He lay there for a moment, staring at the night sky in a daze.

He leapt to his feet and looked around. At the top of the rise, the dark shape huddled over Scott's body. He could hear Scott repeating over and over, "No, no, no..."

Then he saw a sinuous flash of white in the moonlight, and he turned and ran through the field, stumbling again and again in the deep, hard ruts.

He had seen the thing coiling a length of rope around Scott's midsection.

And he was horribly sure what it meant to do.

An overturned glass of gin on the nightstand near Vivian's head sparkled in the moonlight that spilled through the open window. A fat wedge of lime teetered on the lip of the glass. Diamond drops of gin trickled to the floor, the remains of her Halloween treat.

But no trick... not yet...

A faint breeze entered the room, and the smell of autumn leaves, rich with damp earth and wood and rot, floated on it. It stirred the curtains, caressed Vivian's naked legs. She surfaced from her gin-induced sleep long enough to shiver and pull the blanket over them.

As she reburied her head in the pillows and sank beneath the gin, a sound like wet sneakers, heavy and squishy, floated down to her.

A hand clutched her bare shoulder. Where it touched her skin, its cold flesh was soft and disturbingly yielding. A strong odor of mildew and decay, mingled with the sharp smell of cedar, flooded her senses.

Still drunk with sleep and gin, she jerked her head shakily from the pillow, saw the blurred shape of a top hat silhouetted against the window.

A voice, soft and horribly wet, whispered from underneath the hat, spilled past a bloated, rotting tongue.

Vivian, darling, wake up, said the voice, its lips smacking moistly.

I have a new trick for you...

I want to show you how it's done...

For Randy Kalin

HERE

The first time I saw him, he was all motion and energy, pushing over his littermates, straining to get to me, to be taken with me.

To be with me...

Here...

The last time I saw him, he was lying motionless, a pool of dark water in the middle of the country road that runs in front of my house.

Only it wasn't the last time... not really.

I'd gone in for a second, just a second, to pee while I let him out to do the same. I was late getting home from work, and I knew he'd be anxious to get outside. It was dark, no moon, and he was a small, black pug. But I wasn't worried, never gave it a thought. The road, a narrow, gravel thing, heavily cratered and barely graded, was little used. I live on, if you'll excuse the pun, a dead end. The few people who actually use it are those few who actually live on it, and there aren't many of us. Traffic wasn't a concern.

I remember zipping up, my mind wandering over that day at work, what to fix for dinner, what was on TV that night. Nothing more. He'd come in, I'd cook something from my bachelor repertoire, share it with him, and we'd curl up on the couch together, pretend to watch a program or two before hitting the sack.

Not that night...

... not ever again.

I left the bathroom, walked through the house to the back door. The night was cool, and I could hear the river, a dark ribbon twisting through the greater darkness, gurgle just beyond the trees and down the bank at the rear of the property, its waters faintly limned by distant houselights.

Standing there on the little deck leading to the back door, I whistled for him, whistled the short, two-note trill I always gave when it was time for him to come in. Sometimes he'd respond; often he'd ignore it the first half-dozen times until he was ready to come on his own.

Unconcerned, I whistled again... and again... and again. Then, in mounting annoyance—generally I was annoyed with him about something. He was that kind of dog—I called his name, then called it again, louder, sharper.

"Hector! Here! *Here!*"

Then the whistle.

But there was no response.

No pounding of his pads on the driveway, no jingle of the dog tag on his collar.

And my attention, scattered across annoyance and dinner and television, suddenly focused, sharp enough to cut.

I felt something in my gut uncoil, like a length of cold rope.

My mouth went dry, even as something in my brain told me not to make too much of it; he was just sniffing around the neighbor's house or nibbling a treat disgorged from the septic tank or following the scent of a passing possum or any of a thousand things that could have drawn his attention away.

But I grabbed the flashlight and flew out the back door, down the driveway.

Deep into spring, and the trees still wore something between buds and leaves. Otherwise, their naked limbs raked the sky. Clouds mounted in the distance, roiled darkly, ready to spill over the hills on the horizon and into the little river valley where we lived.

It would rain tonight, heavy and hard.

At the end of the driveway, I stopped, took a breath, and raked the cornfield across the road with my meager light. Blunted furrows piled up like waves on a black sea were all that greeted me.

Turning left, I walked onto the gravel road, the beam of light illuminating my way.

That's when I saw it.

Just a pool of water.

Dark water...

Sighing audibly, I continued toward it, sweeping the flashlight before me, certain that what I saw was a puddle left from the recent rain.

Then, the glint of an eye...

I felt a rush of emotion push out from the center of me as I saw that it wasn't water... it was *him*.

"Hector!"

As pugs go, he was taller than most, with long, muscular limbs and a lithe, almost athletic build that, perhaps, one day, would fill out and give him the usual pug look of an ottoman with feet. But now he was only a little more than a year old... just a pup... *just a pup*... and his spare legs and lean body gave him the look of a gangly teenager... which, I suppose, in a way, he was. Dog years and all...

I bent to him, put my shaking hand onto his chest.

Solid, warm... *still.*

His legs appeared whole, unbroken. They were arranged in a kind of repose, as if he had simply lain down in the road to take a nap.

167

"Hector... baby... *no*... come here... back to daddy... come on good boy, come on... here... *here!*"

His eyes were open, unblinking. They stared at me, sad and pitiful, asking me to pick him up, to hold him.

I touched his muzzle. A trickle of blood came from his nose, oozed from the ear nearest the ground.

A car, I guessed...

Not knowing what else to do, I gathered him in my arms, lifted him from the road, as his eyes had asked. I had lifted him in my arms dozens, hundreds of times, and he'd been all flailing paws, squirming muscle. Now, though, he was a rag doll, limp and heavy, and it was then I knew, knew it in my practical brain if not my protesting heart.

He was gone... *dead.*

I lurched across the front yard, the flashlight still clamped in the hand that cradled his neck, throwing a beam that swept back and forth, up and down crazily over the front of the house, as if still searching for him.

My legs gave way at the back door, and I slumped onto the steps. I cradled him in my arms, kissed his cooling black head, his muzzle, pressed the smell of him into me as if trying to capture it. I whispered my love for him, my anguish into his soft ears. I wanted him to hear the sound of my heart breaking, to know that he was loved enough to break it.

How long I held him like that I don't recall, but the cold stickiness of his blood soaking my shirt brought me back. Moving him, my tight embrace of his broken body had made the bleeding worse, and I wore it on my shirt, my pants, dribbled onto my shoes and socks like an accusation.

Hours later, after he'd been buried by my friend Chris, whom I called that night, I looked at myself in the mirror, saw his dark, dried blood across my cheek, my neck, on my hands and arms.

I looked at myself in the mirror for a long while, knowing I should take a shower before trying to go to bed, as Chris suggested before he left—after he'd buried my dog, my friend, my companion. But I didn't want to wash the last of him down my shower drain... didn't want to lose the little part of him I had left, when the rest of him was already cold, already underground, already being rained on.

In the end, I took the shower, but threw the bloodied clothing into my hamper... and haven't removed it since.

When sleep finally did come that night, it came late and more from emotional exhaustion than physical fatigue. I listened to the rain pound on the roof and worried about him getting wet.

And though I missed his back pressed against mine as it usually was when we slept, I kept his collar wound through my fingers throughout the night.

* * *

I didn't sleep much at all, maybe just a little as dawn crept closer to the horizon. But when I did, the only solace I received were images of his sweet face, but not calm and peaceful as he'd been when I'd held him. No, now his face was distorted, his muzzle drawn back from his teeth. His eyes were wide and fixed, grey and cataractous.

And the blood... it had been only a thin trickle. But now, in my dreams, it gushed from his nostrils, his ears, wept from his wide, accusing eyes.

I awoke shaking, nauseous, and rose to sit vacantly in front of the television, watching images of other people's woes, other people's losses.

* * *

"Go ahead and take the day off," my boss told me the next morning. I was sensitive, still am, to that tone in people's voices... you know, the 'it's only a dog' tone that some people give you when you show the slightest inclination to grieve the loss of a pet.

I'd gotten Hector when he was eight weeks, and had raised him since then. It was he and I against the world. I knew it, and I think he did, too. No one was going to tell me that he was *just* a dog.

Another friend I spoke with that morning mentioned that tone, those people. He told me to take their names down and pass them on to him; he'd personally kick their asses for me.

I spent the rest of the morning in bed, lying in sheets that smelled of him, bore his dark hairs. I cried some, more than I ever thought I could—more than I ever thought I *should*.

I hadn't really slept the night before, so I tried to pull the covers over my head, tried to find some piece of sleep that wouldn't confront me with his battered, bloodied body.

And succeeded.

* * *

The next time I saw him was the first time he tried to kill me...

When I awoke, it was strangely dark, and I shuffled to the kitchen for a glass of water.

I glanced at the microwave clock. 7:43 p.m.

I'd slept all day, but felt no better for it.

He wasn't there at my feet, watching me, his eyes darting unsubtly from me to the pantry where I kept his treats. I looked at the space on the floor where he should have been and sighed.

Taking a glass down from the cabinet, I bent to the sink, turned on the water and ran it for a second, waited for it to get cold.

I absently looked out the window as I filled the glass.

Dropped the glass just as absently into the sink...

There, across the river, a blotch on the far bank, etched in dark relief against the bruised, twilight sky...

The glass shattered, but I was already out the back door, not breathing.

I scrambled to a stop where the backyard sloped down to the river, glared into the setting sun.

It simply could not be.

He was there, just across the winding river, no more than 30 feet away on the edge of the opposite bank. I could just make him out, like a dark ghost backlit against the sun. He seemed to be sitting, directly facing me, unmoving.

I stumbled down the bank, clawing at the raw, wet earth, barely able to see through the twilight and my tears. Coming to myself, the cold river water spilled into my shoes, soaked my socks.

I couldn't see his eyes, but I felt their weight on me.

Come! they said.

Here...

I took another step into the river, my shoes squelching in the mud, the water coming up to my shins.

No! Of course it isn't him.

He was dead... buried not more than a few yards away. I could turn to my right and see the disturbed clods of earth that lay atop his body... *had I wanted to...*

But I couldn't cross the river, I knew that. It was deep with spring runoff, choked with tree branches and detritus of all kinds. Its current exerted a powerful pull on my legs even where I stood, less than a foot into its body.

If I tried to cross, I *might* make it... but it'd be more likely that I'd be swept downriver or drown in the attempt.

I stood there, both the water and Hector urging me, tugging at me to come deeper. To break their hypnotic effect, I scrubbed my eyes angrily with the heel of one hand, and phosphenes swam in the air before me, sparkling and nauseating.

But when I opened my eyes again, the shape was still there... *except that it had moved slightly*... ever so slightly... just a tilt of its head... and my heart expanded until I felt it press against my ribcage, as if it might burst through.

That *tilt*... that comical, 'What?' turn of the head dogs do when they hear an odd tone or when they're not quite sure what you've said.

That tilt... I'd seen it from Hector many, many times...

My heart crowded my chest, stopped moving.

I closed my eyes slowly, opened them even more slowly...

He had turned, was moving away into the brush on the opposite side of the river, until he faded into the scrubby darkness and was gone.

I let my breath go in a strangled gasp that was as much a sob as anything.

Turning to the house, I pulled myself from the reeking river mud and climbed the slippery bank, ready to seek the comfort of my bed.

But I walked instead to where he was buried.

Looking down, I saw the grave, the slightly raised mound of dirt.
It was still there, unchanged from the previous night.
He was still there, unchanged, too.
The tears fell, and I went inside.

* * *

I spent days searching the internet, trying to assuage the grief I felt. Days at work were spent in a blur, pretending to get things done, but secretly Googling "*pet grief*" and "*dogs hit by car*" and other combinations of words that, no matter their arrangement, couldn't penetrate the density of my emotions; couldn't seem to shed light on what had happened. Couldn't offer a response to the triteness of *Why him?*

When people came into my office, I clicked away from any one of a dozen Rainbow Bridge web sites, as guilty as if I were cruising porn. Most of the sites were maudlin, saccharine places where people who I might previously have categorized as half-crazed to begin with revealed just how far over the edge the death of their ferret had pushed them.

Nevertheless, I posted to each one, tearing up about Hector's death each time I laid the words down.

And I realized that I was one of them now... had been one of them all along.

We all wanted the same things, this group I found myself suddenly a part of.

We wanted the pet we'd loved to be remembered, not just by ourselves, but by others.

And we wanted to do something, some small thing to honor that love, in the chance... no, the *hope*, however slim, that pet would know, know in a way that perhaps we'd been unable to communicate to it in life, that it was *loved*.

* * *

I saw him again a few days later, as I was driving home from work.

I'd turned onto the road that leads to my house after a long day at work spent trying to catch up on everything I'd been avoiding since his death. It had been a busy, harrowing day, even more so as I realized just how much had slipped past me that week.

The radio was on, an afternoon drive show, and the weather was forecast to be sunny and cool tomorrow. I was not paying attention; having driven this length of road so many times, I didn't think it necessary.

The day was bright and cool, as the radio had just promised tomorrow would be, and something caught my eye keeping pace with the car on the passenger side...

I stomped on the brake, swerved left, and a blur shot out in front of the car, paused.

A squirrel, I thought at first, *or maybe a groundhog or someone's cat.*

I cursed myself for not paying attention, for almost running down an animal just as that unknown driver had run down Hector in front of my house...

The dark shape stopped in a pool of shadow cast by the trees on the side of the road. It was small, a bit larger than a cat, and it stood motionless, facing away from me, looking down the road ahead.

Then it turned its head, looked at me without turning its body.

Hector!

My breathing caught. I reflexively mashed the accelerator pedal. The car jolted forward, scattering gravel behind.

I saw him... *God, it was him!*... tilt his head at me and pull his loose lips into a doggy smile. Then, he turned his head and dashed forward.

Come here!

Breathing hard now, I inched the car closer, watched as he fell back beside the passenger side front tire. I could see him sprinting along the side of the road, through splashes of sun that lit his black fur in vivid blue patches, then into shadow where he seemed to lose substance.

I lifted myself out of me seat, craned my neck to see him.

Lord, lord... it's him... there's just no doubt now...

And as I thought that, he turned his head toward me, still running full tilt, and I saw his eyes for the first time. They weren't sad or empty as I'd seen them last, but bright and eager and full of life, as they'd been when he was...

He flashed me that puppy smile again and... and *winked*, slinging his head sharply to the right, motioning me to follow.

Here!

Then, just as sharply, he veered into the underbrush off the side of the road, disappeared.

"Hecky!" Without thinking, I pulled the steering wheel to the right.

Before I knew what I had done, the front of the car struck a small tree and the front wheels dipped into a drainage culvert.

Luckily, the tree was small, the culvert shallow, and I wasn't going that fast.

I jounced forward, hit the steering wheel with my chest as the car slumped to a stop.

I sat there for a long while, listening to the idling engine, the chirping of birds, and droning of insects, waiting for the full import of what I'd *seen*, what I'd *done* to sink in.

If I had been going any faster, I'd be...

I let out a long, slow breath.

After a few seconds, feeling like a fool, I backed the car out of the ditch and away from the tree, got out to check for damage—a dented front fender and a smashed headlight on the passenger side.

And I knew how lucky I was. I could have flipped the car or hit a larger, less yielding tree.

I could have killed myself trying to get to him.

Maybe, maybe that's what he...

* * *

"Do dogs go to heaven?"

"They do in cartoons," Chris replied, covering a small plate in ketchup as we sat in the local sports bar where we usually had lunch.

The look on my face gave him pause.

"Hector?"

I nodded.

"Well," he said, smashing a red-dripping french fry into his mouth. "I guess I never really thought about it. I mean, if dogs go to heaven, then what about squirrels? Moles? Flies?"

I waited, silently chewing my hamburger and giving him time.

"So, you think they all... you know... go to heaven?"

Swallowing a gulp of ice tea, I nodded.

"Why not? Why doesn't everything that's born, that dies, all go to the same place?"

"*Flies?* Are you shitting me?" he asked, his face scrunching up as if this conversation had taken a turn from sort of uncomfortable to just plain crazy.

"Well, I mean, sure. We're all *born* into the same place. Why wouldn't we all *die* into the same place wherever... *whatever*... that is?" I wiped my mouth with the napkin, settled it back into my lap. "I need to know... to believe... that Hector is there. That he's somewhere safe, loved."

"Heaven?" he asked again. "For a dog?"

"Heaven. Nirvana. Valhalla. The afterlife... *whatever*. I need to know he's okay."

"Why is that so important?"

I waited a minute, pretended to watch the weather report on one of the big-screen TVs.

"Because I keep seeing him. And I think he wants me to follow him... to come to him, wherever he is."

Chris closed his mouth, swirled his tongue around to dislodge something behind his tight lips, played for time. He looked at me hard, though.

"Look, man. Everyone's gotta have their own thing, believe what they want. If you believe he's there, that's great. If you believe you're seeing his... ghost or whatever, great. Who cares what I think or what anyone else thinks? If it makes you feel better, that's great. Just... just don't do anything stupid."

"Stupid?"

"You know… like… to be with him," he said, forcing a fry between teeth that were nearly clenched. "Like that movie says."

"That movie?"

"Heaven can wait, man. Heaven can wait."

I took another bite of my hamburger, mainly just to have something to do with my mouth than make more crazy words. I felt embarrassed, exposed for having told him that I was seeing… *what?* The ghost of my dead dog?

That he was trying to get me to come with him?

… to… where?

Things don't work that way, though,

Do they?

* * *

One week later I saw him again, and it almost killed me.

I sat outside on my deck with a beer, waiting for the time… that damned time a week ago…

The beer I lifted at intervals had gone flat, but the twilight was an explosion of colors, reds and purples and oranges. It was as if the sun, rather than falling beneath the horizon, had simply exploded, spraying the evening sky with its arterial blood.

But that wasn't what I watched.

I kept my eyes on the small, bare patch of the road where he'd been hit, where the car had struck his small body, run it down. Where he had lain, hopefully not for long, in whatever pain or panic God allows a dog to feel in its final moments.

Did he wonder what had happened?

Did he wonder where I was, why I wasn't there to take the pain away, to hold him?

To protect him from it having ever happened?

Only a week… *only a week,* and everything had changed, so suddenly, without warning.

I watched that spot, so bare now, so unadorned, so unremarkable for a place that had turned my life upside down.

What I watched for, I don't know.

Yes… yes, I did.

And there he was.

I didn't need to look at my watch. I knew the time, knew it as if it were the time of my own birth.

More clearly than the two times before, he stood outlined against the stark emptiness of the farmer's field on the other side of the road. I could make him out plainly, even though the light was fading and his coat was black.

I could see his sparkling eyes; the ripple of the wan light on his coat; his short, double-curled tail wagging, eager.

Standing, I went to the deck rail, put my hands on it, gripped it tightly to ensure that I was awake, that this wasn't a dream or a weird fugue state. As if to offer proof, a splinter slipped into the mound of flesh where my thumb met my palm, and I knew I was awake.

Then he moved, and my heart leapt inside me.

It was a playful, puppyish move. He pounced, lowering the front half of his body to the ground, but keeping his head, his eyes fixed on me. Then, he jerked his head, wriggled his rump.

I knew what those moves meant, what they said.

Come to me!

Come here!

Here!

I backed away from the railing, my brain telling me that it wasn't real, that he wasn't there.

But, I mean, really, who ever listens to their stupid, heartless brain?

I stumbled down the steps and across the front lawn.

I was still a dozen or so yards from him, when he turned, dashed into the field about 100 feet, then turned back toward me, lowered his head to the ground again and shook his rump.

Here!

I didn't see the headlights of the truck that bore down on me from the left. All I saw was his small, dark body, so clear in the field, urging me on.

There was a blare of a horn, the skittering of gravel, the whine of brakes.

The car actually struck me, no more than a nudge really, but it brought me around. I turned, as if not really knowing where I was, how I got there, and touched the hood of the truck. It was smooth and warm, and I could feel the engine beneath the metal, like a beating heart.

"Mister, you on something?"

I came around the driver side of the truck, looking back at the field.

Hector was gone.

Distressed, I scanned the field, but couldn't find him.

Of course... of course... because he...

Then, anger.

"You need to watch where you're going," the older driver snapped at me.

"*Me?* I need to watch where *I'm* going?" I spat. "Screw you. *You* need to slow down and watch where *you're* going. I was just walking across the road, and you nearly ran me down."

The man, who was probably more scared than I was, scowled. "Mister, you walked right in front of me. You telling me you didn't see my lights coming down the road?"

I turned to fully face the guy now, anger hot and gelid all at once inside me.

"You're probably the asshole who ran my dog down last week," I snapped. "Why don't you slow the fuck down before you kill someone else?"

Instead of making the guy even madder—and perhaps getting him to leave the truck and join in a little dust-up between the two of us—his face fell, as if I'd accused him of something truly horrible, worse than nearly running me down.

"*Kill your dog?* What a thing to say. Buddy, I didn't kill your dog. Just watch where you're going, that's all."

Insulted, he rolled his window up, effectively ending the conversation. Slowly pulling away, he gave me one stark look in his side mirror. I saw him shaking his head as his car pulled away.

Then all of the adrenaline hit, and I tried to sit there on the side of the road facing the field, but I more fell than sat. I could feel the gravel beneath me, the beer swirling in my blood. My heart began to race and cold sweat leapt from my pores. I swallowed and swallowed, but my mouth was dry.

He'd been here... I knew it... I saw him so clearly, so distinctly. He wasn't a dark shape as he'd been at first, or a blur as he had been when he'd raced the car a few days earlier.

He'd been here and he wanted...

... what did he want?

Here!

Come here!

I'd tried... but it had almost...

Cold swept over me, chilling my sweat-covered body so abruptly that I shivered violently.

That's exactly what he wanted.

* * *

It was daylight when I saw him again, downtown.

It had only been a few days since I'd seen him in the barren field, since he'd urged me to follow him, to come to him.

Here!

And I had spent those two days, in their entirety, thinking about seeing him. But I still didn't know what the meaning of it all was.

What I was supposed to take away from seeing him.

That I was crazy, struck mad from grief?

That I was hallucinating?

That I needed to see him so badly that I was imagining him?

Or was I really seeing him?

I couldn't think. Deprived of sleep, haunted by wakefulness, crushed under the burden of this grief, this guilt, I couldn't hold two thoughts together for more than a few seconds.

Withdrawing into myself, I remained silent at work, holed up at home, didn't go out, didn't have anyone over. Spoke to no one by phone or e-mail.

At work one day, I had to go into the city for a meeting. I had volunteered for it, eager to leave the office and my colleagues, their faces heavy with pity or contempt at what I was going through—*still* going through.

Eager to talk to someone about something other than myself, other than my dead dog, other than my inability to close the incredible loss that had opened inside me.

So, I went downtown, drove my car into the heart of the unaware, uncaring city and found a parking lot. I left my car there, descended the grotty stairwell, with its odors of gasoline and urine, down to the street level, where I lost myself in a sea of humanity, became just a mote within it, drifting like a water molecule in a great ocean of water, unknown, unknowing, unremarkable. No one knew me; no one knew what I felt, or even cared.

Lost, I paused at an intersection, waited for the streetlight to change.

And I saw him again.

The sign said '*Don't Walk*' in bright orange, and I stopped at the front of the crowd of people. The traffic sped through the intersection, and I stared dumbly ahead, waiting for the light to change, for the orange letters to become white and say, '*Walk.*'

Across the street, at the other corner, a similar group of people hovered on their curb, waiting for their light to flash.

I glanced down at the distant curb and saw him.

Hector stood there at their feet, his entire body wagging at the sight of me. I saw his dark brown eyes, the wrinkle of his nose, the poise of his ears.

He looked right at me and barked his silly, low, breathy 'I'm a much bigger dog' bark.

I broke the mesmerizing stare of his eyes and looked around. No one seemed to notice him, a black pug alone on the city streets. No one held him. No leash seemed connected to his...

He was close enough for me to see that there was no collar around his neck.

He barked at me again, and I knew it was him, knew it in my secret, wounded heart.

Here!

I stepped forward, and one foot actually lifted and set itself onto the pavement.

Another bark, and I saw him, finally, prancing on the far corner, weaving in and out of the legs that surrounded him, his gleeful little barks rising above the sound of traffic.

Two things happened simultaneously.

A city bus passed me on the street, so close that I could actually feel the heat of its metal skin through my suit.

A hand grabbed my shoulder, clamped down hard, and yanked me back onto the sidewalk before my other foot had the chance to lift itself.

The light hadn't changed, and the traffic still hurtled by. The bus passed before me, and I inhaled its hot diesel breath as it went by.

Before I turned to see who had grabbed me, I looked across the street, through the traffic, and I saw him still there. But he wasn't excited any more, wasn't barking at me.

He spared one disappointed look back at me before turning and padding his way into the forest of legs and feet... *disappearing.*

"Whoa, buddy," said a large young man dressed in shorts and a t-shirt, his hand still pressing down on my shoulder as if I might dart back out into the street. "Wherever it is you're so hot to get to, you might want to wait."

Thanking him, I crossed the street when the light finally did change, under the man's careful watch, and spent a few minutes searching down a block or two before giving up.

I missed the meeting.

* * *

The last time I saw Hector, he was crossing the field alone...

I sat on the deck again that night, as I did most nights in the weeks that followed his death. Nursing a beer or three, staring off into the distance, to the grey, lifeless spot where his lifeless body had lain, or into the still barren cornfield. Always hoping to see him, just to see him...

And as the sun slid down the arch of the sky, I did see him, standing there across the road, on the very margins of the field. His eyes caught mine, and he playfully lowered his front half, darted his head back and forth. I heard his funny bark carry across the suddenly still air, and my heart ached with what I had to do, with what I couldn't do.

Draining the beer, I walked across the yard to the road. I saw him so clearly, perhaps the clearest I'd seen him since he'd died. His eyes sparkled and his dark coat caught the fiery colors of the sun settling over the field.

I came to the edge of the road, stopped on my side of the street.

He cocked his head at me, barked again.

And I noticed, with mounting rue, that his bark still sounded distant, even though I stood no more than six feet from him now.

But I knew why...

I knelt there, at my side of the road, and looked at him for a second, sketched his face into the depths of my brain.

I did not move near him.

I did not cross the road.

I thought about what that guy had told me after he'd yanked me out of the way of a speeding bus.

Wherever it is you're so hot to get to, you might want to wait.

"I can't," I finally said to him. "I love you, but I just can't."

He cocked his head back and forth at me, at my words, but his eyes lowered, turned away.

"It's not my time yet, Hector. I know you want me to come... I know you want me *there*. And I want to be *there*. Just... not yet."

My legs ached to move, to go to him. My arms yearned to reach out and touch him, to hold him.

But I couldn't. I know what he wanted. I know he wanted me to cross the road, the river, to come to him... to be *there*... now.

Come here...

Here!

Maybe he didn't truly know what that meant for me, but I knew... and I wasn't ready.

"Maybe... just maybe... you could come to me... come *here*." I patted the gravel in front of me with my palms. "Here... here, Hector. Come to daddy, good boy."

He didn't tilt his head or move in any way, and that answered my question.

He couldn't come to me... couldn't come *here* anymore.

I lowered my head and let the tears fall.

When I looked up again, he was right in front of me, inches from my face. I saw every whisker in his muzzle, the gleam of his eye, each hair in his coat.

Surprised, I didn't react.

But he stretched his neck, brought his face to mine, and licked my cheek.

I closed my eyes, feeling my heart break all over again.

I could smell his clean dog smell, his breath, feel his saliva on my cheek.

When I finally thought to bring my arms up, to hug him to me, he was gone. I opened my eyes, and he was back on his side of the road, watching me.

My arms still hung in the air between us, urging him to come back, to be held.

Come here, boy. Once last time...

But I knew he wouldn't... knew he *couldn't*.

Instead, his lips drew back in a smile, baring black gums and white puppy teeth.

And then he was off, dashing away into the field without a look back, fading into the night like the ghost he was.

* * *

It's been more than a year since I saw him last...

Yes, I miss him... but things have gotten... *better*, I guess.

I know he's gone on without me, gone ahead, gone away...

I'm not ready to go to him yet. He knows that now, but he'll wait for me there.

Of that I'm sure. I don't have faith left in many things, perhaps nothing.

But *that*... I have faith in *that*.

And maybe... just maybe, that's enough

I know he'll be there when it's my time to cross, whenever that is.

And I know that he'll be there if I ever change my mind, if I ever do decide that I've had enough.

He'll be there whenever I come, waiting for me in the cornfield across the road or down by the river on the far bank, waiting for me to come to him, to join him.

I'll hold him then, take his kisses and return my own, stroke his dark coat and tell him that I love him. We'll run there, play fetch, stretch out on the soft, cool grass and sleep, his back pressed to mine.

And his *here* and my *there* will, finally, again, both be *here*... *right here*.

It doesn't take his place; it doesn't help the loss... nothing can or will.

But it is a balm...

Sometimes at night, when the air is cool and the wind is soft, and I watch that patch of road where he once lay as dark and quiet as a pool of water, it is a balm...

Dedicated to Hector Taff
Nov. 2007 to April 2009
He was—and is—a good boy.

THE
TONTINE

The wooden box gleamed on the sideboard, the sputtering candlelight captured in the depths of its lustrous, hand-polished amber finish. Like the man who regarded it, the box was a thing of its time: beautiful, strong in its way, delicate in its way. Like him, it was also completely out of place anywhere outside of this small, grandly appointed room.

It was a thing of its time, and its time had passed long ago.

Like his.

He brought his glass over to the armchair, placed it atop the narrow table at the chair's left, sat carefully. Another taper, thin and sputtering, cast fitful red jewels across the top of the table's small surface.

No electric lights now, not for this. Fire, the light of the older world—his world—would illuminate what he did now, what he did here, just as it had when he and the others had made the agreement, had caused this box to be made.

Not that he required any light. His need for light had died centuries ago, gone in a single moment. But this small light, this artificial light would suffice as a reminder of the larger light, the real light, the killing light that he could tolerate no longer.

So, he kept the room dark, deliciously so, lit only by a few of these candles and a small fire that had burned down in the massive stone fireplace dominating the room. Shadows and the ghosts of shadows hung in the corners, draped like cobwebs in the rafters.

Ghosts, he laughed bitterly to himself.

Ghosts.

He felt like one himself. But these days, ghosts—like him, like the box— were a thing of the past. Not even the shadowy corners of this new world could hide them anymore... or him.

Soon, not even this room would serve to hide him.

Even in the gloom, it was possible to see the room was elegantly, sumptuously appointed. Large bookcases filled one entire wall, their shelves lined with leather bound volumes set shoulder to shoulder like the dusty veterans of some antique war. Overstuffed leather furniture huddled near the fireplace, tapestries hanging on either side. Dark, gleaming wood paneling and wainscoting and blood red velvet paper covered the walls.

The small chamber, once one of many, was a refuge for him, a quiet island amidst the gleaming metal and electricity, skyscrapers and airplanes, apathy and unbelief that existed outside in this brave new world. This place was a page torn from an older book, a better book.

He lifted his glass, regarded the thick, red fluid that filled its cut crystals. Its smell came to him, thinner than he would have liked, colder than he would have liked, and he sighed. Touching its rim to his lips, he closed his eyes, downed the drink, replaced the glass. It rang like a tiny bell as it touched the table.

As he shifted his attention back to the box, the door drew open, admitting a thin shaft of the electric light he hated so much. His back to the door, he didn't turn to see who it was or what he wanted.

"How can I be of service, sir?" came the voice of the shadow that stood backlit in the door.

"I asked not to be disturbed, Mr. Gerund, tonight of all nights."

He heard the slightest of sniffs, crisp and haughty, from the shadow.

"But you rang, sir."

"No. I am sorry; I did not. Please leave."

"As you wish, sir."

Again the sniff, and the door closed softly.

Alone again, just him and this box, this tontine, and the ghosts, yes, the rarest of ghosts that clung to him these days. They were all he had left.

The wolf had been the first to go; the prince, the last... at least, not counting him.

Poor Larry, he mused, stroking the box with one sharp-nailed finger. So brutal, so senseless.

Of course, when he died, all of his kind died with him. It was their way. All of them, wherever they were. In the boardrooms of Wall Street or the sunny parks of San Diego or the fens of Bratislava. Day or night, asleep in their beds or curled around their mates in snug, dank dens below the earth.

All dead, all gone, because of some ridiculous college kid with a silver bullet.

He'd heard about Larry's death. He had not been there, but he could imagine it vividly; the extravagant splashes of blood from his death throes. The claw marks on the walls, the concrete. The cries that would have rent the air and caused people for miles around to shudder, draw their shades, pull their children closer.

Ahh, that had been the art of his kind; the violence, the anger, the rage. He was sure that, even in death—no... *especially in death*—Larry had expressed its absolute quintessence, the secret beauty that lies in all violent death. The instinctual gulping of blood and rending of flesh that stripped the attacker to his basic senses and the attacked to his basic constituents.

Ashes to ashes, dust to dust, all helped along by teeth and claws.

In his mind, he could see Larry's human form lying in a Rorschach test of his own blood, his body no longer ridiculously muscled and furred. Just a limp, nude human, smooth and pale as a baby, curled in the pool of its birth.

All because of a small, silver cylinder.

He shook his head ruefully at the utter deadliness of something so small to something so full of life.

It was the same for him and his kind, too, though. Two pieces of crossed wood, a splash of the right kind of water, the tiniest ray of sunlight, and he'd be gone, as well: a wisp of vapor, a heap of clothing, and a pile of ashes.

For a moment, just a moment (*but, ah, weren't they coming ever more frequently these days?*), he longed for that release, the calm it would bring to his mind... maybe even whatever was left of his soul.

He wondered what that release had done for Victor's tortured soul, locked in his hideous, piecemeal body. So tormented, so torn between wanting to be one of them and wanting to punish them for being what he could never be.

When that spark of life had finally fled his scarred, twisted form, perhaps in the second before his borrowed heart stopped beating, did Victor find peace?

Or was it just the fear, the exquisite fear?

That's what had brought them all together, made them compatriots of a sort.

That bond of fear is what had brought about the tontine.

Not just the fear they engendered, but the fear that they carried within them.

Fear of something worse, some fate worse than the curses they suffered under.

If the world held fates such as theirs, certainly it held even worse in abeyance.

The thought had, at one time or another, appalled each of them.

So, they came together, warily at first, surreptitiously to be sure.

The bat, the wolf, the monster, and the mummy.

Laughable, really, he mused to himself, sitting now in this sanctuary, drinking from a crystal goblet. Like a cheap Hollywood movie. All they were missing was Abbott and Costello.

But they had gathered, nonetheless.

Here, in this drawing room in London, before it became their club.

The thin, ascetic Count, with dark, crafty eyes and a feral strength.

The hulking monster, his coat collar drawn up and hat pulled down to cover his puckered, discolored face.

The furtive wolf, nervous, cagey, whose sweat stank of the moon and blood.

And the prince, thousands of years older than even the Count, his wrappings holding together a body that was little more than articulated dust.

Each of them wanting life more than anything, whether it was gobbling it up or possessing some spark of it.

Each of them thrived on fear, made a living, as it were, on fear. Each had become so identified with fear that they were the very stuff of it, howling in every mortal dream, lurking in every shadow, imagined in every dark place.

Funny, then, that fear should bring them together.

Victoria still reigned in England when they bought this bottle, this box.

When they made this tontine.

Like soldiers in a war only they still fought in, they had gripped this bottle, held it tight, sworn the oath.

"The last of us alive, whatever that means to ones such as us, shall drink of this bottle and remember the others, remember the fear, for in the end, that is all we have, all we bring, all we share."

They toasted this epitaph with a glass drawn from the bottle's twin. The Count remembered how the wine had stained the prince's chalky cheeks, his gauze-wrapped neck a deep scarlet, like a spreading blush.

The monster's lip had curled into a deep, disagreeable snarl at the taste of the wine, and he eyed it suspiciously.

Larry, too, hadn't much cared for the wine. He was more of a beer drinker.

Only the Count could truly appreciate it, one of the few things that he could stomach. Because, like blood, the wine was a living thing, and its energy filled the glass. It wasn't the taste he enjoyed; it was the buzz, the crackle of its life as he drained it.

Now, with Larry killed, with Victor reduced to individual pieces kept "alive" in vats of fluid in a secret government lab, with the prince sent back to the Land of the Dead, he was the last one, the last... *alive*.

Funny, now, here at the end, it was him, the only one left: the only one of the four who might even *want* to drink to the health of his comrades.

There were others, to be sure, who had taken their places—others who stalked the fringe of mankind's senses in these bright and shiny new days and doled out what amounted to fear. But he ignored them. They were less elemental than he and his tontine partners—more created by man than born from him.

There was an inbred butcher who wore the stitched together face of his victims and carried a chainsaw. There were two others who wore masks and lurched in the darkness wielding a variety of sharp implements. There was even one who arose from dreams, with claws for hands.

Laughable. To have to hide behind *masks*...

But even those of his kind who existed now were shades without nuance or dimension: hollow shells of desire and hunger, relegated to romance novels and movies filled with smoldering looks and teen angst. His kind had become mannequins of a sort: androgynous, beautiful, with dark eyes and hollow cheeks, lithe forms and red, red lips, and only the finest tailored clothing.

They had become, in effect, the very things they had symbolized, and that was a lessening from which they could not recover. There was little behind this façade now, little to instill the delicious fear that he was accustomed to bringing with him.

They, both those of his kind and those others of this new age, had reduced fear to a smaller thing, a simpler thing.

Fear of pain... fear of blood... fear of *death*.

That was it: the basic fear of life being snuffed out.

A primal fear, perhaps man's first.

The fear he'd brought was the fear *beyond* death—the fear of being lost... of being *undead*.

These... *poseurs* were unable to generate this. They could bring about only the fear of pain, of spattered blood, of rent flesh, of a slow, slow fading, and then...

... nothing.

But what he brought... oh, what he brought was the fear of being reduced to what he was... of being lost to the light, lost to life, but forced to continue within it, *to be abandoned inside it*... that was fear.

That was the fear that the others had brought, too, each in their own way. But with their passing, this fear had passed, too.

Musing, he lifted the box, stroked its smooth skin of wood.

Perhaps this fear died because humanity no longer could wrap its collective mind around the larger fears: loss of soul, being cast out of the light, set on a path outside that of mortal man, yet desiring it, yearning for it, for release.

Perhaps the world had changed, moved past them.

Perhaps mankind could only perceive the smaller fears these days: the fear of bloodshed, of split skulls and open abdomens and slashing knives.

If that were the case—and he was tired enough now to concede this point—then he had reached the end, just as surely as the other three had.

Yet, they were gone now, and he was still here.

He shook his head, laughed, but the laugh was arid and grating.

Still here, after his wife had died, and his children and grandchildren and great-grandchildren and... he didn't even bother to continue. He'd lost interest in hovering around those of his own bloodline and watching their lives long ago.

For all he knew, there were others of his blood now walking the same path he was on, turned by another of his kind.

He felt nothing for them, for their fates. That particular blood tie meant so little to him now. After centuries of drinking from the well of humanity, the blood in his veins was no longer merely the sum of his ancestors co-mingling their blood.

He sighed again, stirred, examined the box.

Ahhh, he thought to himself. *Best just to get on with it.*

His sharp-nailed fingers found the seam of the box, cunningly hidden by its maker (so long dead now), and slipped in to slide it open.

The door behind him opened again, and a wedge of incandescent light oozed into the room, fell over his hand, the box.

"Wait."

The Count froze, not something he typically did.

But there was something about the voice, something sure and commanding and...

Free from fear.

He turned slowly, his fingers tightening their grip on the box.

Three shadows stood in the doorway, and Mr. Gerund hung behind.

"Who are you and why should I wait?"

The three figures stepped into the pool of firelight, and he stood to face them.

Mr. Gerund drew the door closed softly.

"There is no need to partake of your tontine just yet," said the first man. The candles shimmered on his dark, bare skin, bald head. "There are yet worlds of fear to explore."

"Really?" the Count asked, his tone bland. "Do tell."

"I bring the fear of that which is beyond death... the mindless shuffling, the hollow hunger, the compulsion that draws a man from out his grave to feed on those still living."

This figure stepped forward, bared his white teeth in a rictus that might have been a malefic grin. "I am Papa Loa, Father of Zombies."

The vampire narrowed his eyes, betrayed the smallest hint of a smile.

The second figure stepped forward, thin and smaller by far than Papa Loa, gracile and insect like, with delicate limbs and a triangular head. Its large, slanted eyes were pitch black, reflecting nothing of its surroundings.

In a voice that was a reedy whisper, the thing said, "I bring the fear of dreams and nightmares... the loss of self, the theft of memory, of time... of children replaced by changelings. I bring the fear that turns men into cattle."

Stepping fluidly into the light, the being bowed slightly, its smooth, grey skin wrinkling at its waist, at its joints, like rubber. "I am Ebe, the Keeper of Missing Time."

A possibility sprang into the mind of the vampire, a suggestion...

... *perhaps... just perhaps.*

Then the next figure stepped forward.

The wan light revealed a man, a simple, straightforward man with slicked back hair. He was dressed in a dark suit, neat and well tailored. A collared shirt, a tie of red silk. His pants were crisply pressed, his dark shoes shone. A thick gold watch clutched his wrist. In his left hand, he held a briefcase, and the vampire noted that the man's nails were perfectly manicured.

"I bring the fear of ruin, of relentless pursuit, of overwhelming retribution. I bring the fear of mysterious language and occult workings. I bring the fear of powerlessness, of sleepless nights and endless days."

Still the vampire waited for this final figure to reveal its true nature.

The man smiled, revealing perfectly formed, perfectly white teeth, straight and even.

"I am Stanley Zurich, attorney-at-law."

The vampire felt his hand lift from the smooth, cool wood of the tontine box.

He surveyed this new group, so similar and yet so unlike his previous associates.

But it could work, he thought.

It would serve for a time... and that's all he needed.

"Mr. Gerund," the vampire called, tapping the wineglass on the table with the nail of one of his long, thin fingers.

At the crystalline ring, the door opened.

"Yes, sir?"

"Drinks, Mr. Gerund, for us all."

The servant pushed the door open further, walked into the room carrying a tray.

"I took the liberty, sir, thinking that you and your guests might wish something."

Gerund passed the tray before the four men, each lifting a thin glass of champagne. When each had a glass in hand, Gerund inclined his head to the vampire.

"Oh, and Mr. Gerund," the vampire said, nodding toward the wooden box on the side table. "You can place the tontine back in the tabernacle... for a later date. A much later date, I think."

"Yes, sir," Gerund said, carefully taking the box, backing from the room, drawing the door shut behind him.

The vampire held his champagne flute aloft, let its bubbles capture the light.

The three others likewise lifted their flutes together in a toast.

"To us, gentlemen," said the vampire. "To the monsters of the new world... and to the fear we bring.

"Cheers."

THE
MELLIFIED MAN

What is the sweetest thing you've ever eaten?

I won't tell you that, but I'll tell you the sweetest thing that I ever made... the most dreadful thing...

It was Bobby's sweet tooth that did him in.

A common lament, the mumbled apology of every diabetic, every cavity sufferer, every overweight, bad-complexioned kid who stashed candy at the back of his underwear drawer.

Sweets were his bread, his staff of life. It wasn't unusual for him to have an ice cream at lunch... *instead* of lunch, or a piece of cake for dinner.

But he wasn't fat, wasn't even pleasantly plump or husky, as his mother called his brother. He wasn't diabetic, and his teeth were in fantastic shape for a 31-year-old. Bobby Jenkins was, in fact, as close to a perfect specimen as possible for a man of his age. Except, of course, for his sweet tooth… and the fact that he liked guys instead of girls; that—at least, according to his mother—was a mark against him.

He swam, he lifted, he played competitive handball and racquetball at the club, he walked on a treadmill. He neither smoked nor drank, didn't even imbibe red meat or carbs of most varieties.

Ahh, but refined, white sugar was his heroin, his crack, his meth, all rolled into one.

And, like any addict of any substance, he was loath to give it up.

And, like any addict of any substance, his life was dominated by it.

And, like any addict of any substance, his life would be ended by it…

* * *

Bobby was at lunch, poring over papers for a business merger he was shepherding, when he heard of The Alhambra, a new candy store in town. As he was nearby, he decided to swing over and have a look.

The Alhambra was a massive red brick structure, three stories tall and encompassing an entire city block. The front of its first floor was lined with tall plate glass windows that showed the displays inside. A simple, tasteful awning jutted from the entrance, 'The Alhambra' stenciled in flowing, Moorish-looking letters.

Bobby parked his car, fed the meter, walked through the door. Outside, the air was hot, St. Louis summer hot; inside, the air was cool, bursting from an overhead vent directly above the inside of the door.

Two steps inside the door, he stopped, stunned.

He had found his heaven, his paradise, his nirvana…

The inside of the store was done in dark, wainscoted paneling, which covered the walls to about waist height. Textured wallpaper with Moorish designs in reds and golds went from there to the ceiling. Displays and cases were discreetly lit by hanging lamps. Silk bunting covered the ceiling—reds and golds again, but also rich blues and vibrant greens and dark violets.

But the candy… the candy was what caught his eye…

On one side of the long, narrow room were jawbreakers and gumballs of all kinds; licorice whips and lollipops, gummies and stick candy in tall apothecary jars; popcorn balls and candy apples, jelly beans and penny candy of every variety, from root beer barrels to lemon drops. There was even a section with the kind of candy you'd find at any convenience store or gas station.

In the middle of the room, where Bobby stood agog, there were chocolates of all kinds and shapes and colors. Here were chocolate bars, unwrapped, bare and stacked like bullion. Here were ribbons of chocolate so dark it seemed as if they were curled from the very stuff of night. Bon-bons and truffles, chocolate-covered fruit and nuts of every kind, white chocolate, dark chocolate, milk chocolate. The smell of the chocolate alone was intoxicating, heady.

On the other side of the store were items that were less common. Here were pastilles from France, Botan rice candy from Japan, marzipan in a host of shapes, maple candies from Canada, even a case with chocolate-covered mealworms and crickets, sugared ant eggs from Mexico, some kind of candied, dried fish from Norway.

"Ahhh, overwhelmed, are you, sir?" came a voice, rich and baritone, with a blur of an accent. "I am overwhelmed, myself… and I own the place."

Bobby turned and saw a man who was perhaps Spanish, perhaps Arabic. He was a bit shorter than Bobby, spare and lean, with a swarthy, attractive face that looked as though it been carved from the room's dark wood. He was perhaps 45, perhaps 55; it was hard to tell. A magnificent black mustache draped his upper lip and his hair was a dense mop of the same stuff, with a few stray streaks of gray here and there.

"You're like… the luckiest kid in town," Bobby said, still somewhat dazed.

At that, the man laughed, a booming sound that echoed through the store, drawing looks from other patrons.

"I knew we were of a kind when you walked in," he chuckled. Those words and his polite, interested laughter sent a tingle up Bobby's back.

"My name is Afaz Aziz. The Alhambra is mine. Come, what can I show you?" he asked. "More importantly, what can I get you?"

Mr. Aziz said this with all of the tremulous avidity of any drug dealer; and, like any drug taker, Bobby followed him.

* * *

The bag of sweets he'd bought at The Alhambra that afternoon didn't last long. Within four days, Bobby was visiting again, leaving with another bag filled with candy. He didn't want to admit it, but it was as much to see Mr. Aziz as it was to satisfy his sweet tooth.

Week after week, Bobby visited The Alhambra: sometimes twice, sometimes three times a week. Each time, Aziz greeted him warmly, effusively, as if he had been waiting specifically for him.

But Bobby couldn't tell… couldn't *confirm* that Aziz was interested in him… at least, not like that. The man *was* handsy, always touching him, his arm, his shoulder, patting his face, sometimes even taking his hand like a child.

Nothing came from any of this, though, unless one counted the pounds that Bobby was putting on from the rich, exotic sweets he left with. And he always left with something.

* * *

"So, what are you looking for today, eh?" Aziz asked, on a visit a few weeks later. "Chocolate truffles from Madagascar? Hmmm, macadamia brittle from Hawaii? No, hmmm... let me see..."

"I want something different," Bobby blurted, trying hard not to make it sign sound like a pick-up line.

Aziz narrowed his eyes, and for a moment, Bobby felt as if he had blundered, misread the situation, the man.

But Aziz nodded, pursed his lips. "Yes, perhaps we have just the thing for you."

Then, taking his hand, he led him through a thick, velvet curtain the color of a dark sea. Behind the curtain, down a short hallway cluttered with empty boxes and cartons, they came to a door. Aziz, still gripping Bobby's hand (which he was beginning to worry was a little too sweaty), produced an ornate brass skeleton key from a vest pocket, slid it into the lock, turned it.

Aziz pulled him through a bewildering maze of dark corridors. The air had a close, humid feel to it, like warm breath exhaled from a mouth that had been too long closed.

Just as Bobby was about to ask where they were going, they came to an iron staircase that zigzagged up the rear wall. They mounted the rickety thing, which squeaked and swayed under their feet, ascended one flight.

At the top, Aziz opened a door onto blinding sunlight.

Bobby shielded his eyes with his free hand as Aziz drew him through the doorway...

He had nearly gasped the first time he'd walked into The Alhambra; he did gasp now.

They were on the roof of the building, but it was hard to tell.

A magnificent garden spread before them, trees large enough to block the skyline and provide shade from the sun. And even though it was in the high 90s, here, within this lush garden, with its shaded paths and its air filled with mist, it was at least 15 degrees cooler.

Aziz crossed to a path made from paving stones set in the springy grass to a table set near the fountain. The table was under a small structure made of alternating tan and red stone blocks forming Moorish arches, with a dome overhead.

"Drinks!" announced Aziz, clapping his hands as they sat. A young man, dark skinned and wearing white robes, appeared from some hidden door, stopped at Aziz's side. "Haran, we require something to drink as we discuss business. Coffee perhaps? A soda?"

Bobby answered slowly, still a little overwhelmed. "Do you have Coke?"

Aziz laughed. "Do we have Coke? Hah! Coke for Mr. Jenkins and coffee for me."

The young man disappeared, and Aziz watched Bobby gape at his surroundings.

"Beautiful, isn't it?"

"I've heard of rooftop gardens, but this is like a rooftop park. How'd you get all this up here?"

Aziz waved a hand negligently. "Isn't it enough that it's here, that you're here?"

"Of course."

"Then relish it, Mr. Jenkins. Relish the opportunities that life brings you, as I do."

* * *

Haran returned with a silver tray bearing a complete coffee service and a glass filled with ice between two bottles. The boy set everything onto the table, hovered for a moment until Aziz waved him away with a negligent flip of his hand.

"Coke," said Aziz, as Bobby studied the bottles. "Imported from Mexico, where they still make it with real cane sugar, not corn syrup."

Bobby decanted half of one bottle into the glass, where it fizzed and foamed familiarly. One swallow and Bobby knew that he'd never drink another Coke that wasn't made in Mexico. The taste was crisp and glassy, with a sparkling, deep sweetness.

"It's delicious."

Aziz smiled as he put teaspoon after teaspoon of sugar into his small cup of dark, frothy coffee. "I'll have a case waiting at the door. My gift to you."

Bobby sipped at the soda.

"So, what kinds of sweets are you looking for today?" Aziz asked him, his look again becoming serious, measuring.

"Something different, *unique...* that you can't find *anywhere.*"

Aziz wiped foam from his mustache with a linen napkin.

"What would *you* recommend? *What is the sweetest thing you've ever eaten?*"

The Alhambra's owner considered this, poured another cup of coffee. "I won't tell you that, but I'll tell you the sweetest thing that I ever made... the most dreadful thing..."

"The most dreadful?"

"Yes. Have you heard of... a mellified man?" Aziz asked, finishing the sugaring of his second cup of coffee.

"No."

"Ahh," breathed Aziz. "It is the body of a dead man macerated in honey. Arab, Chinese, even Egyptian physicians have used them for centuries to treat certain illnesses, depending on what part is ingested, of course."

"A *dead* man?" Bobby frowned. "People... *eat* it?"

191

"Yes, but only the purest of men can be mellified, only those who have lived clean, healthy lives. It is the rarest, the purest, the most *spiritual* of sweets. And valuable, incalculably valuable."

"Have you... ever...?"

Aziz's eyebrows rose and his face became somber. "If I say no, you'll think I am... pulling your leg. If I say yes, you'll recoil in horror."

"But you said... you said the story was about the sweetest thing you'd ever *made*."

Aziz poured more coffee, shoveled more sugar into it. He stirred the resulting slurry, downed it in one swallow. "When I was younger, I helped my father and uncles make a mellified man. It was a... unique experience, one that has stayed with me."

"What did you do with it... *him*?"

"Why, what we made it for, of course," Aziz said. "For doctors to prescribe to their patients... well, the wealthy ones at least. And to allow epicures like yourself the opportunity to taste a most sublime sweet."

Bobby swallowed. "So, have you... did you..."

"There is only a single piece left of that mellified man," said Aziz, ignoring the question. "The last piece after 45 years. Just the tip of a finger, no larger than a thimble. I have been saving it for the last five years. I think I have been saving it for you, Mr. Jenkins. I think you are the right person."

"*Me*? What would make you think that I'd want to... eat part of a dead body?"

Aziz smiled. "Is cheese just spoiled milk? Is an aged bottle of wine just grapes that have gone bad? No, the process they go through makes them more than just that, just as the mellification makes the flesh more than just flesh."

"Neither wine nor cheese was ever a dead guy. No, thank you."

He rose from the table, turned to find the way they'd come in.

Aziz remained seated, poured more coffee. "And here I thought we were of a kind."

"Me, too," Bobby answered. "Just not that kind."

"I thought you were an epicure of sweets, perhaps the one man who could appreciate the last remaining bite of something rare... something sacred."

Bobby stared at him, said nothing.

"You said you wanted something new, something you couldn't get anywhere. Did you not?"

"I was talking about an everlasting gobstopper or gum that tastes like a four-course meal. Not a chunk of sweetened corpse. Thank you, Mr. Aziz. But no thanks, not for me."

Mr. Aziz still didn't move, and for a crazy, sweating minute Bobby thought that there might be repercussions for saying no. But Aziz merely motioned with his hand. Instantly, Haran appeared.

"Take Mr. Jenkins to the front."

Haran bowed, motioned for Bobby to follow.

They went several steps down the stone path, and Mr. Aziz called to him.

"Mr. Jenkins... think about it... think long and hard. It is a singular honor I offer you," he said. "Oh, and don't forget your case of Coke. Haran will help you to your car with it."

* * *

Two weeks went by.

Bobby buried himself in his work, stayed long hours at the office, put off going back to The Alhambra as long as he could.

But he knew he had to go back... because he had been dreaming about it.

In his dreams, he is at the table in the garden, Mr. Aziz by his side, smiling... smiling...

Before him, on a golden plate is a hand, an entire human hand, severed at the wrist, laying palm up, the fingers curled slightly inward. The hand is a curious deep amber color and sits in a pool of thick liquid the same shade.

In his dreams, he pins the hand to the plate with his fork and slices a thin piece from the mound of flesh under the thumb. It carves like cold butter, the meat draping over onto itself as if carved from a turkey breast. The flesh is golden underneath, dense, almost creamy.

In his dreams, he lifts his fork, golden fluid dripping to the plate, dripping like sparks in the sun, lifts it to his mouth, slides it in...

Just as he begins chewing, the dream ends.

He is left with the ghost memory of its texture, firm like meat, yielding to the gentle pressure of his teeth, liquefying in his mouth...

He is left with a strange taste in his mouth, haunting, evocative, sweet and thick and...

... but it fades... fades...

He has this dream three times before he returns to The Alhambra.

* * *

"Ahh, Mr. Jenkins," Aziz greeted him as he walked into the store. "How nice to see you again. It has been too long. Did you enjoy the Coke?"

Bobby nodded, sweating even though the air inside was, as usual, frigid. "Yes, it was great... delicious. But that's not... I mean... it isn't why..."

Aziz turns to him, and Bobby sees the sparkle in his eye, a slight twitch of his upper lip beneath the fringe of his mustache.

"Of course not. You are here for the mellified man, as I knew you would be," Aziz said, smiling.

"Look," Bobby said, making sure they weren't overheard. "I have questions. I mean... is it... legal? *Dangerous?* Can I afford it?"

193

Mr. Aziz's smile grew wide, and he threw back his head and roared in laughter. "Yes, yes, and yes. All yes. Now, come, upstairs. We make arrangements."

* * *

Mellified man was perhaps the only candy Bobby had ever heard of that required a course of preparation to eat. It wasn't a rigorous course, really... strange, but not rigorous.

"You must take care of your body, keep it in shape," Aziz had said, patting Bobby's gut, which jiggled with the 15 or so pounds he'd put on since discovering The Alhambra. "Especially over the next 27 days."

"The next 27 days?" Bobby had asked. "Why?"

"Because for the next 27 days, you will eat nothing but honey and water. No bread, no meat, no alcohol. Only honey. I will provide all that you require."

"That can't be healthy."

"Bees do it," Aziz had answered. "Honey is the perfect food, perfect. That is why your body must be full of it, saturated with it, before you can ingest the mellified man."

"And how much is this going to cost me?" he'd asked, waiting for the other shoe to drop.

Aziz blinked, frowned, as if he had not considered this.

"Let's say... a thousand dollars."

"A grand? That's it? For something so rare, so unusual? And the last piece of it?"

Aziz had smiled, avidly, like a drug dealer.

"Only because I know you will bring me much business in the future."

* * *

Day 10 came and went, and he felt great, better than he'd have thought; better than he'd ever felt, for that matter. Initially, he'd been worried about getting enough to eat, keeping his energy up, but that seemed to be no problem. He carried a jar of honey in his briefcase, a new one each day, spooned some out each time he felt hungry.

He went to the gym now every day, worked out for at least two hours. In a week, most of the candy weight he'd put on since discovering The Alhambra had come off. Another week, and he was in the best shape of his life.

Where his muscles were noticeable before, now they were prominent, even through clothing. Everything on his body was chiseled, sculpted, from his pecs to the deep ridge of his abdominal shelf, flaring across his lower stomach from his hips, dipping below his navel.

His boss called him into his office to tell him that several people noticed him working through lunch, eating nothing but spoonfuls of honey and a bottle of water. Everyone knew of his sweet tooth, but he thought there might be something seriously wrong.

But Bobby assured him, assured them all (his mother, included) that he was fine... better than fine. He was great. He was in fantastic shape, feeling spectacularly healthy.

"Just a diet, then?" his boss had asked.

"Yeah, just a diet," he said, smiling.

"Okay, well take care of yourself. You're too valuable."

Neither he nor Bobby had any idea how true that was...

* * *

Bobby was shaking so badly by the time he arrived, he couldn't tell if it was anticipation or the fact that every molecule in his body felt like it was vibrating at high frequency.

Haran was there to open the door for him, lead him to the garden on the roof. It was a cool night, summer starting to give way to early fall. Already the sun was low in the sky, painting it roses and blues and dark, bruised violets. Just as in his dream, Mr. Aziz sat at the table under the stone gazebo.

"I am so glad you are here," he said, pulling him into an embrace. Bobby took the man's hug, confused all over again, hugged back. He smelled his aftershave, redolent of sandalwood and leather, his breath of cloves and mace.

Aziz waved him to a seat, sent Haran away, and they were alone.

"So, you are ready for this?"

"Yes, I feel great."

"Excellent. Well, then let us begin..."

"Do you want me to pay you now? I brought cash." Bobby produced a plain envelope.

Again, Aziz seemed surprised. "Of course, that's fine." He took the envelope and secreted it as deftly as a magician in some pocket within his dark suit. He produced a small box from the same pocket, set it onto the table.

"The last remaining piece of the mellified man."

The box was simple, unadorned brass, hinged on one side, about the size of a matchbox. Bobby touched the smooth metal of the box, placed it in the palm of his hand, lifted it. He opened the lid. It took him a second to figure out what he was looking at.

Nestled in crushed velvet was a small, wrinkled thing about the size of a gumdrop.

The intact nail gave it away...

It was the tip, the very tip of a human finger.

It was golden-brown, the color of a well-cooked French fry, moist looking, gelid. The nail was a bit longer than the finger, but it had softened, drooped over its tip.

The smell was larger than the box: rich and aromatic, flowery and almost resinous, sharp.

Bobby was shocked that it made him salivate.

Reaching in, he touched the thing tentatively. It was soft, but not jellied; moist, but not wet; sticky, but not adhesive.

He lifted it from its velvet nest, brought it to his nose.

It was intoxicating, the aroma of every sweet he'd ever smelled—chocolates and licorice and almonds and caramel.

Almost without volition, he opened his mouth, placed it on his tongue, closed his lips, his eyes.

He didn't move, didn't chew, simply let it sit on his tongue and melt...

The taste was indescribable. It warmed in his mouth, sending delicious trickles over his tongue, trickles that tasted of honey, yes, but also of something earthier, something more substantial.

Meat... that was it... meat...

His stomach might have forced him to spit the fingertip onto the table, but he didn't... he didn't because it was so damned delicious.

It tasted of *everything*, everything sweet, everything salty, everything savory...

... and *nothing*... like nothing he'd ever tasted before.

Then he bit down, and the mellified flesh gave way, parted under his teeth with something like the texture of a caramel, dense, resistant at first, but softening.

His eyes still closed, he chewed. His mouth filled with saliva, and he had to force himself not to swallow, lest he swallow the remaining piece of the fingertip and then this would be over too soon.

Then it was over, as the last sliver of it trickled down his throat. There was an aftertaste of musky, spoiled meat that lasted for just a moment. But it was overshadowed by a last, brief explosion of sweet flowers—tasting of sugared violets.

And he thought, thought in that last moment, that this is what flowers tasted like to the bees that made the honey; the essence of the flower, pure and bright and sugary with its perfume.

He swallowed the last of it, looked at Mr. Aziz.

There were tears in his eyes.

"Thank you... good lord... thank you."

"Thank you," Aziz smiled back. "You have no idea the joy this gives me."

Bobby had lost all track of time, had no idea how long he'd sat at the table.

"I feel like... nothing can top this experience. Like this might be it for me and sweets."

"Oh," Aziz smiled, taking the brass box, closing its lid and secreting it back into his jacket. "I wouldn't say that…"

* * *

The next morning, Bobby woke up, feeling strange.

He sat in bed for a few moments, trying to figure out what it was, what didn't feel right.

Then, it dawned on him; the strange, exciting, buzzing energy that had filled him for the last month was gone. It was replaced by a thickness, a kind of turgidity inside him, as if his blood were sluggish, too substantial for his veins.

There was also the taste in his mouth, an unpleasant taste, rotten and carious, as if he had an infected tooth.

It tasted of sweet, dead flesh.

Throwing the covers off, he rose, went to the bathroom, looked in the mirror over the sink. His face looked puffy, his eyes bleary, hung over.

There was something wrong, though… some problem with the bathroom lights.

His skin was a deep, amber yellow. Even the whites of his eyes looked golden, his palms, his finger nails…

Shaking his head, he stepped to the toilet and tried to pee.

Nearly a minute passed. He opened his eyes, looked down. He was not, had not been peeing.

He felt something in his bladder uncoil, and there was a rush of fluid.

Then pain, pain so instant, so powerful that his legs swayed, his knees buckled. His guts cramped, and he felt as if he was passing a rope of fire.

He expected to see blood in the toilet, but what he saw was worse…

Peeing, yes, finally, but it was not the thin, arcing, rushing stream of urine he was accustomed to.

It was a thick, slow-moving, golden stream that didn't so much jet from him as pour like syrup.

And it hurt, dear God, it hurt… too thick, to substantial to pass…

It plopped into the toilet, hit the water and congealed there, forming a golden squiggle that twisted to the bottom of the bowl, curling on itself like piped icing.

As sweat beaded on his forehead, the odor hit him; musky and heavy and sweet…

Shaking as much in agony as in fear, he put a finger in the flow, brought it to his mouth.

Honey… he was pissing honey.

Just as this realization hit, another shockwave of pain rippled through his guts, crumpled him to the cold tile floor.

As he faded into unconsciousness, he thought of the thousand dollars he'd given Aziz.

How he'd thought that was too small a price...

* * *

The candy store wasn't open yet, but he didn't care. He jerked his car to a stop in front of awning, climbed out slowly, lurched to the glass door. Peering through the bars over the windows, he could see that it was empty, the lights off.

"Aziz!" he shouted, pounding on the steel bars and rattling them. "Aziz! Open up!"

People passed on the street, staring. He'd been unable to dress himself, so he still wore the loose shorts and t-shirt he'd worn to bed.

Haran, his eyes wide, unbolted the lock, threw open the bars.

"Mr. Jenkins?" he asked in alarm. "How can I...?"

"Aziz," mumbled Bobby past a bloated and uncooperative tongue. "Must see him."

He pushed past Haran, who drew down the bars, closed and locked the door.

Bobby stumbled through the dark store, bumping into displays, knocking pieces of candy and entire displays over.

"Here," Haran said, taking his arm. "Let me help."

* * *

In the garden, Bobby moved as quickly as his stiffening legs would take him. Toward Aziz, who sat there under the stone gazebo, drinking coffee.

As Bobby approached, Aziz looked up, not surprised at all to see him.

"Atheeth," Bobby yelled, through a hoarse and constricted throat. "Wha ha you done oo mee?"

Mr. Aziz regarded him with delight, his eyes twinkling as they had when he'd first met Bobby.

"Why, you truly were the right person, weren't you, Mr. Jenkins," he said. "We are of a kind."

Bobby found breathing difficult now, his lungs felt as if they were filling with thick fluid.

"Wha?"

"The candy maker and the candy. What... you mean you never *knew*... never *suspected*?"

Bobby felt syrupy tears squeeze from his eyes, dribble down his cheeks. When they touched his mouth, he was not surprised that they were sweet.

"The last piece of a mellified man is used to make a new mellified man," Aziz explained, rising and approaching him. He took Bobby's hand. It was puffy and golden-brown, so engorged with honey that drops of it dewed atop the pores of his skin.

Bobby saw Aziz take a long, wickedly curved dagger from his jacket, hold it to the light.

"This will not hurt... not a bit, you will see."

The knife slipped into his chest slowly, deliberately, and while Bobby could feel it penetrate him, he felt no pain, as Aziz had promised. And from the wound, honey seeped like amber treacle.

Vaguely, he saw Haran wheel in a wooden box, felt Aziz's hands on him, Haran's hands as they eased him down, eased him into it.

"Excuse me, but the wooden casket is temporary only," Aziz apologized. "A few days, after the transformation is complete and you are dead, we will place you in a stone sarcophagus, cover you completely with honey. There, you will steep for an entire year before..."

Aziz reached out, stroked his cheek.

Bobby felt tears track down the sides of his face, pool near his ears.

"You will help so many, so very many other people," he said, his eyes large and moist and almost loving, almost sympathetic.

Bobby tried to say something, to plead, but nothing came out of his mouth now; not words, at least; a gout of honey poured over his chin.

Aziz managed a final smile. "You were a sweet customer, Mr. Jenkins, perhaps the sweetest. Now, you are to become the sweetest thing that I make, the most dreadful thing."

The lid fell over Bobby's face, and darkness enclosed him, darkness thick as honey...

BOX OF ROCKS

Dumb as a box of rocks, my old man used to say. *My old man.* Yeah, he really wasn't my old man, more like my mom's old man or she was his old lady, as they said in the day.

You say—and you're the doctor, aren't you... *the psychiatrist*—you say talking about this will help. How, I don't know, since even thinking about it's so difficult.

But here goes... here goes...

199

* * *

Lucy. The cat. That's what I remember. That's what started it.

Well, she didn't *start* it, really. My stepfather was crazy before... *mean*.

My real dad? He died when I was four. I don't remember much about him. Quiet guy, always smiling. Why do we remember people who die young as always smiling? From what my mother says, his life was ten pounds of crap in a five-pound box.

Box.

Why does that word bother me so much? It sounds ugly, looks ugly on paper.

Anyway, he died. Cancer of the something or other. Quick, no lingering, no loitering, no passing go, no collecting $200.

He was 24; doesn't that suck the big one?

Left my mother with me and pretty much nothing else.

My mom could have ditched me, could have moved on with her life. But she didn't. We were in it together, she told me.

I'm doing this for us.

Goddamn, I love her. I don't know why she won't see me anymore, why she feels so much anger, so much grief for those fucking kittens. I mean, *Christ.* Whatever. I never boxed her around like he did. Never hurt her.

Did I say that again?

Box? Shit...

She was only 21 when my real dad died. She had a job as a waitress at some slop joint: on her feet 12, 16 hours a day for minimum wage, lousy tips and a lot of leers and come-ons. God love her, she hung in there.

For us...

Then she met *him.* Yeah, my stepfather, who the fuck else?

He was a customer, but kept his smart remarks and his hands to himself—at first, anyway. Left her nice tips, talked to her like she was a real person.

She liked having a man to talk to, one who wasn't four years old or pawing at her. One who didn't, you know, *expect* stuff. One who didn't cut and run when he learned that she was a 21-year-old widow with a dead man's kid.

So, she started seeing him, what the hell? She was still young, still pretty. That's not weird, is it? Saying my mom was pretty? He knew it, my stepfather; even knew she was *too* pretty... too pretty for him, at least.

He worked at the coke factory, and I don't mean soda. I mean the ore, the chemical, whatever that shit is. The kind of guy who leaves when it's dark, wears Dickies, carries a gray lunchbox with a baloney sandwich and a bag of chips, a Thermos of coffee, comes home when it's dark again. It was a hard job and it usually left him too tired to hit us... *usually.*

So, yeah, at first it was all ice cream and trips to the toy store and going to grab a burger and playing catch in the yard. Oh, yeah, he was all *father*. And you know? I was too young, too stupid to even know what he was doing. My own dad had died, and I wanted a father, craved one. I'd have taken anyone at that point, you know? Hitler. Ted Bundy. *Anyone*.

* * *

Anyway, it started after my sixth birthday.

There was a little party, a few friends from the neighborhood, my parents. That's pretty much it. No one from his family. I don't know if he even had any; he never mentioned any.

No friends of mom's at the party. By then, they'd picked up things about him we hadn't picked up on yet. And certainly no friends of his. I don't know about family, but I know the man had no friends; I knew that even at six.

I got a bike, real bike, a Schwinn, not some pansy trike. A real one, with a banana seat and reflectors and a wheelie bar and shit. I think he even picked it out for me.

It was the last purely great day I ever had. I sat outside on a card table on the little patio, sat and blew out my seven candles. One to grow on, remember? Ate cake and ice cream until I felt like I was gonna bust. Then he and my mom watched me ride the bike up and down the street. Hell, the bastard had even bought baseball cards to put in the spokes.

Anyway, the next day was a Saturday, and I woke early, but not to watch cartoons like I usually did. No, I wanted to get some riding done early. I dressed, ate a bowl of cereal. Cap'n Crunch. Have you had that since you've been an adult? Tears the fuck out of your mouth. Jesus, I guess we just never cared about that shit as kids. Anyway, I gobbled down a bowl of that, went outside to ride.

I had a blast, you know? Riding the empty streets, making sharp turns, popping wheelies, all the while those damn cards *whack-whack-whacking* in the spokes like a machine gun.

After an hour or so, I went home. But I wasn't paying attention. As I steered into the driveway, my front tire caught in a rut or something. The bike stopped cold. I didn't.

I flew over the handlebars, flew straight into the side of his car parked in the driveway. It was a 1960-something Dodge Challenger, fairly new, midnight blue. *Pristine*. He spent a lot of time taking care of that car, cleaning it, waxing it, washing the whitewalls, the chrome, vacuuming the inside.

I hit the car hard, headfirst, busted my lip and nose, bled all over the place. My head made a dent, an actual dent in the left rear quarter panel of the car, the midnight metal dimpling slightly near the wheel well. Think I even chipped a tooth. Maybe knocked one out. I can't remember. There was a christing lot of blood, though.

Sitting on my little ass where I'd landed, I howled until they came out, until *he* came out. I waited for him to kneel beside me, to wipe away the tears, to comfort me.

Instead, he came out of the house, came out and stopped about halfway to me. He looked at me, looked at the dent, and his face changed. It fell into itself, collapsed. Never saw anyone's face do that. Taking two steps toward me, he lifted his leg, brought it around and kicked me *hard*, like he was punting on the 4th down in the Super Bowl.

His foot caught me square in the back, lifted me off the ground. I mean, I was probably all of 50 pounds soaking wet. And threw me into the side of the car… *again.*

It was so unexpected, so unbelievable, that I had no time to react, no time to say a word before I was slumping down the car, landing with my face against the tire.

"Motherfucker!" Then he kicked me again, and once more, both times his foot digging into my back, into my kidneys. Oh yeah, I wet my pants. Big time. Just let it go.

By the time I heard my mother come out, I was crying so hard I couldn't breathe.

But then, he knelt, took me in his arms.

I was covered in blood and tears and snot, and I was totally out of it, totally confused by what had happened, what he had done.

I actually hugged him, *hugged* that motherfucker, put my arms around his neck and buried my bloody face into his shoulder and cried.

He held me tight, not letting my mother get to me, in case she'd hear anything I might say. In a suddenly calm voice, he told her to get the car keys so that they could take me to the emergency room.

I got six stitches in my forehead and a metal nose cast from where I hit the car the first time. I got another four stitches in my chin and a cast on two fingers from what he did to me. Plus the doctor told my mother I had bruised my kidneys… *deeply*. He prescribed some pain medication and advised her not to be too alarmed if I peed blood for a couple of days. I did, and she was.

It was a bike accident, he'd told them; silly kid got a new bike for his birthday yesterday, crashed into the side of the car.

He never said anything about kicking me, and neither did I. Until now, that is.

* * *

So, we got a cat, literally the next day. I think it was his way of making it up to me. Get the kid a pet. I think he thought I'd ask for a dog. I think that's what *he* wanted. But I was still unsure of him, unsure of how he'd react if I jumped all the way from no pets at all to a dog. So I figured, a cat, hey, they're smaller than a dog, so he wouldn't get that upset, would be less likely to say no.

"A cat?" he asked. "You sure?"

He flipped the cigarette from his lips, ground the butt into the asphalt.

"Well, let's get to the pound and get you a cat."

* * *

That's how I got Lucy, the cat that started all this shit.

Yeah, I know what I said. But, you know, it didn't really get bad until after we got her. After she had the... well... the...

You know... for the life of me, I can't remember what she looked like. Gray, I think.

I don't want to talk any more tonight.

* * *

So, back to where I left off... oh, yeah. Lucy.

We took her home, and she was a good cat. No, a great cat.

For a while, at least, I was happy.

Until I began to notice what he was doing to *her.*

I began noticing how he was with my mom. In fact, looking back on it now, I think he got the fucking cat as much to distract me as to keep my mouth shut.

Was I supposed to be aware of what was going on? Was I supposed to listen to their whispered conversations? Was I supposed to notice the marks on her arms, her legs, the dark circles under her eyes? The way she... *Jesus*... the way she flinched when he came near... *just like me.*

I was six fucking years old and my silence could be had for a $25 cat.

* * *

Sure, over the next few years he hurt me. Usually just a quick backhand. Or maybe a vicious kick when she wasn't looking, or a twist of the arm. Stupid stuff, avoidable stuff if I was paying attention.

Once, though, when I was eight, I came into the house after school, and it was still, quiet. I went into the kitchen to fix myself a peanut butter sandwich before dinner. As I was smoothing the peanut butter onto the white bread, I heard sounds from upstairs; whispered voices, hushed crying.

As I put the bread away, I heard one short, high-pitched screech of pain, almost immediately silenced.

Slowly, cautiously, I crept up the steps, pausing on the landing outside the bathroom door. It was half open, and I could see my own face reflected in the mirror over the sink.

He stood there, my stepfather, his back to me, washing his hands furiously in the sink.

There was blood *everywhere*, spatters of it on the icy white tile.

Tracking down the sink, dripping from the faucet handles.

Even the soap foaming in his hands looked pink and clotted.

But the toilet... there was something in the toilet... *something*...

The toilet was near the doorway, lid up.

I couldn't make out what was inside: a clump, a mass of something, glistening and raw, red with blood that stained the water in the bowl.

It floated there on the surface; a billowing cloud, red and nebulous, spreading from it.

"What the fuck?"

I snapped my eyes from the thing in the water to his face, and it, too, was speckled with blood.

"Don't you fucking knock?"

Saying this, he stepped toward me, lifted his hand.

I think I willed myself into unconsciousness before it crashed into me, before it sent me reeling backwards, tumbling down the steps.

Before I could feel the pain blossoming like a bright flower within me.

Before I could see him standing over me smiling... *smiling*.

Dumb as a box of rocks, that's what he said. What I was... *what I am*...

* * *

I awoke in bed with a lump the size of a Grade-A large egg on my head. My limbs felt as if they'd been twisted out of shape and held there. My back hurt, my ass hurt, and at least one of my ankles felt sprained.

I counted my injuries, trying to remember what had happened. As I reached seven, I remembered the bloody thing in the toilet, the door pushed open.

It was my mom; the yellow light of the hallway backlighting her so that I couldn't see her face.

"Are you awake?" Her voice sounded slurred and shaky, as if she were sleepy, or drugged. "Are you okay?"

I didn't know what to say, didn't know where he was, what he'd told her. So, I just nodded, nodded to her in the darkness and hoped that she saw it, hoped that she didn't ask me again.

God, I wanted to... no, not *tell* her about me... I wanted to *ask* her what it was that I'd seen. What he'd been doing in the bathroom... the blood... the crying.

But I didn't. I didn't.

She told me good night, and drew the door softly closed.

* * *

The cat? You asked about the cat again this afternoon.

I don't know why you, why *everyone* in this entire fucking place is so christing concerned with that cat. I loved that damn cat, but *fuck!* It was just a cat.

When I woke that night, she was there, curled up in bed with me.

I remember the goddamn cat, okay?

Is that really what you're taking away from this?

* * *

After that, well, it seemed as if I always had a large bruise simmering somewhere on my body—across my arms or sides, along my back, or even across my face. He blacked my eyes a few times, but this was back when hitting your kids wasn't against the law; it was a God-given right.

No one said anything. Oh, a few teachers looked at me doubtfully. But no one asked me, no one pulled my mom aside or… well, shit… did *anything*. I was a kid when kids were hit when they mouthed off, hit when they fucked up. Whenever the hitter had a bad day or just wanted to fucking hit a kid.

Life went on, you know. He still worked a lot. I was in school most of the day, so I could avoid him easily—more easily than my mom.

You asked me today about siblings… brothers… sisters…

You know I didn't have any, so I don't know the point of the question. To irritate me?

He didn't want more kids; he told my mom that all the time.

They fought about it; I've told you that already. Why do you keep bringing that up? He'd get mad, crazy mad when she asked him.

Wouldn't it be nice if we gave him a brother, she'd ask. *Wouldn't it be nice to have kids that are part you and part me?*

No, he'd answer. *I don't want the part of me that's already part of me.*

I guess she thought he'd treat her differently, nicer if she had his baby. As if she'd be giving him a kind of gift.

As for me, I couldn't imagine having a brother or a sister that was part of him, even if it were part of my mom, too.

I agreed with him. And I think he knew it.

* * *

So why do you keep asking me about that?

What about the goddamn cat? What is it with the cat again?

You know what happened, what he did to her.

Can you even imagine what he'd have done if… if *she'd*… if *they'd*…

I don't want to think about this anymore.

* * *

My mom got quiet after that. She moped around a lot. She didn't feel well, tired all the time, couldn't eat.

I got afraid, you know, like kids do when their parents are sick.

Except I wasn't just scared of what would happen to *her*.

I was afraid of her leaving *me*, leaving me with *him*.

But she told me she was okay.

I'm doing this for us.

She got so sick that, for a while, anyway, she spent most of her time in bed.

He didn't seem to care, stupid prick. He'd come home from work, eat the dinner she'd made for him (for *us*) and they'd argue some in the bedroom with the doors closed.

No, I couldn't make out what they were saying; it was mostly his voice, strident, angry, and hers, quiet, subdued... pleading.

And I did nothing... nothing.

God, I hate to admit that.

I was eight then, and I had learned my lesson before, when I'd followed those voices up the stairs and into the white, white bathroom, spattered red.

When I'd seen the mysterious thing clouding the water in the toilet bowl.

Dumb as a box of rocks, he'd told me. And I was. I was.

* * *

Yeah, at some point the damn cat got pregnant. She was outside half the time because the stupid prick tossed her out at night when she was in heat.

So Lucy had kittens one night, under my bed. I heard it all night, the panting, the wet, squelching sounds, the licking, the tiny mews.

He and mom were arguing or something, as usual. Lots of loud noises that night, lots of stomping up and down the steps, lots of screaming and... well... other sounds. It covered the sounds of the cat under my bed, and I was glad. Because I knew how he'd be if he heard. I'd get it and Lucy would, too. And so would they.

The kittens, for chrissakes. The kittens.

Anyway, I fell asleep at some point during the night, just passed from being awake to being asleep with no memory of actually falling asleep.

Early the next morning, he came in and kicked my bed, waking me.

"Get up... *now*."

It was still dark, and I was groggy, but he threw clothes at me. "Get dressed and meet me downstairs. And don't make me come up again."

He turned, giving the bed a last kick before going down the steps.

It was christing cold in my room, I remember that. He always kept the furnace set low, but that morning it seemed even colder than usual.

As I shrugged into my shirt, I remembered Lucy.

Falling to my knees, I lifted the edge of the bedspread and looked underneath the bed.

I saw the outlines of a shoe, tangles of clothing, some toys, but no Lucy, no kittens.

I clicked my tongue softly to call her, but I heard nothing.

"Get the fuck down here... now!" He was not quite yelling, but not quite whispering, either.

Downstairs it was dark, too. He hadn't bothered to put on any lights, and he stood in the darkness near the back door in the kitchen.

"Here," was all he said.

I knew he'd found her, knew he'd found the cat... the kittens.

Yeah, I thought of running, bolting out the front door and leaving.

But I couldn't. Above me, still sleeping, was my mom.

I'm doing this for us.

He stood by the back door with an old wooden beer case. He had a few of them that he kept his record collection in. It sat by his feet, closed.

Tossing me my coat, he opened the back door. "Go out there and get as many rocks as you can carry. Big ones. Bring 'em in."

I knew... I knew where Lucy was, where the kittens were. Knew what he was planning. But what could I do? I was only eight, remember?

So I went outside and gathered rocks by the light of the dusk-to-dawn in the alley. Found as many as I could carry from the garden my mom had abandoned—the ones she used to edge the cleared space. The ground was hard, frost-rimed, and I had to yank the rocks out like impacted teeth.

My pockets stuffed, I returned to the door, gave him the rocks. Twice I went back, twice I returned.

The last time he met me on the concrete patio.

"Take an end," he huffed, slinging the box toward me.

It was heavy, christing heavy.

For a moment, I thought I'd lose my grip, and the box would drop, hit the ground, spill open.

Rocks would spill from it... and tiny, furry bodies.

But I held it, and he glared at me, wanting to hit me... oh, he wanted to hit me so badly. But he knew that if he did, I would drop the damn thing.

We walked into the alley. It was very cold and dark, and a light dusting of snow had started to fall. It was barely visible unless you looked up at the streetlight, and then it was like blue powder sifting down.

He grunted, threw his head to the left, and I knew he wanted to go to the woods, to the pond.

We turned onto the gravel road that led behind an abandoned garage. The woods appeared as a dark, indistinct wall that rose up from the night. The trees were bare, angular, but the blowing snow blurred their edges, made them indistinct.

We walked a long time, and I was cold. The box was heavy. I started crying at some point, and he freaked. He told me he was gonna beat the shit out of me.

He knew I knew what was in that box. And it wasn't just the rocks.

Box... rocks...

You're as dumb as a box of rocks.

Jesus... Jesus God... I get it now... holy shit... I get it...

Yeah, fuck... okay... okay... let me get to the end here...

We got to the pond, and there was a gray smudge on the horizon where the sun was trying to come up. The snow fell, harder now, denser...

The pond was gray, too, a huge gray oval. It wasn't frozen, just scummed over with ice.

We swung the box once... twice... three times... and it arced up, out, hit the thin ice, and sank from view with barely a splash. In a minute, even the ripples faded.

I was glad, you know. Glad they were together. I couldn't imagine what it would be like for Lucy if he'd killed the kittens and not her.

I tried to think what it would be like for my mom if he killed me someday. What it would be like for her to be without me... *alone.*

"Stupid bitch. I told her. Told her I didn't want any more. No more."

I didn't know what he meant.

I know that we went home, and my mom was gone.

I know that she'd gone to the police.

I know that they came later and took him, took me.

I know that she came once to the police station but hasn't visited me here in years, years.

That's all I know.

* * *

Okay, fuck this shit. I'm tired of this. If I had matches, I'd burn this entire fucking place down.

I tell you what I know... what I *remember*... and all you do is shake your head, Doc. Shake your head and tell me that I'm making it up... *forgetting.*

You think I'm stupid, like him.

Dumb as a box of rocks.

But I'm not.

I know that he didn't want to have any kids.

I know that.

And I know I didn't have a brother.

I know that, too.

But what do you mean, we never had a cat...?

NOTES

I am excited about this first collection of my work and somewhat daunted that it's taken me 20 years to get to where I am. The much younger man I was when I started writing thought for sure he'd have a meteoritic rise to writing fame. By this point, I was supposed to have been ensconced in an authorial mansion somewhere sorting through fan mail and counting my money. In reality, I don't know which I have less of at this point.

No long, drawn-out stuff here. Just thanks for picking up this book and giving it a read. Hopefully you liked a few of the stories. Maybe they helped pass some time during the day or gave you a reason to keep the hall light on at night. You probably didn't like every story here, and that's okay. Not every story is for everybody, as I have learned. Sometimes the ones I like best are the ones readers like least, and vice-versa. That's the way it goes, and I'm okay with that.

I'd like to thank James Roy Daley and all the folks at Books of the Dead Press for believing in my work and bringing it to a wider audience. If you want more of my work, or news on what I'm up to, visit me at *johnfdtaff.com* and drop me a note or follow me on Twitter *at johnfdtaff.*

Now, here are my the answers to the age-old question of where I got the stories came from... *somewhat... maybe.*

Bolts

This is my Frankenstein story, my homage. It came to me, *complete*, in a dream, from beginning to end. Doesn't happen too often, but when it does, it's like a gift from the God of Short Stories. My girlfriend, Debbie, said that this reads a great deal like our life. Well, except for the whole death and reanimation thing, I guess.

Calendar Girl

Remember date books? Some people used to live out of them before Blackberries and IPads. And while today's devices are much, much smaller, they are every bit as annoying.

But For a Moment… Motionless

Why even try to emulate the master? And Poe is, let's face it, *the* master of the horror genre. He damn near invented much of what we consider *horror* today, in addition to detective stories, mysteries, and even science fiction. How can anyone find it surprising that it may have driven him to drink, may have driven him mad? Those are his words that appear in the story. I wrote this specifically for an anthology that it was *not* accepted for. (I think they were looking for something blunter and more horrific. Oh, well…) I like the idea of responsibility that is central do this story and the hope, however dark, expressed in it.

The Water Bearer

This one is a favorite of my early pieces. Yes, unrequited love. It's a perennial theme with me. But also—and I like to explore this, too—is the idea of what love does to inanimate things. How does human love affect, say, a car or a favorite chair or a house? People say that things can't feel emotions, but speak sharply to a plant for a while, and it's bound to die. So, who knows? This one's a pond… and a jealous one, at that.

The Closed Eye of a Dead World

Aren't windows kind of creepy? I think sometimes they are. Who's looking in your window? Ever look up and see something out the window that doesn't seem quite right? Personally I can't sit with my back to a door or window. Gives me the heebie-jeebies. So, this is my take on a good, old-fashioned monster story. I like the pulpy 1950s feel of this.

210

Snapback

This story is, perhaps, a function of too much *Star Trek*. Time travel stuff gives me a headache, but this story came pretty quickly and pretty definitively. Written for an anthology with a very specific focus, the story lost its home when the antho folded. Well, it turned out that the antho wasn't on the up and up anyway. But I was left with a very specific story that I thought would be a hard sell. It turned out not to be. It sold pretty quickly, and people seem to enjoy it. But because of this experience, I don't like to write stories specifically for themed anthologies.

The Mire of Human Veins

I wrote this for my mom, who is afraid of spiders. Like all my stories, this one started out with an idea, then took a turn that spun it in a completely different direction. This became much more of a dark fantasy tale, but still pretty creepy.

The Scent

I think a lot about the things around us that go unnoticed. The converse of this is true, too... the things that *are* noticed. The things that people notice are peculiar, since all people notice different things—notice them differently—and are affected by them differently. Thus we have the unreliability of eyewitnesses. The differences in how we internalize the things we see, how we peel things away from the reality that our senses provide us and integrate them into our lives never fails to astound me. This guy sees something horrible—truly *awful*. What he takes away from it reshapes a seemingly unconnected, random part of his life. Makes you think about the changes we make in our own lives... and the reasons behind them. This story was going to be part of a longer, literary fiction short story collection I was working on for a while. But, I figured, screw that. I'm a *horror* writer. Why put on airs?

Child of Dirt

How many men, how many fathers have that one thought, however fleeting, however ridiculous: *What if it's not mine?* A woman never has this feeling... at least, I'm assuming so. She gets to feel the child grow *within* her, see it removed *from* her. A man never really has this same certainty, does he? This guy has that feeling of uncertainty, in spades, and it makes him more than a little crazy... or does it?

Orifice

From my erotic horror writing days back in the 1990s when these were, somehow, really popular. Of the several I wrote, this is my favorite because of, again, the unrequited love. But this time it's kind of turned around the other way.

Helping Hands

My attempt to do a *Ye Olde Englande* piece, complete with an alienist, a madman (or is he?) and lots of moody atmosphere and Sweeny Toddish action. Of everything in this piece, it's the fingers snapping as the man falls that really gets to me.

In Men, Black

Wrote this for an anthology, and it didn't make the cut. What the heck. Sometimes it happens. Convinced me not to waste time writing stories for some very specific anthology. What the hell do you do with them if they're not accepted? Stick them in your own damn collection, that's what. Anyway, I thought this was a funny little riff on the whole men in black/mothman legend.

Darkness Upon the Void

I love stories with unreliable main characters. There are a few of them in this collection. I like the friction of not knowing whether the protagonist is *really* seeing what is related in the story or if he's crazy. In some stories, even at the end, this question remains up in the air. Not so in this one.

Sharp Edges

From too many hours spent watching shows like *CSI*, I picked up that there are organized and disorganized serial killers. And I wondered how an organized serial killer might reconcile the messy things he does against a very button-down, careful life. And it came to me: *compartmentalization*. This is what I came up with.

The Lacquered Box

One of the first stories I ever wrote, and it took me nearly 20 years to sell it. Never throw stories out. That's the lesson I learned. Eventually, you might become a better writer and be able to go back and repair what didn't work before. At least, that's what I think I did.

Here

There is a truism in life every bit as definite as death and taxes. You are either a dog person or you're not. There is no real middle ground here. I was not born a dog person; I evolved into one. For the longest time, I was strictly a cat person. Dogs seemed... well... *dumb*. As I grew older and went through some extended down periods in my life, I got a dog, Sylvia, and she converted me. *Dumb* now seems *loving* and *loyal*. A few years after that, I got another dog. He was as unlike the first as is possible, and I loved him dearly. At only a year and half, though, he was killed by a hit-and-run driver. I have never, and I mean *never*, mourned harder for a living thing than I did for that dog, whose name, like the dog in the story, was Hector. This story took me a long time to write, simply because I would sit down, write a couple of paragraphs or a scene, and then become too emotional to write more. But, thank you, Hector: writing this story was cathartic, and opened me to a prolonged writing jag where I cranked out some of the stories featured here. My father read this and asked me what was true and what wasn't, since many of the details of the story were lifted from that experience. Honestly, these days, I can no longer tell.

The Tontine

As a writer of genre fiction, I have those moments when I curse the state of the genre, especially seeing how a venerable horror staple such as the vampire has been... well... *castrated* over the years, for want of a better word; turned into something that better fits teen angst and romance novels. *Yuck*. Who wants that shit? Not me. Give me *Salem's Lot* or one or two of the first Anne Rice vampire books before she went all porno and everything. Got me thinking about how those actual horror staples themselves might feel about the situation... the state of horror, so to speak.

The Mellified Man

Yes, this is real. There really are such things, which just goes to show that some of the weirdest shit out there doesn't have to be created by a horror writer... just integrated into his version of reality. I wrote this for my brother, Bobby, who has and continues to have a tremendous sweet tooth... and is probably too old to be called (or at least *want* to be called) Bobby. Oh, and by the way, I lifted the first two lines, slightly modified (of course) from what are probably the best opening lines of any novel: Peter Straub's *Ghost Story*. I love me some Peter Straub.

Box of Rocks

It's funny, but horror is probably the only fiction genre in which subtlety is an ongoing concern. Neither readers nor authors seem too concerned with subtlety in science fiction or westerns or romance books. But for some reason it is a yin-yang thing in horror. Too much blood or gore or spooks or whatever? Or not enough? Show the body or merely hint at it? Sometimes, subtlety in horror heightens the fear. Look at Hawthorne or even Straub. But sometimes subtlety muddies the waters. Look at James. I thought much about the question of subtlety while writing this story. As an author, particularly a horror author (and perhaps no writer other than a comedy writer can appreciate this), you want the reader to *get it*, to understand explicitly what is going on. And sometimes the fear of the writer is that, unless you're slapped in the face with it, you won't. I'm taking that chance here.

ACKNOWLEDGEMENTS

Thanks to everyone who has been forced, either through obligations of blood or friendship, to read the stories featured here, to comment on them, and talk to me about them *ad nauseum*. Thanks go to my parents, brothers and sisters, teachers, editors. Thanks also to my girlfriend, Deborah Deming, Chris Frisella, Randy Kalin, J.D. Streett, Jonathan Edwards, Tom Lewis, Larry Mudd, J. Travis Grundon, Erik T. Johnson, Sharon Shinn, Diane Kline, Kathy Tongay-Carr, Margaux Medewitz-Zesch, Jerry Rabushka, my Aunt Susan Pardo and Uncle Pat Pardo, my cousins Lori and Lynne, my Uncle Woody, and anyone else I've forgotten or otherwise omitted.

With love to my children, Harry, Sam, and Molly.

CPSIA information can be obtained at www.ICGtesting.com
Printed in the USA
LVOW121311030613

336535LV00002B/80/P

9 781927 112113